CULVER CREEK SERIES BOOK 1

UP THE CREEK

ALISSA GROSSO

GLITTER
PIGEON
PRESS

CAITLIN EMERGED FROM A BLACK, dreamless sleep to screams. Adam's tortured cries sounded almost otherworldly. They turned her blood to ice and made her heart race. She sat straight up, then bolted from bed, blinking sleep from her eyes as she raced toward the door, banging her shin on the dresser as she went. She yanked on the doorknob and almost toppled over when it didn't yield as she expected. Goddammit. Lance had locked the door again.

She spared a glance toward the bed, but her husband wasn't there. Instead he was standing, looking out the window. For a moment she thought she was mistaken. Were the screams coming from outside?

"Lance?" she asked.

He turned to her, but his eyes looked past her at some point on the wall.

"What's going on?" he mumbled, barely awake.

"Adam's having a nightmare," she said.

"Again?" he asked. "Maybe we should just let him sleep it off."

The screams had subsided now, but she could still hear

her son's whimpers from down the hall. Sleep it off? Could Lance really be that clueless? She unlocked the door and flung it open. It bounced almost silently off the rubber doorstopper, which didn't really give her the dramatic exit she was hoping for.

She still couldn't quite wrap her head around her husband just standing there looking out the window while Adam cried for them. Usually Lance was the one who woke up first. Maybe he had already gone to comfort Adam and came back to their bedroom by the time she awoke. He seemed so out of it, though. Well, that's what a lack of sleep could do to a person.

Adam sat on his bed in a nest of tangled sheets. His face was damp with tears and sweat, his dark hair plastered to his forehead. The hippo nightlight cast large, ominous shadows when she stepped into his room. He looked up with a start, then relaxed when he saw it was her.

She sat down beside him and pulled his small body to her, wrapping her arms around him and rocking him gently back and forth. The tears subsided, but he still felt tense.

"Mommy, I'm scared of the bad boy," he said. "The bad boy's going to hurt me."

"Nobody's going to hurt you," she assured him. "You're safe. It was just a dream. Look, you're safe in your bedroom."

At this, Adam pulled away from her a little to study the dimly lit bedroom. Maybe they should get a different nightlight. She had never realized how spooky that hippo light made everything look.

"There were trees," Adam said, "and a river. She was playing in the river."

Caitlin stiffened. Adam noticed it and looked up at her. She smiled at him.

"It was just a dream," she said, as much to reassure herself as him. "It wasn't real."

There were lots of rivers out there, and wasn't Adam just watching a cartoon show with cute animals that had to get across a river? That was probably where that detail came from. Plus, she reminded herself, it hadn't been a river. It had been a creek. She wasn't sure Adam knew the difference between a river and a creek, though. But a little girl playing in a river? No, wait, was that what he had said? He said only "she." For all Caitlin knew, this *she* could have been a girl river otter. Maybe he had been having a cute dream about river creatures.

And a "bad boy," she reminded herself. She remembered his bloodcurdling screams. There was nothing cute about the dream he had. Still, she clung to the "bad boy" detail. Was he talking about a child? If so, then the river was just a coincidence. She wanted to ask him more about the bad boy, but this was the worst thing she could do. He was already starting to calm down, starting to forget the details of his nightmare. She couldn't go dredging things back up again.

"Mommy, can I sleep in your room?" Adam asked.

≈

Lance was fully awake and in bed when Caitlin returned with Adam in her arms.

"Hey there, champ," Lance said. "Have a bad dream?"

"Daddy, he hurt her," Adam said. "He hurt her head. She was bleeding."

Her son's tiny body stiffened again in Caitlin's arms, and she gave Lance an exasperated look as she set Adam down in the middle of the bed.

"We'd already gotten past that," she said in a whispered hiss.

"Obviously," Lance said with a roll of his eyes, "which is why he's sleeping in our bed. Again."

She slid into the bed beside Adam and adjusted the covers, ignoring her husband. She petted Adam's head and made soft, soothing noises.

"Remember, that wasn't real, just make believe, like a movie." She didn't want him to get himself worked up again talking about the dream, but it wasn't just that. She didn't want to hear any more details from the nightmare because the bit about the bad boy hurting the girl's head and the blood felt a touch too familiar.

She stroked his face, and his eyelids slowly drooped closed. He looked so calm and peaceful when he slept.

"I thought we said we weren't going to do this anymore," Lance said. Even whispering, his voice was too loud. She held her finger to her lips. He continued more quietly, "I'm just saying, I think it would be better for him if he sleeps in his own bed."

"It's already after three," she said. "It's only for a few hours."

"That's not the point," Lance said. "He's nearly five years old. We can't keep babying him."

It was like the school argument all over again, and Caitlin didn't want to get into it. Not now. She was still tired and groggy and needed more sleep.

"I want to get him a new nightlight," she said to change the subject. "The one he has makes these creepy shadows."

"A new nightlight," Lance repeated in a skeptical voice. "Sure, that will solve everything."

"The important thing," she said, "is that we have to

remind him that his dreams are not real. That they're make believe. We have to be united on this."

Lance made a dismissive noise and lay back down on his pillow, turning his body away from her and Adam. He muttered something, but his voice was muffled by the pillow.

"Lance, this is important," she said. "We have to make it clear that his dreams are not real. He has to know they aren't true."

He sighed. "What kind of moron do you think I am? Do you really think I'm going to start telling him his dreams about boogeymen are real?" He squirmed around and pulled the covers up in an attempt to get comfortable. She thought he was done, but he stopped shifting around long enough to add, "It's not exactly like you're the foremost expert in dreams."

2

AT AN EARLY AGE, Lance Walker had learned that success in life was all about having the right opportunities. Take, for example, this meeting they had scored with the lead furniture buyer for a national retail chain. If they landed a partnership deal, it could easily double Zooest's profits. Hell, maybe triple them. It was an amazing opportunity, and Doug had secured it all thanks to someone he was chatting with at his country club one afternoon. It wasn't enough to open the door when opportunity knocked, though, you had to first set yourself up so that opportunity would knock, so that it was practically beating down your door.

Lance decided he really needed to take up golf. It was embarrassing that he didn't know how to play the sport. Maybe he and Adam could learn at the same time. It would be a good father-son bonding thing, and it would be good for Adam to start young.

He was worried about his son. In less than a year, Adam would be starting kindergarten, and Caitlin had been fighting him on enrolling Adam in private school. High-tower Day was a prestigious school and only two towns away. It was perfect. Caitlin didn't know this, but he had gone ahead and reserved a slot for Adam in the upcoming kindergarten class two years ago. They needed to commit, though, because the school wouldn't hold his place forever. Well, he would talk to her about that, make her see how important this was for Adam. At the very least, he could paint Hightower Day as the compromise, convince her that it would be far better than sending him away to his own alma mater.

He spared a glance at Corey, who was midway through his pitch for Zooest. Corey was at the point where he was explaining how, in just three years, he and Doug had taken their little startup from nothing to one of the biggest players in the online mattress industry. For a moment, Lance saw not the cool, confident thirty-year-old in the Armani suit, but a thirteen-year-old in a grass-stained lacrosse uniform jogging across the Ryerson quad. Lance wouldn't be here, wouldn't be vice president of sales for a thriving company, if his mother hadn't sent him to Ryerson. If you go to the right schools, you meet the right people, and opportunities abound. That was what he needed to explain to Caitlin.

No, the school thing wasn't really what was troubling him. They could work that out. The nightmares were the more pressing issue. When Caitlin had been pregnant, he used to try to imagine which parts of them would wind up showing up in their unborn child. Would the kid have his hair? Her eyes? He had imagined mostly physical character-istics. He hadn't thought about all the other things lurking in their DNA, until the nightmares began.

They seemed to be getting worse. Two or three nights a week, Adam woke them up screaming. Caitlin didn't want to take him to see anyone. He understood her reluctance. Taking Adam to see a shrink was like admitting there was something broken about their son, and she didn't want to give him some sort of inferiority complex. Still, something needed to be done. This was the sort of problem that needed to be licked early. Nobody understood that better than he did. What did Caitlin know about nightmares, anyway? Of course she didn't understand the seriousness of the situation. How could she?

Someone nudged his arm, and he looked up, startled. Corey smiled at him, but there was annoyance in his eyes. Lance was up, and he had missed the cue.

"Sorry," Lance said. He shuffled through the pitch packet papers on his lap. "To think of Zooest as just another online mattress seller is to miss the point," Lance said. He took a swig from the glass of water on the table beside him to soothe the scratchiness of his voice. He could still feel Corey's eyes on him, and he was pretty sure his boss and old friend was growing more annoyed. He had picked the wrong time to zone out. "Zooest offers something that no other mattress retailer offers, our own patented sleep system. We're selling more than just a mattress. We're selling a good night's sleep."

Across from him, Tom Marks, the retail chain's lead furniture buyer, shifted and let out a little sigh. It was a cue that at some point he was going to tell Corey and Lance that he had heard enough and send them on their way.

"Yeah, your colleague here just said that," Tom said.

Corey delivered a practiced and polite chuckle. Crap. Lance should have been paying more attention.

"Well, it's important," Corey said. "We can't stress it enough."

He gave Lance a playful pat on his arm and a look that said, *Get it together, man.*

Lance felt himself redden as he glanced down at the pitch packet. They had practiced all this back at the office, but he wasn't sure what Corey had already said. Screw it. He didn't need prepared remarks. Prepared remarks were not what had gotten him here. What he had to do was get in their corner, be their equal.

Lance glanced around Tom Marks's office. It was simply furnished with not many personal touches. There was some sort of large crystalline gemstone on the shelf behind Tom. A vacation souvenir perhaps. There was an etched Lucite award, but it was too far away to make out what achievement it recognized. Lance's eyes chanced upon the family portraits in their shiny brass frames. He set the pitch packet papers on the table beside him and leaned forward ever so slightly.

"Do you have kids, Tom?" Lance asked. Beside him, Corey nervously shifted in his chair. This wasn't part of their rehearsed plan.

"A son and two daughters," Tom said. "My oldest just got accepted into Cornell."

"Congratulations," Lance said. "You must be so proud. I have a son. He's going to be starting kindergarten in the fall."

"Well, I'll warn you," Tom said. "The years fly by faster than you can imagine."

"You would do anything for your kids, wouldn't you?" Lance said.

"Of course." Tom looked slightly confused by where this conversation was going. He wasn't alone. Out of the corner of his eye, Lance spied Corey's perplexed expression.

"The thing about fatherhood that I wasn't prepared for

was how helpless you feel when something goes wrong." The secret to lying was to always base your lies on truth, then they didn't really feel like lies. "About six months ago, my son started having nightmares on a regular basis. Nearly every night, he was waking up screaming, terrified. I felt so helpless, sitting there beside his bed trying to soothe him as I wiped the tears from his face. It was killing me to see him suffering like that."

Tom shifted ever so slightly forward in his seat. He was engaged now, had forgotten all about his plan to send Lance and Corey packing. Corey was doing his best to remain neutral and passive as Lance went off the rails.

"His pediatrician said it was just a phase and that it would pass," Lance continued, "but I was desperate. I would have done anything to make sure he didn't have to suffer like that. Then, and I'm embarrassed to admit that it took me so long, but I realized the answer had been right there in front of me the whole time—the Zooest patented sleep system. I mean, I guess I thought of it as something to help retired construction workers with aching backs or stressed executives dealing with insomnia, but our sleep system really is designed to give the perfect night's sleep to every individual. So I created a Zooest Sleep Profile for Adam—that's my boy—and I used our online tool to find him the perfect bedding and room accoutrements to deliver a good night's sleep. Our sleep system designed the perfect bedroom for Adam—from moving his bed away from a noisy vent to replacing his hippo-shaped nightlight, which cast weird shadows. And of course there was the design of the mattress and bedding material based upon his own size and shape. Since we installed his own personalized Zooest Sleep System, he hasn't had a single nightmare."

Lance took a breath to let the story sink in.

"So don't assume we're just another mattress seller," Lance said. "What we're selling is a sleep system tailored to an individual's needs. Every single customer that walks through your doors is a unique individual and deserves their own unique sleeping system, and when you partner with Zooest, you'll be able to give that to them."

Tom nodded. "I'll be honest, we've been looking to expand our mattress offerings, and I've heard some pitches from some of your competitors. The truth is, I wasn't that impressed, but this sounds like something we could get behind."

Though Corey didn't audibly sigh, Lance could still sense the tension that suddenly left his body.

Tom began talking about follow-up meetings and a trial rollout in select stores before they went national, but the deal was as good as done. Twenty minutes later, Lance and Corey were on their way out of the office after having scheduled those meetings, when Tom stopped Lance by resting a hand on his arm.

"How is your boy doing now?" Tom asked. "Is he okay?"

"It's been an incredible transformation," Lance said.

Tom reached into his pocket and slipped out a wallet. He searched inside before pulling out something and handing to Lance. It was a business card, but not his own. This one was purple with a watercolor background. The name on it was Phelicity Green. Her title was listed as Dream Whisperer.

"If he ever does experience any more difficulties, I can highly recommend Phelicity. She's exceptional. Really helped me to heal my chakras and correct the energy flow in my life, and it made all the difference."

"Thank you," Lance said, and he waved the card in the

air before slipping it into his pocket to indicate how grateful he was for this gift.

"That was fucking brilliant, man!"

Corey had just downed his third bloody mary, and all his sentences came out as shouts. Other diners in the steakhouse where they were enjoying their celebratory lunch swiveled around to gawk at the commotion. The attention might have made some uncomfortable, but Lance reveled in it. After all, they were the cool kids in the room.

"That shit about your son and his nightmares? Stroke of genius!" Corey waved his celery stick garnish in the air, and red droplets splattered on the crisp white tablecloth.

The waitress came by to check on them. She didn't actually tell them to keep it down, but it was implied in the way she asked if there was anything she could get for them.

"How about your number?" Corey did that thing where he waggled his eyebrows at her. It was something he had been doing since he was at least fifteen. Back then, the girls at the annual combined school dance had thought it was cute, but at thirty it just made him look pathetic. It didn't help that he was wearing his wedding band.

"Excuse me?" the waitress said.

"Sorry," Lance said. "Don't mind him. He's just a bit giddy. We had some good news earlier."

The waitress left them, but not without a backward glance that brimmed with disgust. Lance decided it would probably be a good idea if they didn't order anything else, because there was a strong risk it would be laced with annoyed waitress spit.

"Some good news," Corey repeated with a bark of a

laugh. "Understatement of the year! Hey, sorry, man. I had no idea that Marks character was going to be such a weirdo, but you picked up on it, didn't you? That's why our planned speech didn't work, but you saw that, didn't you? Genius!"

"Sometimes you have to improvise." Lance didn't add that improvising was pretty much what he had been doing his whole life.

"Healed his chakras," Corey muttered. "Weirdo. Hey, what was that card he gave you anyway?"

Lance fished the business card out of his pocket and passed it across the table to Corey. The glossy purple coating caught the light as Corey read it.

"Phelicity Green," Corey said. "Dream whisperer. Yeah, I bet she healed his chakras. I wouldn't mind healing her chakras, if you know what I'm saying."

Lance did that thing where he smiled and sort of half-laughed, but he noticed more glares from the others in the restaurant. It was probably time to get the check.

"We should get back to the office," Lance suggested.

Corey waved the idea away as if it was absurd.

"Hey, did you see this?" Corey asked, still looking at the business card. "Says she's in Culver Creek. Isn't that your old stomping grounds?"

The floor fell out from under Lance. He felt like he was tumbling off a skyscraper after being punched in the gut. The house of cards he had so meticulously constructed began to fall in on itself.

"Culver Creek?" He managed to squeak out the words through a suddenly dry throat. "No, I never lived in Culver Creek."

"No, I know you're from Atkins, but isn't Culver Creek near there?"

"Oh, yeah," Lance said. The relief took several seconds

to make it to his racing heart. "I mean, kind of. Not that far, I guess."

"Small world." Corey flipped the business card back to Lance, and it skimmed into a red bloody mary droplet. "Where's that waitress? I need another drink."

"We should get back." Lance wiped the business card on his napkin and shoved it back in his pocket. "Hey, I'm gonna hit the john."

L ance splashed cool tap water on his face and patted it dry with a couple of paper towels. He had almost lost it back there. Stupid. Thankfully, Corey was mildly inebriated and probably hadn't noticed a thing, but that was just luck.

Then there was the meeting earlier. He had almost screwed that up completely. He had saved himself, and it all came right in the end, but he had come very close to ruining things. Way too close. He needed to get it together.

He wasn't getting enough sleep, not quality sleep. He couldn't function without sleep. It may have been a line from Zooest ad copy, but that didn't mean it wasn't true. Something needed to be done about Adam's nightmares. Caitlin was dead set against taking Adam to a shrink, but this problem seemed to be above the pediatrician's pay grade.

He fired off a quick text to his mother. He had already discussed his concerns about Adam and the bad dreams. His text said he wanted to try taking Adam to a psychologist but that Caitlin was resistant to the idea, and he wondered if she had any advice. He hesitated for a second before hitting the send button. Maybe this was the sort of thing more worthy of a phone call than a text, but he didn't have time for that.

He needed to get back out there. If he left Corey alone for too long, he would order another drink, or worse, attempt to grab the waitress's ass or something. He hit the Send button and headed out of the men's room.

3

CULVER CREEK, Pennsylvania, population 14,335. It was home to the Everluster Paint factory and the Rixby Potato Chip plant. The town was named for the body of water that wound through it. The creek was barely more than a trickle of water much of the year, though it swelled up after heavy rains, and during the spring rainy season it resembled a raging river. On a few notable occasions it had overflowed its banks and flooded homes and businesses in and around Culver Creek's downtown.

Right now it was somewhere in between, thanks to the rain they had the previous day. Sage Dorian stared at the water as he sat in his department-issue car eating a tomato-and-Swiss sandwich.

Culver Creek's two factories meant that the small town would always have a certain number of transients, and that led to the occasional problem, but for the most part this was a quiet, working-class town. Major crimes were nearly nonexistent, except, of course, for that one—the one that made Culver Creek famous in the crime forums.

A nineteen-year-old unsolved murder was the reason he

had up and moved to this sad little town in the middle of nowhere. When he thought about it too much, he'd start to wonder if he was as mentally stable as he pretended to be. He feared the answer. Moving to a strange town because of a little girl he'd never known who had gotten killed there nineteen years ago was hardly the most impulsive thing he had done. He owed his whole career to an obsession with web sleuth crime forums that stemmed from an entirely different unsolved murder.

It was how he had wound up in law enforcement, first as a uniformed officer and then as a detective in a small Pennsylvania city. He had job security and just enough work to keep him from being too bored. But he'd thrown it all away when he saw the job posting that someone from the web sleuth forum had shared with him.

Two weeks later, he headed to the town, which was somewhat notorious on the forum, for a job interview.

F ive months ago, Sage Dorian sat in the Culver Creek police department trying his best not to sweat through his interview suit. Rayanne Lawrence drummed her fingers on the desk as she reviewed his resume. Culver Creek's chief of police didn't rate a big shiny office, but it was her own private space, which was more than any of the other officers in the department had. Her fingernails, like her hair, were cut short and practical. Sage guessed her to be around thirty-five. He attempted to do his best Sherlock Holmes on her, trying to read her life story in the condition of her skin and the way she wore her clothes.

From the way she held herself, he got the impression she hadn't grown up with much. Maybe she was raised by a single mom. Was she from Culver Creek or a nearby town? If she was from here, she would have grown up in one of those apartment buildings downtown or maybe one of the sad little houses near the town's two factories. He had been in Culver Creek all of twenty minutes, but he had spent a lot of time reading up on the town via internet forums, and he got the impression of a closed-off town that didn't trust outsiders much. For them to make Rayanne Lawrence, a woman, chief of police, she would probably have to be from here. She would have worked her way up from the bottom. He liked this about her. He felt a kinship with her.

"So, I have to ask," she said after a few moments, "why are you applying for this job, Sage?"

She spoke in the blunt, direct way of a cop. He knew he wasn't wrong about her working her way up the ranks. He also knew this wasn't just some canned job interview question. She was genuinely mystified why someone with his background would leave a city police department, where he was on track to be promoted to lieutenant and later captain, to come to this backwater burg and take what was effectively a dead-end detective job. He knew the right answer was not that he was looking for a challenge.

Folded into the smallish chair that sat across from Rayanne's desk, Sage shifted in an effort to get comfortable. He found that most furniture seemed to be constructed for someone of a smaller stature.

"I think it would be a good fit for me," Sage said.

Rayanne nodded speculatively as she gave him an appraising look. A support bar in the chair dug into the backs of his thighs, and it took every ounce of his willpower not to shift around again. He didn't want to give the impression that he was squirming beneath her gaze. It felt like this was what she wanted, and for one conspiracy-theory moment, he entertained the thought that she had deliberately chosen this too-small chair for the interview because she wanted him to be uncomfortable. Of course, that was absurd. She wouldn't have known how tall he was until he showed up here.

"I'm just wondering if you'll find the pace of things here a bit slow for your liking," Rayanne said. "We don't have too many murders."

He wondered if she was baiting him.

"If memory serves," Sage said, "wasn't there a notorious murder in this town some years ago?"

She raised one eyebrow at him, and her lips twitched into what could have been called a smirk.

"You've done your homework."

"Comes with the territory," he said.

"Well, I don't want to burst your bubble, but that was probably the last exciting thing to happen in this town, and that was nearly twenty years ago."

Was it weird to describe the murder of a little girl as an "exciting thing"? Sage thought the word choice made him even more uncomfortable than the chair he was sitting in, but the murder had occurred long before Rayanne was a cop. Temporal distance could make people forget about the human victims of old tragedies. He wondered what the cutoff point was when a murder victim ceased to be a human and became a sort of mythical figure. He figured it had to be more than six years. Six years hardly seemed to be any time at all.

As if she could read his mind, Rayanne asked, "Where do you see yourself in five years?"

I want to have caught my sister's murderer, he thought, but of course he didn't say that out loud.

"I'd like to be in a position where my work makes a difference, where people are more than just numbers."

"The town council has mandated that the department add a detective to our staff," she explained. "There was a series of incidents, nothing too serious, but they all happened to occur right in a row and no arrests were made." She ticked them off one by one on her fingers. "A series of businesses downtown were burglarized, a woman was attacked while walking home from work one night, and then someone stole some equipment and fixtures from the park. As crime waves go, it was fairly mild. So if that's the sort of police work that would suit you, the job is yours."

A month after he got the job, he had solved the three crime wave cases. Well, the one—the missing park equipment —had already been solved. That had been local teens messing around, and since some of the guys on the force knew some of the kids' parents, they had handled things quietly without arresting anyone. Sage traced the downtown burglaries to a meth addict living in one of the apartment buildings in town. That took less than half a day. Finding the woman's attacker required a little more digging, but in the end it all stemmed from a love triangle and a case of mistaken identity.

Sage had been on the job five months, and Rayanne Lawrence had been right about the slower pace. Detective work in Culver Creek was boring as sin, but that was all about to change. This morning he had asked and Rayanne had granted Sage permission to tackle Culver Creek's notorious cold case, the murder of Lily Esposito.

But it was a different murder on Sage's mind as he

watched the creek and finished his sandwich. Last night he dreamed about Melodie. His sister showed up at his front door, much the way she had shown up at his college dorm room the last time he saw her. In his dream, she kept trying to tell him something, but her voice was too quiet or there were too many other noises for him to hear what she said. He awoke frustrated, never having heard her words. Well, he didn't need a dream interpretation guide to know what that meant.

Memories of the last time he had seen his sister started to come back to him, and he crumpled up the last few bites of his sandwich in the paper wrapper and shoved it into a plastic shopping bag. He didn't have time for that. He had a murder to solve.

4

CAITLIN WALKER HAD NOT HAD a dream in over nine years. It was hard to believe she had experienced nearly a decade of beautiful, dreamless sleep, but maybe that was why she could still remember bits and pieces of the nightmares she had when she was younger with such vivid clarity. There was another explanation; a memory popped into her head of her mother seated at their kitchen table frantically scribbling down Caitlin's words in a notebook as she dutifully described her latest dream.

It was better if Adam didn't describe his nightmares. *Better for who?* Caitlin ignored the voice in her head. This wasn't about her comfort. This was about not making the dream real by describing it. It would be that much more difficult to forget once he framed it with words.

Certainly that was the case for Caitlin, who had spent the better part of the morning obsessing over the dream Adam had described to her the previous night, or at least replaying a scene in her head that looked an awful lot like the ugly dream Adam had described. The creepy shadows could not obscure the little girl standing beside the creek, the fear on her face as she looked up at the big rock bearing down on her. Caitlin saw the girl's crumpled form lying in the mud beside the creek. She saw the blood that ran down her pale face. Adam said there had been a bad boy that hurt the girl, but that wasn't right. It was a man, Caitlin was sure of it.

Her phone pinged with a notification, and she abandoned the memory and returned to the real world. She glanced at the phone to make sure it wasn't any kind of alert from Adam's nursery school. It wasn't. She saw her mother-in-law's name on the display and decided she could safely ignore it. Raquel was probably busy planning her latest party and wanted to brag to Caitlin about the menu she had ordered from the caterer or some other inanity.

Instead Caitlin returned to her work, or in this case the blank screen she had been staring at for the better part of the day. The graphic design firm Caitlin worked for was generous enough to allow her to work from home most days. This was perfect because it meant she didn't have to hire a babysitter for Adam or send him to daycare. And in an ideal world, it meant that the three days per week he had his full-day pre-k, she had hours of distraction-free time to get work done. Distractions managed to find her all the same. Even in a quiet house, she was capable of distracting herself by worrying about Adam and the nightmares that plagued him on a near daily basis.

"Enough," she said to her empty office, and reread the project notes for what must have been the tenth time.

They were working on an ad campaign for a state lottery commission. It was a huge account and a major score for the agency. Caitlin was honored and proud that Brittney had entrusted her with the ad design, but stupid doubts and her old sense of inferiority were interfering with her ability to create. Then there was the slogan. "Dreams come true." On the surface it was a simple, maybe even banal slogan, but every time Caitlin read it, she found herself taking it literally. That image of the little girl lying dead in the mud came back to her, and it was all she could see. She tried to conjure up visions of someone gleefully driving an expensive car or waving from the window of a palatial home, and for a moment she saw these things, then the dead little girl chased them from her mind.

Maybe she should tell Brittney she wasn't the right person for this ad campaign. How would she put it? She could say she wasn't feeling it. She knew how well that would go over with her business-minded boss. Plus, if she turned down a major project like this, they would be that much less likely to give her big accounts going forward. No, she had to knuckle down and get this done. She wouldn't get distracted by the slogan. She would leave that part until the end, get everything else set first.

She took a deep breath and got as far as opening her artwork folder when her phone rang. Unless it was the school, she wasn't picking up. She looked at the display. Oh, good. It was her mother-in-law. Was she calling because Caitlin hadn't responded to her text message quick enough? Caitlin had asked Lance on more than one occasion to tell his mother not to bug her during the day when she was working, but it was useless. Raquel didn't seem to understand that what Caitlin did was actual work and not some sort of quirky hobby. Maybe it had something to do with the fact that Raquel spent her days surrounded by women who were fellow members of the Flower Arranging Society or the Lunching Ladies or any of the dozen or so social clubs she belonged to.

She should let it go to voicemail, but now her concentration was broken and she was annoyed. She grabbed the phone and gave it an angry swipe to answer it.

"I'm working," Caitlin said. "This better be important."

There was a moment of silence before Raquel said, "Caitlin? Hello?"

Caitlin sighed and reined in the anger enough to at least make a half-hearted attempt at civility. "Yes, I'm here. How can I help you, Raquel?"

"Oh, good. I hope I haven't caught you at a bad time," Raquel said. Before Caitlin could say that it was in fact a very bad time, Raquel continued, "I was just speaking to Lance, and he told me about the problems you've been having with Adam and his nightmares."

A new wave of anger overtook Caitlin. Apparently while she was hard at work (she ignored the little voice in the back of her head that reminded her that she had accomplished absolutely nothing all day) her husband was spending his day at work calling his mother so he could discuss their personal life with her.

"It's really no big deal," Caitlin said. "Adam's pediatrician said as much."

"Well, it's been my experience that you can't really trust these small-town doctors."

Caitlin resisted the urge to snap and tell know-it-all Raquel that the pediatrician in their affluent New Jersey town was Harvard-educated and highly respected.

"Raquel, we have everything under control," Caitlin said.

"Oh, I'm sure you do," Raquel said. "It's just I was speaking to someone the other day at the club, and he's a psychologist who specializes in sleep disorders. I think you should at least take Adam in for a consultation. What could it hurt?"

"He's four years old. He had a few bad dreams," Caitlin said. "He doesn't need a psychologist."

"And that will probably be what Dr. Franklin concludes too, but you at least owe it to the boy to take him in," Raquel said.

"Right, well," Caitlin said. "I'm kind of in the middle of a project here. So I've got to go."

She clicked off the phone before Raquel had a chance to say anything else. Her hands shook with rage when she tried to return to work. Plus, when she looked at the clock, she noticed she had less than fifteen minutes before she had to leave to pick Adam up at school. There was no sense in starting anything now.

~

She was still steaming from Raquel's call when she got behind the wheel of the Land Cruiser. There was plenty of time before she needed to be at the school, but she didn't have the patience to deal with other drivers. She beeped at anyone who didn't hit the gas the second the lights turned green and anyone else who mildly annoyed her.

A psychologist was the last thing Adam needed right now. She understood that better than anyone. He shouldn't be made to feel like there was something wrong with him. Taking him to a shrink would send the wrong message. It would only make him focus on the dreams, which was exactly what Caitlin didn't want him to do. There was nothing a psychologist could do to help anyway. Caitlin should know. She broke down and went to one a decade ago.

Caitlin went to see her campus psychologist after Delia

Chambers. Of course, she didn't know the girl's name until she read the newspaper article about the brutal murder. It was the only new information the article had given her. She already knew all the other details and then some about the horrible crime.

The psychologist spoke with a soft voice and did his best to radiate understanding and compassion, but he was light-years away from grasping Caitlin's predicament. When she explained how upset she was after Delia's murder, the psychologist assured her she wasn't alone.

"My office has been unusually busy lately," he said. "A lot of students and faculty have been shaken by this event. What you're feeling is perfectly normal."

"But do any of them feel like they should have done more to prevent it from happening?" Caitlin asked.

"No one could have known what was going to happen," the psychologist said.

"I did," Caitlin said. "I had a nightmare."

The psychologist misunderstood her. He thought she meant she had a nightmare after the news broke. "A lot of students have been having nightmares and interrupted sleep, but you're doing the right thing by opening up and talking to someone about what you're going through."

She debated trying to clarify things, but she knew it was pointless. This guy wasn't going to get it.

"If you're having difficulty sleeping, I can write you a prescription for a sedative," the psychologist said.

Caitlin didn't want to go to sleep. She had been deliberately forcing herself to stay awake and avoid her dreams. It meant she found herself falling asleep during class or nodding off while studying.

After a few weeks of that, it was taking a toll on her grades and her immune system, but she had trained herself not to sleep at night, and now despite her sheer exhaustion, when she laid her head down at night, sleep refused to come.

She considered taking the psychologist up on that sedative prescription, but instead she went to the drug store in town and perused the collection of over-the-counter sleep aids. The large variety was a bit overwhelming. She grabbed a package more or less by chance. She would have grabbed one of each package just to try them, but that wasn't in her budget.

So it was then that Caitlin began to experiment with drugs in her junior year of college, but these weren't the recreational narcotics favored by many of her peers. Her experimentation was limited solely to over-the-counter sleep aids. She tried them all, both individually and in combination. She was several weeks into her experiment when she discovered Pacifcleon. It was a miraculous and amazing product.

It was the only one of the many sleep aids she had tried that consistently delivered a deep, dark, completely dreamless sleep. It was pure heaven. The drug changed her life. On Pacifcleon she became a new person. She was self-assured and confident. It gave her a new perspective on things, and she became more energetic and hopeful. She could never go back to the way things had been before.

She made sure she always had a ready supply in stock, which used to be no problem. Back when she was in college, it seemed every store with even a modest pharmacy section stocked those little blue-and-green Pacifcleon boxes. Even the little convenience store gas station around the corner from her college sold the stuff.

By the time she was married, Pacifcleon's popularity had dwindled. She could still pick it up at Rite Aid or

Walgreens but was less likely to find it on grocery store shelves or in other general retailers. The writing was on the wall, but like an idiot she ignored it. She had been lulled into a false sense of security.

It was about two years ago when she went into the Rite Aid in town and found they were sold out of Pacifcleon. That was unsettling, but worse than that, there no longer seemed to be a space on the shelf for it. There was a Walgreens in the next town over. They had just two boxes, both marked with clearance stickers. She bought them both, then she went to the CVS down the road and found one more box.

She looked up the website for the company that made the pills and searched it extensively. She couldn't find any information about Pacifcleon or any other sleep aids. In an emotional state, she fired off an email to the customer service address. The corporate reply made her cry.

"We regret to inform you that we have ceased production of Pacifcleon. There are no plans to bring this product back to market."

At least she had the foresight to go on a drug store shopping spree. She hit every store within a thirty-mile radius and was rewarded with what amounted to a fifteen-month supply. It seemed like plenty at the time, but she regretted her lack of further foresight soon enough. Why had she limited herself to thirty miles? Why hadn't she covered the whole state or multiple states? Hell, she could have turned it into some cross-country expedition. Of course she had a two-year-old son and a husband who would never understand her need to make a pharmacy-chain tour of the country. So she had hunkered down with her measly fifteen-month supply and set up an eBay alert. She bought just about every box of Pacifcleon that enterprising resellers listed, but it was not enough. It could never be enough. She had stretched her fifteen-month supply into a thirty-eight-month supply, but that was nothing in the grand scheme of things.

She only hoped that before she ran out, somehow someone would decide to start producing her precious Pacifcleon again. Maybe they would change the name, but if she was lucky, they wouldn't alter the formula. This was the slim hope she clung to fervently.

She pulled into the nursery school parking lot a full ten minutes early. Was Pacifcleon the answer for Adam? She was pretty sure the drug wasn't recommended for children, and the single pill was likely too big of a dosage for her small son. Of course, pills could be cut in half, and this was something she had considered for herself. It wasn't an ideal solution, but if she cut back to half a pill a night, she would suddenly find herself with a six-year supply. Then again, if she started sharing her pills with Adam, that would do away with her surplus. But that wasn't really her concern. She didn't like the idea of drugging her son. It was all fine and good if she decided to self-medicate, but she wasn't going to force this on Adam.

On the other hand, she saw how tense he had looked when she went in to check on him last night. What she wouldn't give to be able to save him from the fear and ugliness, to give him the peaceful sleep and confidence she had found for herself when she was twenty-one. She wanted to save him from all those years of suffering.

The only other solution was to ignore the nightmares as much as they possibly could, to play it down. If they made it clear the bad dreams were no big deal, then maybe the dreams would somehow lose their power.

5

LANCE STEPPED into the house from the garage, and Caitlin sprang out from the kitchen with a wild look in her eyes. She had been waiting for him. There was a time, early in their marriage, when such a greeting might have preceded a passionate lovemaking session, but those days of carnal spontaneity seemed to be behind them. He might not have been able to tell just what that look was in Caitlin's eyes, but he knew it wasn't lust.

"I'm surprised you didn't decide to swing by to visit your mother on the way home," Caitlin said.

Lance tried to decipher the remark. His mother and stepfather lived in Atkins, Pennsylvania. It wasn't exactly a place he could swing by on his way home from work, nor had he ever done so. Was Caitlin suggesting he was late getting home? It was true he had been working some longer days lately, but he had texted her to let her know he was on the way.

"Sorry, the traffic was bad," he said in an attempt to placate her. He still had his jacket on. He hadn't taken more than two steps into the house.

"Don't try to change the subject," she said.

"And what exactly is the subject?" He managed to edge past her. He set his keys in the little dish on the hallway table and went to the coat closet. She followed so close on his heels that he had to take care not to elbow her as he slipped off his jacket. He hung it on a hanger and placed it in the closet, then turned to look at his fiery-eyed wife. He tried to defuse the situation by saying in a half joking, half serious way, "Hi, honey, how was your day?"

"Oh, I'm sure you'd love to know so you can give Raquel a full report."

Damn it. His mother had called. He had specifically instructed her not to, but when had his mother ever done as he asked?

"She cares about you," Lance said. His mother had been the subject of more than one argument, and a big part of the reason was that Caitlin seemed to think Raquel didn't really like her. Perhaps at first his social-climbing mother had regrets about Lance's choice of a partner, but she had come around and saw that Caitlin was a supportive wife and a good mother.

"Well, maybe that's what I can tell Brittney when she asks where the project I was supposed to finish today is," Caitlin said. "My mother-in-law cares about me. That should go over well."

"Look, I'm sorry," Lance said. He slipped past her again and went into the kitchen. He flipped through the slim pile of mail on the counter while Caitlin watched him from the doorway. There were no pots on the stove, and the oven was cold.

"It's like she doesn't even understand that I work for a living. She must think I hang around here all day eating bonbons."

"She doesn't think that," Lance said. "She just—"

"Loves to stick her nose in where it doesn't belong?" Caitlin supplied. She saw him glancing around the kitchen. "Yeah, well, you can thank your mother for dinner not being ready. I've been trying to finish up that project I was working on when she interrupted me."

"She shouldn't have called you when you were working," Lance said. "I'm sorry about that. I'll talk to her."

He hugged Caitlin and smoothed her hair with the palm of his hand. It had the desired effect. She softened in his arms, and he could feel some of the tension leave her body. He kissed her lightly on the lips and, when he pulled back, was surprised to see tears glistening on her cheeks. An uneasy feeling came over him without warning.

"Where's Adam?" he asked. It suddenly seemed strange and worrisome that his son hadn't come running to greet him when he arrived home.

For an instant there was a look of panic on his wife's face, then she relaxed. "He's up in his room playing with his trains."

"I shouldn't have texted her about Adam," he said. "I'm worried about him, and I was just hoping she could help."

Caitlin made a dismissive sort of snort noise. "She gave me the number of some shrink who belongs to her country club."

"Well, maybe we could—" Lance began but didn't get to finish.

"I'm not taking our son to a shrink," she said, "and I'm not about to take parenting advice from a woman who sent her eleven-year-old son away to boarding school so she could shack up with her new boyfriend."

"That's not how it was," Lance said, but he knew with Caitlin's current mood it would be a waste of time to attempt any further explanation. "I'm going to go check on Adam."

~

C aitlin didn't know the full story about why his mother sent him to Ryerson Prep, mainly because Lance hadn't told her. To do so, he would have to explain how he spent his first twelve years in Culver Creek. He would need to explain that strange summer—the way he and the rest of the kids in his small Pennsylvania town had been on a sort of house arrest. The bikes and skateboards stayed locked up in garages. Trampolines and above-ground swimming pools went unused. Everyone seemed to be waiting around with held breath. He could still remember his mother standing at their front window for what seemed like hours, chewing on her fingernails as if she expected the boogeyman to show up at their door.

Though never a fan of school, he had actually been looking forward to the start of classes that year, when his mother dropped her bombshell news on him. There was a pamphlet sitting by his place at the table that night. Boys in ties and blazers beamed at him against a backdrop of perfect fall foliage and old stone buildings. He stared at those pictures as she spoke her incomprehensible words.

"Private school?" Lance asked, confused. At the time, his biggest concern was the uniform. He wasn't going to go around dressing in those dorky clothes like the boys in the brochure. He could already hear the taunts and jeers from the other kids in the neighborhood when they saw what he was wearing. He wasn't exactly the most popular guy to begin with, but something like this would be a complete disaster. "Wait, will there be a different bus?" Lance asked. "Will I have the same bus stop?"

His mother sighed and shook her head. He recognized her look of impatience. It was the way she looked at him when she thought he was being dense.

"You won't take a bus," she said, and from the slow deliberate way she spoke, he guessed she had already explained this, that he had missed it while he stared at the stupid brochure. "Ryerson is a boarding school. You'll live there."

He crumpled up the brochure and threw it at the wall. He stormed off to his room.

A few short weeks later he sat in the passenger seat of his mother's car as she drove through the wrought iron Ryerson gate. He thought it was the end of his life. It would take him a full year to recognize that it was the beginning.

Lance was painfully aware that he had nothing in common with his fellow Ryerson classmates. Fearing the ridicule that never really came, that first awkward semester he kept to himself, answered in monosyllables when spoken to, and more or less tried to be invisible. He hit the jackpot with his first-year roommate. Maxwell had allergy-related breathing issues and slept with a special air mask with a pump whirring away all night. To drown out the sound of the pump, Maxwell wore a pair of earplugs to bed each night. It meant Lance could have thrown a raucous party on his half of their shared room and his roommate would never have been the wiser. It meant Lance's secret remained safe.

Lance had a vague plan that he would go home for Christmas break and simply never come back. That plan fell apart almost at once, when his mother picked him up at school and announced that she had rented a North Carolina beach house where they would spend their Christmas break.

"Remember that summer when we went to the Outer Banks?" his mom said in a perky voice as she steered her old, tired Volvo out of the Ryerson gates. "That was a lot of fun, wasn't it? I thought we should go back, and you wouldn't believe the deals you can get on a beach house during the winter."

It turned out that maybe the reason his mother had gotten such a good deal on the beach house rental was because the Outer Banks were not nearly as fun to visit in the winter as the summer. A lot of places were shuttered for the season, and the weather was something short of desirable. Still, Lance was happy not to be at school, and he figured when the holidays were over, they would head on back home to Culver Creek.

It was the day after Christmas when his mother dropped her latest bombshell. They sat at the kitchen table while a furious rainstorm raged outside. His mother explained that she had sold their house and, even more shocking, she was going to marry Tucker Rixby in the spring. Lance thought she was trying to make some sort of joke, but when he looked into her eyes, he saw how serious she was.

"Your boss?" he asked. "The one with the bad breath?"

"Well, he's not technically my direct supervisor, and anyway, I won't be working there anymore. I'll be leaving my job at the end of January."

His mother had worked as a receptionist at the Rixby plant for as long as he could remember. It was part of her identity. She was his mother, and she was an administrative worker at Rixby. That was something she had always stressed with pride, making an effort to set herself apart from the lowly factory workers in their grubby coveralls.

"Isn't Tucker Rixby old? Are you in love with him?" Lance asked.

His mother fake laughed. "Tucker's barely ten years older than me, and he's a sweet, caring man. He's going to make a wonderful stepfather."

He noticed she hadn't answered his question about being in love with Tucker. He noticed something else as well, something that had escaped his notice before. The earrings and necklace his mother had been wearing were new and looked expensive, and he had never seen any of the clothes she had worn over the past few days. These too appeared to be expensive.

It was possible she had made money from selling their house and treated herself to new clothes and jewelry, but he also knew Tucker Rixby, one of the heirs to the Rixby fortune, was loaded, and Lance suspected that this and not love was his mother's motivation for marrying the man.

Rain lashed the windows as Lance sat there trying to process all this information. Had this been his mother's plan all along? Was this why she had sent him away to Ryerson? And where had the money come from to pay for his private education? Had Tucker Rixby paid for that as well? Maybe it was Tucker who had suggested the idea. Maybe he had sent Lance away so he could have Raquel all to himself.

On the surface, it looked like a plausible theory. It was what he had believed for a time, and so he could understand why Caitlin thought his mother had packed him up and shipped him off to school like he was some sort of pesky inconvenience. He knew now that it was love for him and not Tucker that drove her into that marriage and her decision to send him away to school, but there was no way he could easily convey this to his wife.

~

L ance poked his head into Adam's room. The boy was sitting with his back to the door in the middle of the floor, surrounded by train tracks and his assorted Thomas toys.

"It's okay, Ashima, I can help," Adam said in a quiet voice as he pushed one of the train engines toward another, making chugging train noises along the way. Lance's heart swelled with pride and love. He would do anything for this boy, and though it wasn't his fate, if marrying his stinky-breathed old boss was the only way he could have given his son a better life, he would have done it.

He owed it to his mother to set things right with Caitlin, to make her see that sending him away to school had been a selfless act on the part of his mother, not a selfish one. Lance shifted, and a floorboard squeaked. Adam jerked his head up and spun around, then smiled when he saw his dad standing there.

"Daddy!" Adam yelled. He ran over and wrapped his little arms around Lance's legs. "Want to play Thomas with me?"

"Sure thing, bud," Lance said, and even though what he really wanted to do was change out of his work clothes, he joined Adam on the floor in the midst of the tracks, where his son brought him up to speed on the doings and antics of the various engines.

By the time Caitlin made her way upstairs twenty or so minutes later, Lance and Adam were embroiled in a massive effort to save poor Thomas from the yeti (a recruit from Adam's Imaginext toys) who had him trapped in a cave. She smiled at the two of them crawling around on the floor.

"So do either of you two have any ideas what you might feel like for dinner?" she asked. "And keep in mind it's after seven, so it's not going to be anything complicated."

Without looking up from his trains, Adam muttered, "Bananas and olives."

"Interesting idea there, bud," Lance said, "but I've got a better plan. How about we all go out to Chequers?"

The local burger joint wasn't a usual weeknight destination for them, but he considered it a bit of a peace offering to Caitlin.

"Can I have curly fries?" Adam jumped up, having forgotten all about poor Thomas and his predicament with the yeti.

"Sure thing," Lance said, and he raised his eyebrows in Caitlin's direction. "Curly fries for all!"

"It's pretty late," she said. "I could make something quick."

"You've already worked hard enough today." He untangled himself from Adam's toys to give his wife another hug. She kissed him on the cheek, and he knew his olive branch had been accepted, which in his opinion was much better than bananas and olives for dinner.

6

THE CULVER CREEK police force had not had a detective on staff at the time of the Lily Esposito murder, and it showed in the case file. The records were a mess and largely incomplete. In an effort to make sense of the chaos, Sage spread the papers out over his desk. Despite being focused on his work, he felt the eyes of his colleagues on him.

Maybe Sage hadn't gone out of his way to make friends with his coworkers, but it wasn't as if he had done anything to inspire the animosity the other police officers directed at him. He knew it wasn't really a personal thing. They resented Sage and the idea that an out-of-towner had joined their ranks and felt the implication was that they were just a bunch of dumb locals not up to the task of solving crimes. Nobody said this, of course, but Sage was pretty good at reading moods.

"Shuffling papers there, eh?" said Rod Smith, one of the more outspoken officers. "Guess, that's what they pay you the big bucks for."

He nodded to his cohorts, and they all laughed like a pack of teenage boys. What Sage wanted to say was that if the Culver Creek officer who had handled this murder investigation had done a better job of it, Sage wouldn't have to waste his time cleaning up the mess, but he knew better than to say anything so provocative.

The Lily Esposito investigation had been headed up by an Officer Bill Brighton. He was long since retired. Sage had looked him up. The state police had also had their own investigation going, and though the two agencies were supposed to be working together, Sage got the impression there had been a bit of friction there. In any case, it seemed to have only added to the chaos of the files.

"Anyone of you know Bill Brighton?" Sage asked.

"I know Bill," Steve Arlo said. He was one of the oldest members on the force. "What about him?"

"You know where I could find him? There were some questions I wanted to ask him," Sage said.

"Questions about what?" Steve asked, suspicious.

"The Lily Esposito murder," Sage said.

"That's what they got you working on?" Rod said. "Well, damn, way to be current and on top of things."

This earned him another round of laughter from his cronies, but Steve ignored the hubbub and gave Sage Bill's contact details.

Brighton's wife led Sage down the steps of the bi-level home and opened the slider door to the patio. Sage stepped out into a small but well-maintained backyard. Not far from a broken-in Adirondack chair, a gray-haired man carefully refilled a bird feeder with seed. Bill gave him a nod but stayed focused on his task.

On the phone, Bill had not seemed eager to delve back

into the old investigation, but he told Sage to come by and pay him a visit. Sage got the feeling Bill saw him as some sort of annoying mosquito bothering him here in his backyard oasis.

"The weather was perfect that morning," Bill said as he scooped more birdseed from the container by his feet and poured it into the feeder. "The sun was shining, but it wasn't hot yet. The air was clean and crisp. That's what I think of anytime we get a day like that. I think of that awful morning."

Satisfied the birds would have enough to eat for a while, Bill attached the cap back to the feeder, then put his scoop into the container of seed by his feet. He grunted as he hefted the tub off the ground. Sage offered to carry it for him, but Bill batted his arm away. They walked back to the patio, and after Bill set the tub down, they sat in a couple of aluminum patio chairs.

The call from Honoree Esposito had come in at five minutes to six, shortly after she discovered that her daughters were not in their bedroom or anywhere else in the house. On the 911 recording Sage had listened to at least a dozen times, her voice sounded frantic.

"Goyle and I headed over to the creek," Bill said. "He's gone now, Ray Goyle. Had a heart attack a few years ago." Bill looked out at the backyard, but his eyes looked like they were seeing something much further away, an awful morning nineteen years ago. "Honoree said the girls liked to go down there sometimes to try and catch crayfish."

Sage was still getting to know Culver Creek's geography, but he knew the spot along the creek where Lily Esposito had been killed. He had spent several minutes standing there studying the landscape, watching the way the water flowed over the rocks where the creek made a slight jog to the right.

"Goyle spotted her first," Brighton continued. "It was just a flash of color in the water where there shouldn't have been anything, part of her pajamas sticking out of the water. We ran in and pulled her out, laid her down on the bank, but nothing could be done. She had been in there for hours."

The report from the medical examiner listed the official cause of death as drowning but noted that the blow to the head had been severe and might have been enough to kill her even if she had not been dumped into the water.

"It was only after we pulled her out that we saw the other girl, Jade. She was sitting right there, only a few feet away, but she was so still I thought she must be dead too." Bill shook his head at this. "She was in shock of course. I don't think she ever really recovered."

In the notes Sage read through, Jade stopped speaking after her sister's death. She likely had seen the whole thing. At any rate, there was a very good chance she knew who had murdered her sister, but she hadn't been able to provide the police with any information.

"Do you think it could have been her?" Sage asked. From what he could tell, the police had been very delicate with the girl. Well, they had to be, but still, had anyone even thought to investigate her? At the very least, her behavior seemed suspicious.

"Jade?" Brighton asked as if Sage had just suggested it was little green space aliens that were responsible for the murder. "No. It wouldn't have been possible. She was just four years old and small for her age. The blow to the head was pretty severe. It was from someone much bigger and stronger than a tiny four-year-old girl."

Sage knew Brighton was probably right. He had read the coroner's report. Whoever had struck Lily Esposito would have likely been standing facing her, bringing the weapon down and striking her where the top of her skull met her forehead. Based on its irregular shape, the weapon was presumed to be a rock, but it had never been found. Sage wasn't surprised. He had seen that spot of the creek. It was full of rocks. Any one of them could have been the murder weapon.

There was something else in the coroner's report, not stated but implied. Whoever had killed Lily Esposito had stood there facing her. She had not tried to run away. There were no signs that she had struggled with her attacker. The girl knew her murderer. Sage was sure of it. His mind flashed momentarily to his sister Melodie before he shifted his attention back to the case at hand.

In his head, he heard Honoree Esposito's frantic voice on the 911 call. It sounded exactly like what you would expect a mother who had just found out her children were missing would sound like. It was almost too perfect.

The police report indicated that the girls had climbed out their first-floor bedroom window sometime after ten that night. It was not the first time they had done so. Once, a neighbor had called after seeing the girls escape, and Honoree had gone outside to apprehend them. Another night, she heard a noise from their room and caught them in the act. Why were the kids so determined to escape their home?

And another thing. The girls could have been missing for as much as eight hours before their disappearance was reported.

"Why did it take the mother until six in the morning to report them missing?" Sage asked.

Bill acted like he hadn't heard the question. He pointed out at the recently filled feeder, where a finch was now perched.

"That's Pete," Bill said. "He likes to keep all the other birds in line, make sure everyone takes their turn and behaves nicely. He's like a bird cop."

Sage was not interested in avian members of law enforcement.

"Wouldn't she have heard the window open?" Sage asked.

"Honoree had just come home from working a double shift at Rixby," Bill said. "She crashed pretty early."

"And she didn't hear the kids leaving? She was only in the next room over, right?"

"There was a bathroom in between," Bill said, watching the birds at the feeder.

"Still, you would think—" Sage began before Bill cut him off.

"It was hot that night, so she had an old box fan going in her bedroom window. You ever sleep next to a box fan?"

Sage acknowledged that he had.

"Well, then you know how loud those things are," Bill said. "You can't hear a television blaring in the next room, let alone two little girls sneaking out a window."

"But why were those kids so determined to run away from that house?" Sage asked.

"They weren't running away." Bill turned away from the bird feeder to give Sage his full attention. "They were just kids having fun. I did the same sort of thing when I was a kid."

Sage felt like the family angle hadn't been explored closely enough by the police. He couldn't be sure that

Honoree was guilty, but the fact that the police hadn't really treated her as a suspect bothered him.

"It's just—" he began, but Bill cut him off again.

"She had been having trouble sleeping." Bill let out a sigh that it seemed he had been holding in for twenty years.

"What do you mean? After the murder?" Sage asked.

Bill waved away his question. "She was working some extra shifts at Rixby, trying to bring in enough money to keep up with the mortgage. Her schedule was all messed up, and she wasn't sleeping well."

"So then she would have been awake when the girls left," Sage said. His annoyance had crept into his voice.

"She had started taking some sleeping pills. Some over-the-counter stuff," Bill explained. "I don't remember the name. It's in the case notes somewhere. Anyway, that stuff really knocked her out. She probably could have slept through an earthquake, let alone a window opening two rooms away."

"And can anyone corroborate this? Did her doctor prescribe it?" Sage asked.

"It was over-the-counter," Bill said. "She blamed herself for what happened. She never forgave herself for taking those pills, for sleeping through everything."

"Yeah, but—"

"She didn't do it," Bill said in a clipped, angry tone.

"Well, then who was it?" Sage had been trying his best to keep his frustration in check. He came out to Brighton's place prepared to give the retired cop the benefit of the doubt. The files were a mess, but Sage realized that Bill had been in over his head with the murder investigation. Plus, there was the confusion with the state police taking things over. He wanted to give Bill a chance to prove he wasn't completely incompetent. Instead, retired Officer Brighton seemed to be confirming every bad opinion Sage had of him.

Bill had the chance to catch the killer when all the leads were fresh, and instead he had botched everything up. But did this frustration he was feeling have anything to do with Lily Esposito? Wasn't it possible he was thinking of another police investigation, another dead girl, another unsolved murder? He shook off the thought. Now was not the time.

Bill had turned back to watching the feeder, where a few more birds now joined the finch, but Sage could see that faraway look in his eyes again. He was back there, back in 2001. There was sadness in Bill's eyes, a certain way his face sagged. Sage got the impression he wasn't alone in his frustration. It was a long time before he spoke, and when he finally did, his voice was so quiet it was almost a whisper.

"It was someone we missed, someone who must have been right there under our noses the whole time, but he slipped by us," Bill said.

"I saw a police sketch of a suspect in the file," Sage said. "Who was that?"

Bill glanced back toward the house, and Sage's eyes followed. A curtain in the kitchen window fluttered. The retired cop turned back to him, but there was a strange look in his eyes.

"That was our only lead," Bill said.

Sage couldn't say what it was, but he got the distinct impression that there was something Bill was keeping from him.

"It was a psychic who provided us with the description."

"A psychic?" Sage tried to keep his tone level, but there was no disguising his disappointment.

To have made crucial mistakes in the investigation

was one thing, but for Bill to actually waste time with some purported psychic was more than Sage could stomach.

Bill nodded, and there was something in his expression that Sage did not like. This man was hiding something. He was sure of it.

∽

Sage's microwave dinged to let him know dinner was ready. He stuck the frozen pot pie on a plate and carried it to a kitchen table scattered with pages from the Lily Esposito file. After his meeting with Brighton, he had gone back through the thing hoping to group together anything that had to do with the alleged psychic. He didn't need that nonsense getting in the way of his investigation. Facts were what solved crimes. Truth was what he cared about, not woo-woo stuff.

His mother went to a psychic a few times. For all Sage knew, she was still giving money to that charlatan. No doubt she wouldn't tell him after the way he had reacted.

A few months ago, Sage had gone back home to help his mother with a leaking kitchen faucet. It was a thing his father would have helped with before, but he had moved out more than a year prior. Maybe their separation would have happened anyway, but Sage couldn't help but feel that their marriage was one more thing that the unknown murderer had killed.

Sage had his head under her kitchen sink and a wrench in his hand when his mom casually mentioned that she had been a few times to see a psychic.

"Debbie at the bank recommended her," his mom said.

"You would think someone at the bank would have

better financial sense," Sage said as he tightened the nut and shimmied out of the cabinet.

"Oh, Lorena is very reasonably priced, cheaper than that useless therapist I was seeing," she said.

Sage placed the wrench back in the little toolbox, then tried out the sink and left it running long enough to wash his hands.

"Lorena had a lot of insightful things to say," his mom said.

"I'm sure." Sage splashed some water on his face, then turned off the tap and dried himself off with some paper towels. "She tell you who the killer is, by chance? That would be some useful information."

"She said Melodie wants us to know how much she loves us," his mother said.

Sage threw the paper towels in the trash and sighed before turning to face his mother. "Ma, that's the kind of BS those sort of people feed to you. They prey on your grief and are trying to make a quick buck."

"Lorena's not like that," his mother said confidently. She patted the chair beside her at the table.

She had set out a cold can of soda for Sage, and he took her up on the offer, popping open the cap and guzzling about half the can of cold, sweet beverage before sitting down.

"Just maybe don't give this Lorena any more money," Sage said. "You know with Dad moved out, you've got to think about your expenses more."

His mother ignored this advice. "She said something else too. She said she got the feeling that Melodie had a premonition about her death. That she tried to tell someone about it. I couldn't think of anything, but maybe. Well, I was wondering, did Melodie say anything to you before . . ." His mother let her voice trail off as she waved her hand in the air to avoid having to directly mention Melodie's murder.

Sage, who was about to take another sip of soda, froze with the can in midair. His hand tensed enough that the aluminum can flexed in his grip. He made a concerted effort to lower the can calmly without spilling it.

"See, this is what I mean," Sage said. This came out louder than he intended. "This woman's got you going around accusing people of ignoring some message that Melodie was trying to deliver."

"I'm not accusing anyone," his mother said defensively.

"This is what they do, these psychics," Sage said. "They make these vague sort of statements, because they know how people are. They'll read things into them. I mean, anything can look like some sign or some message if you analyze it long enough."

His blood was pumping, and he was too fired up to sit at the table. He stood up and started walking across the kitchen, even though he had nowhere to go.

"Sit down," his mother insisted. "It's no big deal. I just went to see Lorena a few times, and you're right, I can't afford to keep spending money like that."

"It's getting late," Sage said. "I've got to get going."

"Now? I thought you were going to stay for dinner."

"I can't," he lied. "I've got to get back."

That afternoon, before he pulled out of his mother's driveway. He spent several minutes sitting in his car taking deep breaths and trying to calm his racing heart. Mostly he tried to not think about the last time he had seen his sister alive.

7

CAITLIN STOOD at the bathroom counter and slipped the blister pack from her current box of Pacifcleon and pushed out the evening's pill. There was a week's worth remaining in this box, and five more boxes were stashed at the back of the linen closet, but they wouldn't last forever. She needed to track down more. She would check eBay again in the morning. As she put the box back into her drawer, she noticed the expiration date on the flap. It was nearly a year past its recommended date. She wondered if the date really mattered. Would the pills lose their efficacy at some point? Most likely she would run out long before that ever happened, but she didn't want to think about that.

Adam had another bad dream the previous night, and she had slept through it. Lance was the one who had gone in and comforted Adam. She felt guilty about the whole thing even though Lance tried to reassure her that it wasn't all that bad.

"He was back asleep in minutes," Lance had said.

Still, she should have been there to comfort him. She should have at least heard him. It made her hesitate just a moment before swallowing the pill. It chased away dreams, but it also made her sleep soundly—so soundly that she didn't always hear her son crying out in distress down the hall.

Well, maybe they would get lucky and there would be no nightmare tonight. At least she could guarantee that she wouldn't have one. She swallowed down the pill and went into the bedroom.

Lance was already in bed. The door was shut, and Caitlin could see that Lance had gone and locked the door. It was one of his quirks. It made no sense to her that the same man who routinely left his car unlocked in a crowded parking lot would also lock their bedroom door inside their own house. She had always found it a weird but tolerable habit. Since Adam had started having his nightmares, though, the locked door bothered her. She had said something to Lance before, but he didn't listen.

"I don't want to keep the door locked in case Adam has a bad dream," she said.

"I'll wake up and go to his room if he does," Lance said.

"Or I might," Caitlin said.

"Unlikely," Lance muttered.

She could remind him that just last week she had been the one who woke up and went to Adam when she heard him screaming, but she still felt guilty about last night. How had she not heard a thing?

"Still, there's no need to lock the door," Caitlin said.

"Fine, whatever," Lance said.

She went over and unlocked it. Lance didn't exactly sigh, but he exhaled a little louder than normal. It reminded her of her father.

∿

C aitlin missed her father. She missed so many things about Raymond Gordon Pendergast. She missed the cherry-tinged scent of his pipe tobacco. She missed the way he would sit in that worn-out recliner in their living room playing endless games of solitaire on a little folding tray table. His quiet, easy-going manner had been the perfect balance to her mother's loud hyperactivity. Growing up, Caitlin had always seen her father as an ally. They were kindred spirits, doomed to live in a household dominated by loud, brash Luanne Pendergast. Only later did it occur to Caitlin that her father had, for whatever reason, elected to spend his life with Luanne, whereas she had no choice in the matter.

This was also around the time she realized that his customary way of dealing with her mother's erratic mood swings and crazy plans was to sigh and shrug things off. How would things have been different for her if just once her father put his foot down and stood up to Luanne? What if he had intervened at the very beginning—the first time she had one of those terrible dreams?

When Caitlin was four years old, she had a nightmare about her Grandma Mimi. It was vivid and horrifying. Even now, twenty-six years later, she could still recall snatches of it if she closed her eyes. She remembered the sound, a horrible screeching noise, metal on metal. She saw broken glass and then vividly bright red blood. It stained her grandmother's pink blouse. It dripped onto the ground. It was the sight of that blood that made her wake up screaming and sent her running into her parents' bedroom. Her mother soothed her and comforted her and told her it wasn't real, but her mother was wrong.

Two days later, Caitlin was eating a bowl of Froot

Loops at the kitchen table when the phone rang. Her mother set down the towel she had been using to dry dishes to take the call. Caitlin watched the stricken look on her mother's face. She turned slowly to face her daughter, and there was both awe and fear in her expression.

Grandma Mimi had been in a car accident. Another car had run through a stop sign and crashed into hers. She was in the hospital with broken ribs and a lacerated spleen.

"It's just like your dream," her mother said as she drove them to the hospital later that morning.

Her grandmother had two black eyes and a bandage around her head when they stepped into the hospital room, but Caitlin was relieved to not see any blood.

"I'm going to be just fine," Grandma Mimi said when she saw the worried look on her granddaughter's face. "It takes more than a little car accident to take this old gal down."

After that, her mother made it a point to ask Caitlin about her dreams each morning. At first, Caitlin enjoyed telling her mother about the harmless dreams she could recall from the previous evening, but then there were the dark, ugly dreams. The ones she didn't want to relive again. Although it wasn't a particularly awful dream, she had a dream about her father suffering an injury, and then a few days later while trying to hang up a shelf, he cut his hand. It was nothing serious, but her mother claimed it was proof that Caitlin had a gift.

Luanne bought a notebook, and she would write down the dreams Caitlin described each morning. Caitlin soon tired of the exercise, but her mother was insistent. And her father? Caitlin recalled the disapproving sighs and his sense of dissatisfaction with the whole business, but those had little bearing on her mother's crusade.

It was more than a year after she had the dream about her grandmother that Caitlin had the awful dream about the woman with the red hair. Caitlin had never seen the woman before in her life, but she could see her clearly in her dream. What she could also see clearly was the violent struggle with the man with the beard, and then the worst part of all, the gun. The explosive sound was even louder than the horrible screeching from her Grandma Mimi dream, but just like that dream, there was blood. Lots and lots of blood.

Caitlin woke up screaming. Her mother was there to comfort her, but she hadn't come empty-handed. She had her notebook, and in the dim glow from Caitlin's bedside lamp, she scratched out notes, frowning at the words on the page.

"A woman with red hair? A man with a beard? Who can that be?" her mother asked.

Caitlin didn't know, but soon she would. It was a few days later when the news came out about the murder that had occurred in their quiet suburban town. A domestic argument had turned deadly when a man turned a gun on his ex-girlfriend. Her mother showed her the pictures from the newspaper.

"That's them, isn't it?" her mother asked. "That's the man and the woman from your dream."

Caitlin recognized them right away. She was horrified, but her mother seemed delighted.

"Don't you see what this means?" Luanne said. "You can see the future! You're like a superhero."

When Caitlin was in elementary school, her mother became a regular at the off-track betting place a few towns away. She would search for horses with names that matched things Caitlin had described in her dreams. Sometimes the connections were a stretch. In one dream, Caitlin described seeing a small man, and her mother bet on a horse named Pot of Gold under the assumption that this small man must have been a leprechaun. Sometimes the horses would win, and Luanne saw this as confirmation, but it seemed that just as often the horses lost.

The horses were Luanne and Caitlin's secret until the day Luanne bet the $300 that was supposed to pay for the new water heater on a horse named Canadian Pride after Caitlin had a dream about a moose. Canadian Pride came in dead last. Luanne had no choice but to tell her husband what had happened to the water heater money. It finally happened. Her father did more than sigh and shrug.

Though her parents were behind their closed bedroom door, she could hear her father's stern shouting. It was memorable because Raymond Pendergast never raised his voice, but the other thing Caitlin remembered was that even then, when he could have put an end to the whole dream business once and for all, what he chose to focus on was Luanne's gambling. He forbade Luanne from betting on any more horse races. Caitlin knew this would not end Luanne's fascination with her dreams.

Was it fair to blame her father for his failure to call an end to Luanne's endless recording of Caitlin's dreams? Couldn't Caitlin have stood up for herself? It's true she was just a child, but she could have refused to participate in Luanne's scheme. She didn't have to share all her dreams with her mother. So why did she?

Was it because she felt uncomfortable lying to her mother? Caitlin liked this explanation, but she knew it wasn't true. Even by the age of ten, she was quite accomplished at lying to Luanne, whether it was simple fibs like saying she had completed her homework or cleaned her bedroom when she hadn't, or more serious lies like the one she told about that scrape on her knee that hadn't come from tripping in the kitchen but from riding her bike down the road at night, when she was supposed to be in bed, or that time she ate all the cupcakes for the bake sale and blamed it on her friend Mara Mooney. Caitlin had no problem lying to her mother, so why didn't she lie about the dreams? Maybe it was partly about the attention. Her mother loved her and patiently listened to her stories about school or her favorite television shows, but there was definitely a different level of attention that Luanne paid to Caitlin's descriptions of her dreams. It did make her feel special to have what her mother felt was an amazing gift.

Caitlin had always felt more comfortable talking to her father. He took things in stride and seemed to genuinely listen to what she had to say, except where dreams were concerned. He never came straight out and said he didn't care about her dreams. That wasn't his way. Instead he indicated his impatience with the sort of sighs that he generally reserved for Luanne.

Where dreams were concerned, Luanne was Caitlin's ally. Luanne was the only one who really understood how significant Caitlin's dreams were. Still, Caitlin was miles ahead of her mother in understanding how her dreams worked.

Long before Canadian Pride lost that race, Caitlin had realized her mother was all wrong with the horse betting. Not all of her dreams came true, but when they did, they were never the nice, happy dreams. It was only ever the dark, frightening ones that came true.

Caitlin's dreams terrified her. They were graphic, horrifying nightmares, but they were more than just nightmares. Her dreams were real things. The burden was too great to carry on her own. Sharing them with Luanne was one way to lessen the load. The other thing about her dreams was that she only ever had these psychic dreams about someone close to her—a friend or relative or someone in close physical proximity—someone in town or close by. Sometimes she wondered if it was because even if she didn't recognize these people, it was someone she had come in contact with at some point. Maybe she had passed by them in the grocery store aisle or they had been walking through the park when she was there riding on the swings.

At least that was how it had always been, but then she dreamed about the little girl.

Lance didn't understand that Adam's dreams were more than just harmless nightmares, and Caitlin fully intended to keep it that way. If there was some way she could stop her son from ever having to experience another terrifying dream, she would, but short of drugging him, the next best solution was to convince him that his bad dreams were nothing to be scared of, that they weren't real. She would never force him to divulge the details of his dreams to her while she jotted them down in a notebook. She would never heap praise on him for having some supposed gift. And under no circumstances would she ever drag him to some police station in some godforsaken Pennsylvania town to help solve a murder.

8

LANCE AWOKE naked in the bathroom. He had a dizzying moment of panic before he assured himself that it was in fact their bathroom. The reason he didn't recognize it at first glance was the state of disarray it was in. Bottles and tubes of every sort were strewn about the large counter. He counted seven towels in various wadded-up states on the floor. He stared at the dark mass in the sink until he realized it was his clothes. For some reason, a pair of his jeans and a navy blue polo shirt had been left to soak there. He pawed at the soaked clothing and saw that his socks and underwear were in there too. Scratch that. One sock. Where the hell was his other sock? And why were the rest of his clothes in the sink? Obviously he was trying to wash them, but why?

He sniffed at his wet clothes in the sink. They had a metallic sort of odor. Was that blood? A wave of dizziness overtook him, and he grabbed the counter for support. He needed to get ahold of himself. Besides the wet clothes in the sink, was there anything alarming in the bathroom? He looked around. Well, a huge mess, but mostly it just looked like he had raided the linen closet and flung stuff everywhere. There was nothing here to make him panic, but he knew what he needed to do.

It took him a few seconds and several deep breaths before he worked up the nerve to open the door into their bedroom. The light from the bathroom spilled out into the dark room, revealing Caitlin still sleeping soundly in the bed. She was sleeping, wasn't she? He held his breath as he watched, and only released it when he finally saw the comforter moving slowly up and down with her breathing. Everything was fine. He could relax.

Then he looked across the bedroom and saw something that made his blood run cold. The bedroom door was wide open. He remembered Caitlin insisting they leave the door unlocked despite his protests.

He raced down the hall to Adam's room. Belatedly he remembered that he didn't have any clothes on, but he didn't care. He just needed to make sure Adam was safe. The floor creaked as he stepped into his son's room, and Adam stirred in the bed. Out the window, Lance saw the indigo sky of early morning. The sun would be up soon, which meant Adam and Caitlin would wake up. Lance had a disaster of a bathroom to get cleaned before then.

~

L ance threw on a pair of sweatpants and a T-shirt before heading back into the bathroom to survey the damage. He had made a huge mess, but he figured he could clean it up before Caitlin woke up. The problem was he didn't remember where everything had been, and even if Caitlin wasn't the neatest person in the world, she would still be able to see that things were out of place. She would have questions. He needed to have an answer.

So he struck upon a solution. He would give the bathroom a thorough spring cleaning. His cover story would be that he couldn't sleep and decided the bathroom was long overdue for a thorough cleaning. It wasn't even a lie. There was all kinds of crap they hadn't touched in years shoved to the back of their linen closet. Did they really need hundreds of half-used mini bottles of hotel shampoo?

He loaded his sopping wet clothes and all the towels scattered about the bathroom into a laundry basket and carried them down to the laundry room. If he started the load now, it might wake Caitlin and Adam. So he left them in the basket. He ran the risk of Caitlin walking into the laundry room and finding his clothes inexplicably drenched, but he decided this was unlikely.

He carried a big black trash bag upstairs to the bathroom and set about emptying the linen closet of anything that looked vaguely like trash. He chucked in all but a handful of the hotel shampoos and soaps. Then he found a mostly empty bottle of mouthwash so old that the plastic had started to turn yellow. According to the date stamped on the back, the stuff had expired four years ago. This gave him a new mission, and he began checking expiration dates on every package he came across. Cough syrup, ibuprofen, and a bottle of nasal spray went into the trash. Then he hit the mother lode. Shoved to the back of the closet were boxes of Caitlin's sleeping pills. Judging by the expiration dates on the boxes, she must have forgotten about them years ago. He tossed them all into the garbage bag.

When the closet had been purged of all its extraneous contents, he set about rearranging the remaining items neatly before refolding and stacking all the towels so they looked like they belonged on a department store shelf. With the organization task complete, he grabbed a spray bottle and paper towels to clean all the surfaces. When he was finally done, it was light out. He took a step back and surveyed his handiwork. Was it too much? Had he gone overboard?

Caitlin was still sleeping soundly when he hauled the full trash bag out through the bedroom and downstairs to the garage. He realized it was garbage day. Well, that was a lucky coincidence. It made his early morning bathroom cleaning seem just a touch more justified. He grabbed a second bag and went around the house emptying all the bins before wheeling the filled container out to the curb.

The wheels made a thunderous noise on the pavement. It was enough to wake the dead, let alone his wife and son. So when he headed back inside, he went straight to the laundry room to get the load started. He dumped everything into the washer and added the detergent—but wait! Had he checked the pockets? He hauled his pants back out and searched them. He turned up a quarter, a paperclip and a business card. He dropped the pants back into the machine and started it before he took another look at the odds and ends in his hand.

Was that blood on the corner of the business card? His heart began to race as he turned it over, but then his eyes fell on the words *Culver Creek*. It was the dream whisperer's card, and that red stain wasn't blood but tomato juice from Corey's bloody mary.

He was surprised he hadn't thrown the card out. Maybe he was meant to keep it. Maybe he was meant to call her. Caitlin had specifically said no shrinks, but this woman wasn't a shrink at all. This morning's panic was still fresh in his mind. He couldn't go on like this. Even if he was able to convince Caitlin to lock the bedroom door, that wouldn't stop the bigger issue—Adam's nightmares. Sure, right now that was all they were, but it was only a matter of time before the nightmares turned to something else.

In his head he saw a linoleum floor splattered with blood and felt the pain in his bloodstained fist. Moreover, he felt the confusion and utter helplessness. He didn't want Adam to ever have to feel that way. Could this dream whisperer woman help? Maybe. At least it was better than doing nothing.

He heard someone coming down the stairs and shoved the card into his sweatpants pocket before heading out into the kitchen.

9

SAGE SPENT most of the day dealing with a stolen car case that didn't require a modicum of actual detective work. The victim already knew her worthless ex had taken the vehicle, and sure enough, when they located it, there he was passed out behind the wheel. Unfortunately for the car's owner, a large maple tree now resided where the engine should have been. The busted radiator was still steaming when the police arrived on the scene.

By the time they made it back to the station and got all the paperwork completed, it was after four. Sage kept a close eye on the time. Steve Arlo plopped a stack of forms down on his desk for him to sign off on.

"That's the last of it," Steve said.

"Thanks," Sage said as he quickly began to scribble his signature in all the right spots, glancing again at the clock as he did so.

"Not quite quitting time yet," Steve said with a little bark of a laugh.

"Got a meeting with a witness scheduled," Sage said.

A worried look passed over Steve's face as he glanced at the pile of completed paperwork. "About the stolen car?"

"No, not that," Sage said quickly. "This is about the Lily Esposito murder."

Steve nodded. "That's a relief. For a second there, I thought I was going to have to redo all this."

Culver Coffee was one of the few thriving businesses on the small town's main street, and so Sage had chosen it as the spot to meet up with Maura Gautner, who had worked at Rixby with Honoree years ago. She smiled when he walked in. Even without a uniform, she made him right away.

"You have very good posture," was her response when he asked.

All he had told her on the phone was that he had a few questions about her former coworker Honoree. Maura hadn't been interviewed by police during the original investigation, but as Sage started digging, her name turned up a couple of times. Besides working with Honoree, she had on more than one occasion given Honoree rides to and from work, and possibly had also helped Honoree locate the apartment that she and Jade had moved into a few months after the murder.

Maura still lived in Culver Creek but no longer worked at Rixby. She had a part-time position at the grocery store. "It's better than the factory, but only just," she had told him on the phone.

"We worked in different parts of the factory," Maura said. "I only ever saw her in the break room or at church on Sundays."

"Did you know her before her daughter was killed, or only after?" Sage asked. He scalded his tongue on the cup of too-hot green tea in front of him.

Maura shuddered a little at the word *killed*.

"I knew her before too," Maura said. "That's when she started coming to St. John's. My sister taught the girls Sunday school."

"They attended church regularly?" Sage asked.

"More than just the holidays, if that's what you're asking," Maura said. "It was just Honoree and the girls, though. Rick was never there."

"That was her husband? The girls' father?"

Maura nodded. She sipped the coffee in front of her.

"I was under the impression he didn't live with them," Sage said.

"Honoree eventually had enough and kicked him out," Maura said. "I guess that must have been a year or so before the murder. She should have ditched him long ago. He was a drunk and couldn't hold a job."

"Did he ever hit her? The girls?"

"Well, you don't really know what goes on in someone's house, do you?" Maura asked. "I definitely wouldn't have put it past him."

There was almost nothing about Rick Esposito in the case files. Had the police even considered him a suspect?

Sage thought of the morning's encounter with the drunk ex and the stolen car. People didn't make the best decisions when inebriated. Could Rick Esposito have gone on a bender and done something to harm his own daughter?

"Do you think he could have murdered Lily?" Sage asked.

"Rick?" Maura frowned. "It's hard to imagine how anyone could do a thing like that, let alone her own father, but if he was liquored up, not acting like himself . . . I don't know. Maybe."

"A neighbor in the apartment building Honoree and Jade moved to said you used to drive her to work," Sage said.

Maura nodded. "She had car troubles a lot and didn't always have the money to get it fixed. She missed a lot of work after Lily died, and then those heartless bastards at Rixby laid her off. Really, who does a thing like that?"

"What about Jade?" Sage asked. "Did you know her at all?"

"That poor child," Maura said with a shake of her head. "That awful night, Honoree really lost both of her daughters. Jade was never the same after that."

"I guess there were too many memories here for Jade. That must have been why she left."

"Left where?" Maura asked. Less than a second later, Sage saw a look of regret flash across her face.

"Does Jade still live here in Culver Creek?" Sage asked.

"What, now? Oh, I don't think so. I mean, I wouldn't know, would I? I lost touch with Honoree after she was fired. Tried checking in on her when I could, but I got the impression she wanted to be left alone."

Sage studied Maura. There was something she wasn't telling him, something about Jade.

"You sure you don't know where Jade is?" Sage asked.

Maura pushed her coffee cup away even though it was still half full.

"No, like I said, I lost touch after Honoree got fired." She looked out the window at something. Sage followed her eyes but saw nothing. "I didn't realize how late it was. I have to get going. I have to get dinner started."

After she got up, Sage glanced at his phone. It was just after five.

As Sage stood up to leave, he heard someone call his name and turned around to see Steve Arlo at the counter.

"Guess I'm not the only one who can't stand to drink that swill at the station," Arlo said.

Sage offered up a half smile as a response. He was pretty sure if he confessed that his to-go cup was filled with green tea and not coffee, he wouldn't be helping his image any with the rest of the Culver Creek police force. Working with him today had proved that Steve was a nice enough guy, but no way was he going to keep some juicy tidbit like the fact that Sage was the kind of weirdo who drank green tea to himself.

"Nice work today," Sage said.

"Hey," Steve said. "It's Cubberson's birthday today. The guys were going to head over to the Creek Tavern to have a few rounds of beer in his honor. Why don't you join us?"

Sage appreciated the olive branch Steve was offering. He had a pretty good idea Steve hadn't cleared this with Rodney or the others, and he could already picture the looks of disgust on their faces when he sauntered in to spoil their fun night out. In the interest of diplomacy, he considered accepting, but he knew it would be suicide. If he was worried how green tea would go over, he couldn't imagine how his colleagues would react when he ordered a Coke instead of a Budweiser.

"Thanks," Sage said. "Another time maybe. I've got some things I need to take care of tonight."

He hoped his excuse didn't sound too hollow.

"Sure," Steve said.

As he walked out of the coffee shop, Sage felt Steve's eyes on him.

≈

S age parked in the little pull-off near the creek, then followed a path worn smooth by the feet of fishermen who came down to this spot to do some angling. The sun was getting low in the sky, and he imagined this would be a scenic spot to watch the sunset, but for him the natural beauty was eclipsed by the knowledge he was only feet away from the spot where a little girl had gasped her last desperate breaths, only to fill her lungs with creek water.

They found Jade in a catatonic state only a short distance from where her sister lay dead in the water. Had she seen the whole thing? By all accounts she became non-verbal after the incident, but Sage had checked the school records, and Jade had continued to attend school up until her mother died in her junior year of high school. After that, the girl seemed to drop off the map.

She must have eventually started speaking again. Why hadn't the police ever gone back and interviewed her? Surely she must have remembered something from that night. Those he had talked to said Jade was never the same after Lily's murder, that it had left her irreparably damaged.

Well, murder could do that, couldn't it? What would he be doing right now if Melodie had never been murdered? He imagined himself living in some swanky apartment driving a luxury car with some bigwig corporate career, but somehow he didn't think that would have been his destiny. Maybe he wouldn't have become a cop, but something told him he wouldn't have been living a substantially different life.

And his parents? Would they still be together if Melodie hadn't been killed? Their relationship had always been strained. As far back as his middle school years, Sage could remember lying awake in bed as he listened to them arguing from the other side of his wall. He had wondered then if they would get a divorce, and if they did, which one he would have to live with. Had he and Melodie been the glue holding their parents together, and once she was gone the bond became too brittle? Or maybe it was the stress of the whole thing—the murder investigation, that constant feeling of expectation. He could recall the three of them sitting around in that house waiting for the phone to ring and deliver the answers they all so desperately craved.

The murder was the worst part, but the not knowing was its own special hell. That sort of thing might have been enough to destroy a perfectly happy marriage, let alone one that was on the rocks.

Was it that much worse for Jade, who had been with her sister the night she was killed? Surely she must have felt helpless and even partly responsible. Then there was the fact that she was most likely an eyewitness. Did she have no recollection of that night? Or was there another reason she had never spoken to the police?

Bill was sure Jade had not killed her sister, and Sage was inclined to agree, but what if the medical examiner had gotten things wrong? Could Lily have been sitting or squatting in the water when she was attacked. If so, her younger sister might have then been able to strike her from above. Maybe it was an accident. Jade could have been carrying a rock that was too heavy for her tiny arms, and as she struggled to hold onto it, the wet rock slipped through her hands and hit her sister in the head. But the autopsy report made it clear that Lily had been hit with force, a rock dropped from just a few inches above her wouldn't have been capable of causing the sort of injury she sustained.

Did he want it to be Jade because it would have fit so neatly? It would explain all of Jade's strange behavior, but so would watching your older sister have her skull bashed in right before your eyes. Murder could have a devastating impact on families, but it didn't make those relatives murderers.

He thought of a post on the web sleuth forum by someone who used the handle DaddysLilGirl. She was the first to suggest Sage Dorian had murdered his sister. His diminished academic performance, in her opinion, indicated his guilt. And why, she wanted to know, had he decided to go into law enforcement? He had been tempted to respond to the post and refute her various points, but that would have meant outing himself and revealing his identity. So he had kept quiet.

But what DaddysLilGirl and those who agreed with her conclusions failed to understand was the day that unknown person killed his sister, they had murdered part of him as well. How could he possibly go on living the same life when he wasn't the same person anymore?

He might be one of the few people out there who could relate to and understand Jade. He wanted so desperately to talk to her.

It was his assumption that when Jade disappeared after her mother's death, she had left town. With no surviving family members here, she would have wanted to put as much space between herself and this awful town as she could. That made perfect sense to Sage, but Maura's reaction made him wonder if he had gotten this wrong.

Maybe Jade hadn't left town right away. How long had she hung around for? Could she still be here? He doubted this. Culver Creek was not so large a town, and he hadn't been able to turn up anything on Jade since after her mother died. He should have pressed Maura. She knew something about Jade. Maybe at the very least she could give him some hint of where Jade had gone after she left Culver Creek.

He pulled his phone from his pocket and called her. It rang but went to voicemail. He did his best to sound kind but firm in his message, but he didn't think it mattered. She wasn't going to return his call.

Sage stood outside his car and studied the small strip of asphalt. To call it a parking area might have been too generous. It was nothing more than a strip of pavement adjacent to the shoulder of the road. There was room for two cars max.

The parking area was significant because it was the nearest creek access to where Lily had been killed. The surrounding area was residential. This little strip of pavement and the short path that led down to the creek was town property. The murderer had either walked down this little path to the creek or had done as Lily and Jade had most likely done and cut through a backyard to get there.

The terrain on the opposite side of the creek meant that the killer almost certainly came from this bank. Navigating the narrow path or one of the backyards in the dark suggested to Sage someone local, someone who knew the area well enough to find their way around in the dark.

No one recalled seeing a car parked in the pull-off that night, but Sage had read the interviews closely. While no one could recall seeing a car there, there was also no one who could say with certainty that the parking area had been empty. Sage slowly turned around. There was only one, maybe two houses that would have really had a clear view of the parking area, and then only from certain windows.

How likely was it that they would be looking out them in the middle of the night?

Someone could have parked in the parking area long enough to walk down to the creek and murder Lily and leave without anyone ever noticing, but why? And how would the killer have known Lily and Jade would be down at the creek? Had they arranged to meet the girls there? Was it just dumb luck?

Lily would have tried to run away from a stranger she met at the creek. She wouldn't have stood there facing them. His skin prickled as he stood there looking at his car parked on the shoulder, but he wasn't seeing it. He was seeing Melodie's little Kia, pulled off at the side of the road less than a hundred feet from where they had found her body.

She had been working the closing shift that night. She was killed sometime between ten fifteen and eleven p.m. Her car had been in working order, so why would she have pulled off the road and gotten out of it? Could she have stopped to try to help what she assumed was another motorist in distress? He knew his sister and couldn't see her doing something so foolish. Not that late at night, anyway. She would have called for help, perhaps, but she wouldn't have stopped her car and got out, unless it was someone she knew, and that was the thing, wasn't it? Like Lily Esposito, Melodie had been facing her killer. She hadn't tried to run away.

"There's something I need to talk to you about," Melodie said to him. He could hear her voice like she was right there, and like history repeating itself, he ignored her phantom voice. He stepped into his car, slammed the door after him and drove away like he could escape his past mistakes.

10

BRITTNEY'S OFFICE looked like it had come straight out of a catalog. Her desk and the bookcases held a small assortment of accent pieces, giving it just the right amount of color, but the whole room had an impersonal feel. Caitlin had never really noticed the lack of photographs and mementos in her boss's office before, and realizing it now made her feel pity for Brittney, who had devoted her life to her business. The pity didn't last long.

"I don't suppose you know why I asked you to come in here today," Brittney said. She sat behind her desk. Caitlin sat in one of the expensive but uncomfortable chairs across from her while Adam played quietly on the floor beside her. She had picked him up from school a little early so she could make it to this afternoon meeting on time.

Caitlin had misread Brittney's neutral tone on the phone and assumed the meeting was to discuss some new, upcoming project, but now she wasn't so sure. She shook her head because she felt too nervous to speak.

"Look, you're a hard worker, and your work is good, top-notch," Brittney said. "I've always thought so."

"Thank you," Caitlin said, still confused about where Brittney was going with this.

"But I think you also understand how important this business is to me, and how I can't afford anything that jeopardizes our accounts," Brittney continued.

"Of course," Caitlin said. Beside her, Adam asked her something, but she tried to silently signal to him that now was not the right time.

"Last week, you mistakenly sent an email to our liaison at the lottery commission that should have been sent here to the office," Brittney said.

Panic seized Caitlin. She had no recollection of making this error, but she realized it was a real possibility. She searched her memory for emails she had sent last week. Could she have made some sort of disparaging remark about the lottery people or the campaign? But nothing came to mind.

"I'm sorry," Caitlin stammered. "I didn't mean to."

Brittney waved the comment away. "It was no big deal, nothing damaging in the message. This time."

Adam was on his feet now, tugging on Caitlin's sleeve to get her attention. She couldn't gracefully ignore him. She held up a finger to pause the conversation with her boss and turned to her son.

"What is it?" Caitlin whispered to him.

"I'm tired of playing with my dinosaur," he said.

Caitlin dug through the tote bag she had brought with her and found some paper and a box of crayons, which she handed to Adam. Satisfied, he sat back down on the floor and began doodling.

"Sorry," Caitlin said, turning back to Brittney.

"Right, well. It's not the first mistake I've noticed," Brittney said. "And I'm worried that the next time you mistakenly send an email like this, it will be far more damaging."

"Honestly, it was just a stupid mistake," Caitlin said. "It won't happen again." She glanced at Adam humming to himself as he colored quietly. "We've been having a difficult time lately. It's Adam. He's been having these nightmares."

Brittney nodded in a way that Caitlin supposed was meant to be sympathetic, but it felt hollow.

"You know, I was going to say that you looked exhausted," Brittney said, "but I didn't want to be rude."

Caitlin nodded slowly. The truth was, thanks to her Pacifcleon, her sleep hadn't really been affected by Adam's nightmares. She slept soundly and tended to get a minimum of eight hours of solid sleep each night, but no way was she going to mention that now after her young, perky boss told her she looked tired.

"It's just a phase, I'm sure," Caitlin said, glancing again at Adam. He pressed so hard on the paper with the red crayon in his fist that she was sure it would break.

"You know, sometimes you just can't do it all," Brittney said. "You have to pick between being a mother and having a career."

Caitlin tried to tamp down the rage that began to boil inside of her. What did childless Brittney know about being a mother? And what kind of antiquated, sexist bullshit was this women-can't-be-mothers-and-have-careers philosophy of hers?

There were a lot of choice words Caitlin could have said, but all that came out was, "Are you firing me? Is that what this is?"

"No, absolutely not." Brittney acted mock-horrified at the very suggestion, even though that had clearly been the implication of her words. "But I can't stress enough that we can't afford to have any more errors like this. Maybe for now it's best that you don't email the clients directly, at all, just in case. We can do everything through an intermediary here at the office."

"It will take more time." Caitlin didn't often have reason to email clients, but when she did, it was usually to ask a quick question about a design she was working on. Having to do this through a third person here at the office would just add to the time it would take to get a response.

"It will," Brittney said, "but for now I think that's the best solution."

Her sentence was light, but still Caitlin bristled at the idea of being punished. Brittney began talking about some upcoming projects they would be working on, but Caitlin barely heard her as she silently fumed. It was only when Brittney rose from her desk that she realized the meeting had mercifully concluded. Caitlin stood as well, then leaned down to gather up Adam's things.

"Come on," she said to him. "We've got to get going."

"I drew you a picture," Adam said.

He handed her the masterpiece he had been working on, and at first glance all she saw was a page full of crayon scribbles, but soon the drawing resolved itself into an all-too-familiar picture. Her attention was drawn first to the intense red scribbles. Blood, she saw now. It spurted from the top of the little girl's head. It dripped from the rock held in the tall man's hand. It ran into the blue squiggles of water. Beyond this was another girl, a little shorter than the bleeding one. Caitlin could clearly see the tears on the girl's face. In an instant she was seeing not Adam's drawing in front of her, but the image that was so seared in her memory. This was exactly how it had looked, but how could Adam have known this? She knew how. He was drawing a picture of his nightmare, but why would he have a night-mare about this now?

"Caitlin?" From a million miles away, she heard Brittney saying her name. "Is everything okay?" Brittney asked.

Caitlin finally looked up from the drawing. She shoved it quickly into her tote bag, creasing its corner in her haste, not that this was a drawing she would be hanging on the refrigerator.

"Fine," Caitlin said. "We've got to go."

She bustled Adam into his windbreaker, but her hands were shaking too badly to zip it, and she left it undone as she led him out of her boss's office.

"Don't forget to stop in with Tonya and fill out that updated form," Brittney said.

Caitlin nodded even though she had no idea what form Brittney was talking about, and she had no intention of going to see Tonya. She just wanted to get the hell out of there.

As Caitlin drove home, her mind was a million miles away, or more accurately, nineteen years away. She was ten years old, but she could remember it as if it happened yesterday. She awoke in the dark with her heart racing from a terrifying dream. None of her psychic dreams were especially pleasant, but this one had been truly awful, maybe the worst one yet.

In her dream, she had watched a little girl get attacked by a man wielding a rock. They had been beside some sort of river or stream, and she had watched the girl collapse to the ground and saw with frightening clarity the way the blood flowed from the wound on her head and ran into the water. There was another little girl there as well, and she stood there silently, frozen with fear, her eyes wide as saucers.

Caitlin wanted to go back to sleep and forget all about the awful dream, but the dream didn't want to be forgotten. She tossed and turned until the sky turned to the purply-blue of early morning. The house was still silent, but she rose and dressed before heading downstairs. When she couldn't find anything good to watch on television, she put her *Little Mermaid* tape into the VCR, but even Ariel couldn't distract her from the frightening nightmare.

She didn't want to tell her mother about the dream. She didn't want to speak or think about the awful, ugly thing. So when her mother came down and made breakfast for her and inevitably asked if Caitlin had any dreams the previous evening, she shook her head no. Was it the way she shook her head? Was it the haunted look in her eyes? Whatever it was, her mother was not fooled by her denial. She knew Caitlin had a dream, and she wanted to know all about it.

Caitlin let her cereal turn to soggy mush in the bowl as she shared the details of the frightening dream. Her mother jotted them down in her notebook, and though she made an effort to remain impassive, Caitlin noticed the little shudder that went through her when she described the attack.

"Who was the girl?" her mother wanted to know. "Did you recognize her?"

For the second time that morning, Caitlin shook her head, but this time she was being honest. She had never seen the girl before. Her mother wanted to know what the girl looked like.

"She had dark hair," Caitlin said.

"Was she your age? Could it be someone you go to school with?"

Caitlin shook her head to both questions. The girl was younger, definitely.

"She looked like maybe she was in first or second grade." Caitlin closed her eyes and pictured the terrible dream even though she really didn't want to, and she noticed another detail. The dress the girl was wearing had ruffled cap sleeves and an illustration on the front, and Caitlin realized it wasn't a dress at all. "I think she was wearing her pajamas," Caitlin said when she reopened her eyes, "a nightshirt."

Her mother dutifully noted this detail in her notebook. She pressed Caitlin for more details about the man in the dream. What did he look like? Did Caitlin recognize him?

Caitlin hadn't spent as much time in the dream looking at the man as she had the little girls, but she had caught a glimpse of him. Except for the fact that he was wielding a rock as a weapon, he didn't seem that scary at all.

"Did you recognize him?" her mother asked. "Maybe he's the dad of one of the kids you go to school with."

To Caitlin this seemed like a strange suggestion, but just like with the girl, she was sure she had never seen him before. Caitlin was relieved when her mother finally ran out of questions. She thought it was all over, but in truth it was only beginning.

Because that night her mother was watching the news when she saw the story about the little girl in Pennsylvania who was killed in a brutal and shocking murder. The news story offered scant details, but the school portrait of the little girl with the dark pigtails and the information that the murder had occurred outdoors near a creek, in the middle of the night, made her shout Caitlin's name.

Caitlin looked up from the picture she had been coloring to see the all-too-familiar face on the screen.

"What's going on?" her father asked as her mother ran to grab a pen and paper to write down the phone number to call for tips.

"Caitlin saw the murder," her mother said, "in her dream."

Her father looked over at Caitlin, and his look was both sympathetic and concerned. Maybe if he had spoken up and said something right then, everything would have been different, but as usual he said nothing, and within seconds Luanne had their cordless kitchen phone and was dialing the tips number.

Caitlin slammed on her brakes, and the Land Cruiser lurched to a sudden stop, but it was a fraction of a second too late. The bumper had connected with the fender of the small black car. She blinked in surprise as she tried to make sense of what had just happened. She knew the intersection well. They were just a couple of blocks from home. Had she not seen the black car before proceeding through the stop sign? But as she tried her best to recall the last minute or so, she had the sudden awful realization that she had gone straight through the intersection without stopping.

Someone rapped on her window, and she jumped. She stared at the woman standing there in surprise.

"Are you okay?" the woman asked. Caitlin nodded her reply.

The driver of the black car stepped out, and he was swearing and waving his fist in the air. Two other cars had pulled over to the curb, and now their drivers stepped out to assist. One of them, a large man, intervened before the angry, shouting driver made his way over to Caitlin. The woman at Caitlin's window said she should move her car out of the intersection and wait for the police, which she did.

"What's going on?" Adam asked in the backseat.

"It's going to be okay," Caitlin assured him, and she hoped she was right.

11

AT DINNER, Caitlin said she didn't want to talk about her accident. Well, maybe *said* was the wrong word. It was more like she snarled the words in an angry, under-her-breath sort of way. Lance thought she meant she didn't want to talk about it in front of Adam because she didn't want to upset him. Lance thought it was sort of like the way she insisted they stress to him that his dreams weren't real, as if he was going to go around telling his son that the monsters in his nightmares were real. Sometimes Lance thought his wife assumed he was an idiot.

But now that Adam was safely tucked in his bed and they were sequestered behind their closed bedroom door, he felt it was safe to bring up the little fender bender. He waited impatiently in bed as Caitlin puttered endlessly in the bathroom. He roasted beneath the too-thick comforter, and he flung it back to try to cool off.

"This comforter's too warm," he said in a voice loud enough for her to hear in the bathroom. "What happened to the old one? That one was better."

"That one was ugly," Caitlin said, at last emerging from the bathroom.

"It looked fine to me," Lance said. One downside to having a graphic designer as a wife was that Caitlin was always picking form over function. Sometimes it was maddening. She rolled her eyes at him as she went over and unlocked the bedroom door. That was the other maddening thing. "I don't see what difference it makes if our door is locked," he said. "It's not like Adam ever gets out of bed and comes looking for us."

"Well, what's the point in keeping it locked?" she asked.

The argument was valid, and he couldn't explain to her why it was better to keep the door locked. It didn't really matter. He would wait until she was snoring away, then get up and re-lock the door.

Caitlin climbed into bed and pulled the bulky comforter up over her, which meant she pulled it up over his legs as well. He reminded himself that Caitlin had a rough day, and there really was no point in starting an argument over bed linens.

"Hey, so what happened this afternoon?" he asked.

"What happened?" she asked, like she didn't know what the hell he was talking about. She was testing his patience, and honestly, it didn't help that he was trapped under the blanket of molten lava.

"The accident," he reminded her, unable to keep his annoyance out of his voice.

"I said I didn't want to talk about it," Caitlin said.

"So that's it? You're not going to tell me anything?" His voice was on the verge of shouting.

"I made a mistake," she said. "I rolled through a stop sign. I'm a fuckup of a mother who endangered the life of my child with my carelessness! Are you happy?"

She angrily lay down on her pillow with her back to him, yanking the covers over her, which actually exposed half of Lance's leg to mercifully cool air.

"No, I'm not happy," he said, careful to stay calm. Had he brought on her angry outburst with his near shouting? "Look, you're not a fuckup. It was just a little accident. No one was hurt. I mean, even the cars barely had a scratch on them, right?"

He waited for a response, but Caitlin didn't say anything. Instead he heard a muffled whimpering noise. Shit, was she crying? He couldn't believe he had made her cry.

"Look, I'm sorry if I sounded angry," he said.

"What if the timing had been different?" Caitlin asked. "A second later or a few seconds earlier? The other car could have crashed into us. Adam could have been hurt or worse." Her sniffles turned into full-out sobbing, and Lance felt helpless. He petted her shoulder as she cried herself to sleep.

Lance knew something was wrong the second he opened his eyes. He didn't know where he was, but he wasn't in his bed. He also wasn't alone. The muffled whimpering noise was vaguely familiar, and in an instant he was back at Ryerson, kneeling on the hard linoleum dormitory floor, his fists sore and raw from pummeling Eric Pitt. He felt sick.

The queasiness brought him back to reality, and with a sudden shock, he realized where he was and what he was doing. He recognized the dim light filling the room. It was Adam's nightlight, and the whimpering was coming not from Eric Pitt but from his own son, and—oh God, what had he done?

He let go of what he was gripping as he realized it was his son's neck, and he jumped back from the bed as if it were on fire. His hands didn't ache like they had all those years ago, but he felt a stiffness in them not unlike the feeling he got after tightly gripping a screwdriver or the steering wheel. But the thing he had been gripping wasn't an inanimate object. Seconds ago, his fingers had been wrapped about his son's small, fragile neck. For how long?

"Adam," Lance whispered urgently. He heard only whimpers in the silence. "Adam?" He said it again, more tentative, on the verge of tears himself.

"Daddy?" Adam finally answered, his voice so small and scared in the darkness.

The darkness. Lance went over and fumbled around on the wall before finding the light switch. He turned slowly to face his son, scared of what he would see.

"Please don't hurt me, Daddy," Adam said. "I'm sorry for crying. I won't do it anymore, I promise."

"No, you didn't do anything wrong." Lance sat down on the side of Adam's bed. He reached to brush Adam's damp hair from his face, but the boy shied away from him. Sadness stabbed Lance's heart, but he forced himself to look at his frightened son. He was relieved to see no blood. There did seem to be some faint red marks on Adam's neck. Would they turn to bruises, or were they light enough to fade away?

Even as he was basking in the relief that things did not appear to be too bad, a little voice at the back of his head reminded him that if he hadn't woken up when he did, he could have killed his son. What if next time he wasn't so lucky? There couldn't be a next time. He had to make sure of that.

"It's okay." He wasn't sure if he was trying to soothe his son or himself.

"Daddy, you were hurting me," Adam said.

Lance realized that even if there were no telltale bruises, Adam was sure to tell Caitlin about what happened, and how would he explain that? His deep-sleeping wife would no more understand that than she could Adam's nightmares.

What was so frustrating was that this was all her fault. She was the one who insisted on unlocking the door. He meant to get up and re-lock it after she fell asleep, but he must have drifted off before he had the chance. He couldn't let that happen again, and she need never know about this.

"No," Lance said, "you were having a bad dream. I came in here to try to wake you. It was all just a dream. It wasn't real."

Adam blinked several times. His cheeks were damp with tears. Lance reached out to wipe them away, and this time Adam didn't shy away, though his expression remained uncertain.

"You hurt me," Adam said quietly.

"Just a dream," Lance promised him.

Adam seemed to accept this. His small body relaxed as he lay back down on his pillow, and for the second time that night, Lance stroked an upset family member's shoulder as he waited for them to fall asleep. He rose when he felt his own eyelids growing heavy and heard Adam's steady sleep-breathing.

So long as Adam kept having his nightmares, Caitlin was going to insist on keeping their door unlocked. He had to make sure he got up to lock it after she fell asleep, but could he rely on that? All it would take was one time. He couldn't allow that to happen.

So what could he do? Maybe he could impress on his wife the importance of locking their bedroom door. Perhaps it was time to tell her everything. She would hate him. How couldn't she? What's more, she would blame him for Adam's nightmares, and as Lance glanced down at his now-sleeping son and noticed those reddish marks his hands had left on the boy's neck, he realized he couldn't confess everything to Caitlin right now.

He felt so utterly helpless as he watched his son sleep. Was this how his own mother had felt? He recalled how it had been for the two of them in that sad little house in Culver Creek. He heard Corey reading out the town's name as he studied that business card, and Lance knew what he had to do.

In the morning, he would call the dream whisperer. Caitlin had said no doctors, but the so-called dream whisperer wasn't a doctor. Caitlin wouldn't approve, but she didn't have to know.

He would take Adam to see the dream whisperer. Maybe she had some wacky new-age cure for his nightmares. Adam would stop having bad dreams. They could sleep with their bedroom door locked again. Everything would go back to normal. Everything would be fine.

12

SAGE AWOKE IN A PANIC, and for a second or two he was convinced he was in his college dorm, but the layout of the room was all wrong. Then the last shred of his dream melted away, and he saw that he was in his Culver Creek apartment. As the dream disappeared, so too did Melodie. She had been about to say something, but he woke up too soon. He closed his eyes and tried to return to the dream, but that wasn't the way dreams worked. With sleep and the dream out of reach, he rose from bed and wandered into his living room, where he had tacked up a map he'd sketched out of Lily Esposito's neighborhood on butcher paper. It took up one whole wall of his not especially large living room.

The previous night before going to bed, he had cross-referenced all the witness statements taken after the murder with the addresses of each of the witnesses on the map. He had thought this monumental task would bring clarity to the confusing case, but as he studied his handiwork in the dim, gray early morning light, it all just looked like useless busy-work. He was just spinning his wheels, nothing obvious was jumping out at him.

He had marked a star by one of the houses and now tried to remember why. The house was on a different street than Lily's, but the backyards were nearly adjacent. He consulted the witness statements to refresh his mind as to why there was a star there, and then he remembered.

The starred house belonged to Raquel Walker, who had told police she saw a suspicious vehicle the day before Lily's murder. It wasn't much, but the house was close enough to Lily's that maybe it might have been something. He felt like he was grasping at straws. Something about the description of the vehicle nagged at him. Raquel wasn't sure of the make or model of the older blue sedan. "A real beater" was the phrase she had used to describe it.

Something about it seemed significant. Did it match the description of the vehicle belonging to Rick, Lily's estranged father? He flipped through the papers from the old case that now filled every surface of his living room until he found the one with the information on Rick, but no, Rick drove a pickup truck.

There had been another description of a car like the one Raquel Walker had seen, wasn't there? He was sure it was in the files somewhere. He wasted forty-five minutes combing through the mess of papers before he decided to shower and get ready for work. It was as frustrating as his dream.

～

It figured that the one morning he was late, his boss was there waiting for his arrival. Rayanne Lawrence didn't need to glance at the clock or a watch as she stood beside his desk. He could read the disappointment in her eyes.

He stammered out an apology, but she cut him off.

"I need you to go down to the high school," she said. "There was an incident last night."

Before he had a chance to ask what sort of incident, she returned to her office. So, he learned the particulars from Principal Brim as they stood in front of a trophy case now taped over with plastic.

"There was glass everywhere," Brim said, waving his arm to indicate the stretch of hallway. "I had the janitor clean it up first thing, for safety reasons."

Sage pulled back a corner of plastic and peered into the display case. He hadn't seen what it looked like before, but judging by the sparse contents, he guessed that more than a few trophies had been stolen. Crude graffiti marred some of the photos left behind in the case.

"Do you think it was students?" Sage asked.

"Former students," Brim said. "I can give you their names and a copy of the security footage."

Sage wondered why Lawrence had sent him here. This wasn't something in need of any detective skills. He followed Brim back to his office, where the principal handed him the list of four male suspects and a USB stick with the security camera footage. Sage glanced at the list, and one of the names leapt out at him.

"Kevin Arlo," Sage read. "Is he—"

"Steve's son." Brim nodded. "Steve's a nice guy, but Kevin . . . well, let's just say this isn't the first time there's been trouble with him."

"When did he graduate?" Sage asked.

"A couple of years ago," Brim said. "Since then he's been hanging around this town going nowhere fast. Culver Creek's not exactly awash in opportunities. The kids who don't go away to college tend to spend their time getting drunk and acting like assholes."

Sage almost said the description could probably apply to the kids who went away to college, too, but he didn't want to make it sound like he was dunking on Culver Creek, because from his experience, the phenomenon was more of a universal thing.

Wisps of last night's dream came back to him, and they blended with his actual memories of that weekend Melodie came out to see him at school. Sage might not have been breaking into high schools and vandalizing trophy cases, but like Kevin Arlo and his pals, he had been a drunken asshole. He could see the look of disgust in his sister's eyes, and it felt like someone was taking a knife and stabbing him in the gut.

With a start, he realized Brim had asked him a question.

"Sorry, what?" Sage said.

"Can you arrange for them to be given community service hours?" Brim asked. "It's about time they started giving back in some way."

"That's all up to the judge," Sage said.

~

When Sage found Kevin Arlo hanging out in his buddy's backyard in the trailer park out by the highway, the young man denied everything.

"You're on camera," Sage said.

"So," Kevin said. "Do you know who my father is?"

"Yeah, I do," Sage said. "You want me to call him and have him come down here?"

"You can't do that," Kevin said. "I'm an adult."

So that was the kind of logic he was dealing with. Sage had better things to do with his time than deal with oversized juvenile delinquents, and he knew it was only because Kevin was Steve's son that he was even here in the first place. He really wasn't in the mood to deal with this today.

He hated Kevin Arlo because he was the sort of loser who contributed nothing to society, but that wasn't it. What he really despised was how much this arrogant, self-centered jerk reminded him of himself.

"If you don't wake up soon, someone's going to get hurt," Sage said. "You want that on your conscience?"

"Are you threatening me?" Kevin asked as he leaned forward and fixed Sage with a defiant stare.

"Would it make a difference if I was?" Sage wished someone had been there to give him a wakeup call, but he realized that was exactly what Melodie had been doing there. The problem was he had been as thick and senseless as Kevin Arlo. "Look, it will make things easier all around if you just come down to the station with me."

"What, now?" Kevin asked. "I'm in the middle of painting my truck."

He waved a hand at the pickup parked behind him, covered in a still-wet coat of gray primer. Sage blinked at Kevin's truck, but he wasn't really seeing it. What he was seeing were police notes in Bill's not quite illegible hand, a car with a homemade paint job, an empty can of gray primer spray paint found beside a driveway. The car hadn't jumped out at him when he reread the notes this morning because the color was wrong.

"Come with me now or I send your father back here

with a warrant to arrest you," Sage said. "It's your choice."

Kevin jumped up from the plastic lawn chair and practically ran to Sage's car.

That night at his apartment, Sage flipped back through the old case file. He lost track of how many pages he had gone through before he found it, but his heart skipped a beat as he read the information scrawled there: 1986 Pontiac Grand Am, belonging to a Mr. Bud Ivan.

Sage went over to his hand-drawn map to locate Bud Ivan's address.

"Bingo," he said aloud in the empty apartment.

13

CAITLIN STILL FELT groggy as she helped Adam get dressed. She had gotten out of bed roughly an hour ago—right around when Lance was leaving for work—but she felt barely awake. She noticed red marks on his neck as she slipped his shirt on. They didn't look that bad—the skin wasn't broken, at least—but they worried her.

Could he have done it to himself during one of his nightmares? She tried to picture him clawing at his own skin during one of the bad dreams. It was one explanation, but she didn't think it was the only one. It was possible he hadn't been asleep at all.

∾

The first time Caitlin harmed herself was in college. She was fully awake when she deliberately tore her skin with a pair of dull scissors, but a dream was to blame.

For over a week she had been having a frightening nightmare. It was the same dream each time—a young woman attacked in an ill-lit parking lot. What she saw in terms of details varied from night to night, which was why it wasn't until the third night of the recurring dream that she recognized the parking lot. It was the one between one of the dorm buildings and the student center. She went there the next afternoon just to be sure. She shivered as she stood there examining the lot. Even in the light of day, it felt like a creepy place.

She didn't recognize the woman in the dream, and she never got a good look at her attacker. All she had to go on was the location. She walked down to the campus security office and tried to explain to the security guard manning the desk that they needed to keep a guard posted at the parking lot by the student center.

"Has something happened?" the guard asked. He barely looked up from the game of computer solitaire he was playing.

"Something will happen," Caitlin said, but she was pretty sure if she told him she was getting her information from a dream, she would lose any chance she had of convincing the guard to do anything. "It's not safe over there."

"Could you be more specific?" the guard asked as he slid digital playing cards around on the screen. "Is there a light out? An uneven sidewalk?"

For all Caitlin knew, there might have been a light out or an uneven sidewalk, though she hadn't noticed either. Something told her neither of those safety hazards would prompt any kind of immediate action. So she fudged the truth a bit.

"I've seen someone over there a few times," Caitlin said. Technically this was true. It was just that she had only seen this in a dream. "He looked suspicious, just sort of hanging out in the shadows there."

This was enough to cause the guard to turn away from his computer screen.

"Did he say anything to you? Did he try to follow you?" the guard asked. Caitlin shook her head. "What did he look like?"

Caitlin did her best to describe the shadowy figure she had seen in her dream. It was Culver Creek all over again, but the difference here was she was ahead of the game. Maybe with her report and her frustratingly vague description, they could actually catch this guy before anything happened. She allowed herself to believe this.

She wasn't so much surprised as she was crushed when the news broke less than a week later. She wanted to blame the campus security guards for not doing more to prevent the senseless tragedy, but deep down she knew she bore the full responsibility for that innocent woman's murder.

How could she have possibly thought that telling one solitary security guard was going to be enough? She should have gone to the police. What about the dean of students? Even if no one in a position of authority was willing to listen to her, she should have organized some sort of student version of a neighborhood watch. They could have made sure that parking lot was under surveillance. Instead, she had done the bare minimum and foolishly hoped this time everything would turn out different.

Stabbing her arm with a pair of scissors until she bled might not have solved anyone's problems, but it helped to ease the burden weighing her down. She considered it her penance. Often it was her mother's voice she heard as she stabbed the scissor blades into her flesh. Luanne's chipper voice filled her head, reminding her she was like a superhero or telling her she had a gift. That was how Luanne had always seen it—a gift, not a curse.

Once again, though, Caitlin had been given the opportunity to be the superhero, and like always she had failed,
squandered her precious gift. Those angry marks on her
arm wouldn't bring the dead girl back to life, but they did in
a roundabout sort of way cure Caitlin of her peculiar
malady.

If it weren't for the marks on her arm, an astute
professor wouldn't have referred her to the campus mental
health center, and if it weren't for her therapy sessions, she
might never have discovered her miracle drug of choice
—Pacifcleon.

∾

"**D**addy is a bad man." Adam's voice wrenched Caitlin
back to the present. She adjusted his shirt, but she
wondered if she should try to find one with a higher collar.
What would his nursery school teacher think if she saw
those marks?

"What did you say?" Caitlin asked absently, his words
finally starting to penetrate the tangle of thoughts taking up
space in her head.

"Daddy's a bad man," Adam repeated.

Was this something from his nightmare? It must be.

"No, he's not," Caitlin said. "Remember what we talked
about. Dreams aren't real, right?"

Adam nodded his little head, but she could tell by the
look on his face that he wasn't convinced.

∾

Caitlin had the house to herself and her mother-in-law wasn't pestering her with phone calls, but she still couldn't focus on her work. Those marks on Adam's neck and his talk about his nightmare had rattled her. He was too young to be dealing with this sort of thing. Though, had she ever been old enough to deal with this thing?

She pulled up a new tab and did a Google search for Pacifcleon. It was one of her regular internet distractions. Some people procrastinated by reading social media posts, others played mindless games; she spent her time searching for discontinued sleeping pills. To each his own.

Her search proved fruitless. It didn't mean that tomorrow or the next day she wouldn't find someone on some corner of the web selling some expired boxes of her miracle drug, but it seemed like the stuff was getting more and more difficult to track down. Well, of course it was. Pacifcleon hadn't been manufactured in years. There was no need to panic yet. She had plenty of the stuff in reserve, but it wouldn't last forever, and now she felt the sudden need to take inventory of her stash. She wasn't getting any work done anyway.

When she opened the linen closet, she remembered Lance's bizarre decision to reorganize the bathroom. Lance tended to be a bit of a neat freak, and she couldn't help but feel that his early morning bathroom cleaning had been some sort of personal attack on her and her sometimes disorganized ways. Still, she had been impressed. He had done a good job organizing things, and she was pleasantly surprised at how much less cluttered the linen closet looked.

Now, though, she realized a drawback to his mad organizing. She couldn't find things. Maybe she wasn't especially organized, but at least she knew more or less where everything was. Now, forget it. The only thing she really cared about, the most important item of all, was nowhere to be found.

She tried to get inside Lance's head. Where would her neat-freak husband have decided to put her stash of sleeping pills? She had never exactly kept them hidden from him, but she always tried to disguise the fact that out of necessity she bought the stuff in bulk. He might have questioned her decision to continue to consume a discontinued, expired drug. Of course, he would have come across the stash in his organizing raid, but where would he have put the pills?

She searched the linen closet quickly, then turned her attention to the vanity drawers and cupboards, but other than her nearly empty current package, she hadn't found a single Pacifcleon package. What the hell had he done with them?

They had to be in the linen closet somewhere. She must have missed them. She began to methodically go through the contents of the closet shelf by shelf, undoing much of Lance's organizing in the process despite her best effort to be neat. But as she neared the last shelf, she gave up any attempt at neatness whatsoever and resorted to strewing the contents of the closet every which way in a frantic attempt to locate her missing pills.

Ten minutes later, she was on the phone with the Zooest receptionist, who told her Lance was in a meeting.

"Can you interrupt him?" Caitlin asked. "I need to speak to him. Now."

The emphatic tone of her voice convinced the receptionist that this was an urgent matter, and less than a minute later Lance was on the phone breathless, asking her what had happened.

"I need to know where you put my Pacifcleon," Caitlin said, "when you cleaned the bathroom."

"What?"

"My sleeping pills," she said.

"What?" Lance repeated. "Sheryl said it was an emergency. Wait, didn't you take one last night?"

"Not the opened package," Caitlin explained. "I had a whole bunch more."

"Why do you need these now? Don't you have to pick Adam up at school soon?"

Caitlin pulled the phone away from her ear for a moment to check the time. Crap. She had spent more time than she realized ransacking the bathroom. She needed to go pick up Adam. She heard Lance's tinny voice coming through the speaker and pressed the phone back to her ear.

"Wait, were these the packages that were expired?" Lance asked. "I threw those out."

"You what!" Caitlin's voice was so loud it startled her. "What do you mean you threw them away? You didn't even ask me about it?"

"Caitlin, they were really, really old," Lance said.

"So! They were still good."

"Look, can we talk about this later? I've got to get back to that meeting."

She was too angry to reply. She ended the call.

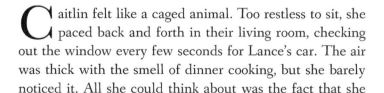

Caitlin felt like a caged animal. Too restless to sit, she paced back and forth in their living room, checking out the window every few seconds for Lance's car. The air was thick with the smell of dinner cooking, but she barely noticed it. All she could think about was the fact that she had less than a week's worth of sleeping pills and no idea how she was going to find any more of her miracle drug.

Even if she was able to track some down online—and she didn't see how, as apart from a quick interlude to pick Adam up at school, all she had spent the remainder of her day doing was searching for Pacifcleon—the likelihood that she could have it shipped to her house in less than a week's time was slim. Out of desperation, she had ransacked the lone garbage bag in their pail, even though she was sure the garbage had already been collected after Lance's cleaning spree.

When Lance's headlights turned into their driveway, she ran to the door, fists clenched at her side as rage-fueled adrenaline made her jittery. It took him an interminable amount of time to leave his car and open the door, but when he did, she was ready. She attacked him with a volley of words that made him take a step backward into the garage.

"What gives you the right to throw away someone else's possessions? You didn't even think to ask me first? I was right in the next room!" Spittle flew from her lips as she shouted.

"Just calm down," he said. "This isn't the end of the world." He stood in the doorway. "I'll go to the store and buy some more, okay?"

"Ha!" was all she said.

"In fact, if you want, I'll go right now. The car's still warm."

"There's no point," she said. Her rage had died down to a simmer. Lance's offer was a perfectly reasonable one. Of course he didn't know she had long since bought up every package of Pacifcleon in a twenty mile radius. Wasn't this as much her fault as it was his? She heard Adam's footfalls on the stairs and saw the way she had her husband pinned in the doorway. What was wrong with her? "Come inside," she said.

"No, I'll go get your stuff," Lance said.

"You can't buy them at the store," she said. It was time to come clean, to tell him the whole story of the drug she was so dependent on. "They discon—"

"What's that smell?" Lance asked.

"What?" she said, confused by the sudden change of topic.

"Mommy, the oven's on fire!" Adam wailed.

She spun around just in time to hear the glass in the oven door shatter. Lance shoved past her as he ran to place himself between his son and the flaming oven. Lance grabbed the fire extinguisher they kept under the sink and wrestled the pin out before dousing the oven and the remains of their dinner in white foam. Caitlin clutched Adam as she watched the flames extinguish.

She had been too busy searching for expired sleeping pills to cook anything from scratch and resorted to baking a frozen pizza. It was a feta-and-spinach-flavored pie, so she reasoned it was borderline gourmet. She glanced at the clock. When had she put the pizza in to cook? She was drawing a blank. It felt like it wasn't that long ago, but could she have cooked it so long it caught fire?

Lance examined the wreckage in the smoking oven.

"There's no pan," he said. "The cheese must have dripped down and caught fire."

"There's a pan," Caitlin insisted. "I always use a pan."

"Cait, I'm telling you, I'm looking right at it and there's no pan."

She walked over and peered over his shoulder. There was no pan beneath the now mostly black pizza. How had she forgotten a pan? Well, she had been preoccupied.

Everything would be okay. The only casualties were a not very inspired dinner and the oven door. A shiver of fear went through her as she saw the cracked glass in the door. What if the glass had exploded and shot across the room? It could have easily injured Adam or worse. She wouldn't have been able to live with herself. She needed to pull herself together, and she knew the only way she was going to do that was if she replenished her Pacifcleon supply.

14

LANCE GLANCED in the rearview mirror and saw Adam in his car seat in the back happily singing a little song to his stuffed kangaroo.

"Just you and me, right, kiddo?" Lance said. "Having a fun boys' day together."

"Mmmhmm, Daddy," Adam said without looking up.

That's what Lance had told Caitlin, and she seemed to welcome a Saturday all to herself. Things had been tense since the night of the flaming pizza, and Caitlin seemed out of sorts. Maybe she had been under too much stress with work. He envied the fact that she could work from home, but it had to be difficult balancing work with taking care of Adam and the house. She had that big project she was working on for the lottery commission, and probably that more than him throwing out some expired sleeping pills had been at the root of her outburst the other night.

She hadn't said any more about the sleeping pills, and he hadn't dared to bring it up, but maybe today while they were out he could stop at a Rite Aid and pick some up. He couldn't remember the name of the stuff she took, but maybe he would recognize it when he saw it.

Lance had been vague about what he and Adam had planned for the day. So it wasn't like he was lying to her. He had never specifically said he *wasn't* taking Adam all the way out to Culver Creek to see some dream psychic.

"We'll have a fun boys' day," Lance had told her. He liked the idea of he and Adam doing their own thing together. They would have to do this more often. It gave Caitlin a nice break, and it was a good chance for he and Adam to do some male bonding. He would be the father he'd always wished he had.

No one would ever mistake Culver Creek for a posh town, but there was something almost charming about this old town that seemed so far removed from the hustle and bustle of modern life, or maybe that was Lance's own nostalgia coloring his opinion. He had been under the impression that he had no memories of the town where he spent the first twelve years of his life, but as he drove toward the center of town, he recognized some of the different sights and landmarks. There was the elementary school he had gone to, and the public library where his mom used to take him for story time.

The road went around a bend, and sunlight sparkled like gemstones on running water. It was the eponymous Culver Creek, and just like that, a memory kicked off in his head.

He couldn't remember how old he was, but he and another boy were standing ankle deep in the running stream. Their feet were bare, and their jeans were rolled up to their knees. The water was icy cold. A few feet away on dry ground stood a third boy with a stopwatch in his hand. It was a challenge to see who could stay in the still-frigid early spring water the longest. A small crowd had gathered on the bank—other boys and girls from the neighborhood. They shouted and laughed as Lance and the other boy fought to keep their numb feet planted in the ice-cold water —Allen, that was the other boy's name. He lived two doors down from Lance, and they used to ride bikes together all the time.

Allen let out a yelp and splashed toward the shore. Lance was declared the victor, while Allen shouted that a fish bit his toe and it wasn't fair. Lance wasted no time running toward the shore to pull his dry socks onto his soaked feet. Lance's memory jumped ahead to later that day, when his mother caught him trying to secretly strip off his wet clothes in the bathroom, but no, that wasn't right. That must have been a different time, because the clothes he was wearing were different—summer clothes, not spring clothes.

"Turn right, Daddy," Adam said from the backseat.

Lance snapped back to reality and realized Adam was mimicking the GPS directions that he hadn't been paying attention to. He missed the turn and had to turn around and backtrack. They were already running a few minutes late, but he suspected a dream whisperer wasn't the sort of person who would worry too much about punctuality.

The dream whisperer's office was on the second floor of a tired old building a block off the town's main drag. The ground floor space was leased to a lawyer, and

Lance and Adam had to climb a creaky, dimly lit staircase to reach Phelicity Green's door.

"Where are we?" Adam asked. "Is this a haunted house?"

"No, of course not," Lance said. He hadn't explained this part of the day to Adam, and he knew he had to choose his words wisely. Adam could very well repeat anything he said back to Caitlin. "Daddy just needs to stop in and see someone for work, but after we talk to her, then we can go do something fun. Do you want to do something fun?"

Adam nodded. They reached the top of the stairs. The door was locked, but an index card taped to the wall instructed him to press the doorbell. They waited a few seconds.

"Nobody's home," Adam said. "Time to do something fun."

"Hang on there, bud," Lance said, and at last he heard someone approaching the door. There were a few more seconds of waiting while it seemed several locks were being undone, and then finally the door swung open and a woman with an unruly mane of hair and a purple tunic top with a long greenish-colored batik skirt stood there staring at him. Lance noticed right away that her feet were completely bare.

"Sorry we're late," Lance said.

"Oh, no worries," she said. "Come in."

She waved them into a room even more dimly lit than the stairway. As his eyes adjusted to the darkness, he saw a tiny room cluttered with shelves filled with assorted rocks and crystals and various figurines.

"You must be Adam," the woman said, leaning down to talk to Adam at eye level.

"Yes," Adam said. "Do you work with Daddy?"

Lance regretted his little white lie.

"Heh-heh, no, sport, I didn't mean to confuse you like this. I don't work with this nice lady." Then to Phelicity he added, "Sorry."

She gave him a slight nod, but he noticed the way she was studying him. Was she trying to determine what sort of parent would confuse his child with dumb lies?

"There's a mat here where you can leave your shoes," she said to them. It was said in an offhanded way, but he understood it was meant as an instruction. So he slipped off his own shoes before bending down to remove Adam's as he wondered what kind of new-age nutjob factory this place was.

At Phelicity's instruction, they sat on a rug on the floor because clearly this woman wasn't using her dream whisperer income to buy furniture. Lance regretted his decision to come here. This was not his sort of thing—crystals and the cultural appropriation of Eastern philosophy. As Phelicity launched into some mumbo jumbo about dreams being a portal to another realm, which was all going way over Adam's head, Lance realized that this quackery was never going to be able to do anything for Adam and his nightmares.

Would it be rude to leave now? He could pretend to get an important text on his phone. It was another lie, and another tale Adam could tell Caitlin. So in the end, he struggled to arrange his legs comfortably on the mat as he breathed patchouli-scented air and listened to Adam dutifully tell the dream whisperer about his nightmares.

Lance had heard Adam talk about his dreams before, but it was like he was hearing the words for the first time. Maybe it was something about all the crystal energy in this room, or more likely it had to do with being in Culver

Creek, dredging up memories that had lain dormant for so long, but as Adam described a girl in a river who was hurt by a bad man, Lance was struck by how much the story resembled the one that had been on everyone's mind that last, awful summer he spent in Culver Creek. That year, a little girl who lived down the road from him was senselessly murdered, and it filled the entire community with fear.

As Adam described an attack on a young girl in frightening, graphic detail, Lance wondered where the boy could have come up with such ugliness. Was Caitlin allowing him to watch inappropriate television shows? No way was he picking up the stuff he was describing from Thomas or any of the other cartoon shows he watched. Lance noticed the serene expression on Phelicity's face had slowly morphed into one of horror, and the color seemed to have drained from her skin.

"Okay, Adam," Lance said with a touch of a chuckle to defuse the dark mood in the room. "That's probably enough for now. I think we all get the picture." He tried his best to offer the woman a friendly smile, but she still looked horror-stricken. She was probably assuming he was the one letting his kid watch violent television; that or she had decided Adam was some sort of psychopath.

"Adam, maybe you can tell me some more about this bad man in your dream," Phelicity said. She acted calm, but Lance heard the tremble in her voice.

Adam looked over at Lance as if to ask his permission before speaking more about the dream, and Lance decided this was his cue. From his cramped position on the floor, he wrestled his phone out of his pocket and pretended to read a message on the screen before slipping it back into his pocket.

"I'm sorry," Lance said as he began to rise from the

ground. "Something's come up, and we're going to have get going."

"But you can't go," Phelicity said. "I haven't had a chance to—"

"Sorry," Lance said. "I'll still pay you for the full session."

Over the phone she had quoted him $100 for the initial session, and he had been smart enough to bring cash, no questionable credit card charges for Caitlin to quiz him about. He peeled the bills from his money clip and handed them to her as he led Adam to his feet.

"But—" Phelicity said, flustered.

"Is it time to do something fun?" Adam asked.

"Well past time," Lance said.

"What?" Adam asked.

"Yes," Lance said. "Come on, let's get your shoes on."

As he fought to get shoes back on his son's feet before putting his own on, he regretted ever taking them off in the first place. It was difficult to leave quickly when one had to first put on footwear.

The memory hit Lance as soon as he stepped into the ice cream parlor. He had been here before with his mother. He remembered the pastel-colored walls and the swivel seats and that sickly sweet smell in the air. It was strange to him how so many things were coming back to him as he traveled around Culver Creek—stuff he hadn't thought of in years.

After they left the dream whisperer's, he took Adam to play a round of miniature golf, and as they teed off at the first hole, he remembered going to the mini golf place for a classmate's birthday party. The familiar obstacles and the video game noises that emanated from the arcade dredged up memories he thought had been lost forever. And now here at the ice cream parlor, he felt a dizzying sensation as his childhood memories merged with the present day.

"Daddy, I want 'nilla," Adam said.

"But they've got so many different flavors to pick from. Why don't you try something new? Look, they've got banana. You like bananas."

"'Nilla," Adam insisted.

Lance sighed but capitulated, ordering a vanilla cone for Adam and a cone with a scoop of peach and a scoop of mango for himself. They sat down at a table by the window, and Adam was as taken with the spinning chairs as Lance had been as a boy.

"Less spinning, more licking," Lance said. "It's all going to melt if you don't eat it quicker." He watched in dismay as streaks of white ice cream dribbled down Adam's face and began to form a vanilla-flavored lake on the table. Caitlin always ordered Adam cups of ice cream instead of cones, and Lance now saw why.

So he had made a few mistakes on this father-and-son day together. Ordering a cone instead of a cup was the least of it. Certainly the whole dream whisperer thing had been a colossal mistake. He saw the look of abject horror on Phelicity's face as Adam described in way-too-graphic detail his horrible nightmare.

"Hey, bud," Lance said, "we can't be telling everyone all about our dreams, okay? You know the way your bad dreams frighten you?"

Adam nodded. There was ice cream smeared all around his mouth and streaks of it on his shirt.

"Well, when you tell all the scary parts to other people, that scares them too."

"Dreams aren't real," Adam said before slurping some more soupy ice cream from his cone. Lance estimated maybe twenty percent of it actually ended up in his mouth.

"Right, exactly," Lance said. "So there's no need to tell people all about them, right?" Lance grabbed a wad of napkins from the dispenser on the table and began to spread them on top of the vanilla puddle. "Besides, it doesn't really make for good conversation. People don't want to hear about other people's dreams. It's about as exciting as describing watching paint dry."

"I like painting," Adam said.

"Sure, painting's fun, but watching it dry is boring, and talking about watching it dry is even more boring. See what I'm saying?"

"Are we going to do painting next?" Adam asked.

"Next we're going to find a bathroom and get you cleaned up," Lance said. "Then we're going to head back home, because I bet you Mommy misses you."

15

BUD IVAN HAD BEEN BROUGHT in three separate times for questioning after Lily Esposito was murdered. The house he rented sat right on the creek, literally a stone's throw from where Lily's body had been found, and Ivan was no stranger to the police. He had a string of convictions that stretched all the way back to an assault charge when he was eighteen. At the time of Lily's murder, he had only been in Culver Creek less than a year, and he still managed to pick up a drunk and disorderly. He was a prime suspect, with a recently repainted car.

Bud Ivan had an alibi for the time of the murder, but it was a weak one from what Sage could see. He had been drinking at a bar, a place called the Raven's Nest, and though he had definitely been there that night, there was some discrepancy about just when he had left. The bartender placed him there later than the customers did, and Sage wondered how good the word of any of them were. From what he could see, the main reason the police eliminated Bud Ivan from the suspect list was that sketch drawn from the psychic girl's description. Long-haired, scruffy Bud Ivan looked nothing like the clean-cut man depicted in the drawing.

The car, the rap sheet, and Ivan's proximity to the creek made him a likely suspect in Sage's book, but then there was what he found out when he did a little digging. Bud Ivan no longer lived in Culver Creek. His current address was inside a state penitentiary, where he had wound up after he was convicted of murdering a child. Sage was decidedly confident as he made the drive out to the state pen, sure this was going to be a clear case of game, set, match.

❧

A haggard-looking Bud Ivan slouched in the chair across from Sage in the small interview room. Ivan narrowed his eyes in a menacing way but otherwise seemed completely apathetic.

"I'd like to ask you some questions about when you lived in Culver Creek," Sage said.

"Culver Creek?" Ivan said. "That's ancient history, man. I can barely remember what happened last week, let alone twenty years ago."

"You remember that a little girl was murdered maybe fifty yards from your back door? You remember that?"

"Sounds familiar," Ivan said, still slouching, sneering.

Sage stared at the man with disgust. What a worthless excuse for a human being.

"You followed the girls out there that night," Sage said. "Or you saw them and waded out into the creek."

"Nah," Ivan said. "Check the notes. I had an al-i-bi." He enunciated each syllable of that last word just to be extra obnoxious.

"A weak one," Sage said. "And then you went and repainted your car."

"It's a crime to paint a car?" Ivan said.

Sage's blood started to boil. Ivan's attitude was infuriating. Some dirtbag just like this had murdered his sweet, kind, caring sister without giving it a moment's notice, and all Sage wanted to do was wipe that smug smile off of Ivan's face. Instead, he slammed his hands down on the table.

"Why?" he demanded. "Why did you do it?" His voice was loud in the small room. He spared a glance over his shoulder at the guard by the door, who peered in the little window to survey the situation.

"Paint my car?" Ivan asked.

"Murder Lily Esposito!" Sage roared.

This finally got Ivan to sit up. His gaze was level and calm as he looked across the table at Sage.

"Look, I may not be a saint, but I ain't no monster who goes around murdering kids."

"What about," Sage paused to consult his notes, "Tammy English."

"Tammy?" Ivan said. "Tammy weren't no kid. Look, she told me she was twenty-two, and would a kid go and screw around behind your back with your goddamn stepbrother? Anyway, that's who I was aiming for, that shit-weasel stepbrother of mine, but my fucking hand slipped."

Sage cursed himself for not looking more into Ivan's case. He got so excited when he saw that the man had been convicted for killing a child, he hadn't looked further.

He looked over and was surprised to see mean, nasty Bud Ivan had a few tears running down his scarred and wrinkled cheeks.

"Tammy," he said. "It's her own fault. If she hadn't been such a stupid slut, she wouldn't have got herself shot."

Sage watched Bud Ivan unravel before his eyes. His tears became sobs, and then through the crying he repeated Tammy's name again and again. He was criminal scum to be sure, and though he might have some regrets about killing his underage girlfriend, Sage couldn't really muster up any pity for the man. But he knew that as worthless as Bud Ivan might have been, he wasn't the man who had murdered Lily Esposito.

~

T he sun was low in the sky as Sage walked across the parking lot to his car. The big, ugly penitentiary building loomed behind him. He was no closer to finding Lily Esposito's murderer, and the meeting with Bud Ivan left him with a bad taste in his mouth and the desire to take a long, hot shower.

Ivan's tear-soaked retelling of the murder of his underage girlfriend played on repeat in Sage's head. What if Melodie's murder had all been some huge mistake? What if whoever shot her was aiming for someone else instead? For the longest time, this was the only thing that made any sense to Sage. Then he had discovered the web sleuth forums and had become a cop, and it quickly became apparent that just about everyone had some secret life, and he came around to the idea that whatever had gotten Melodie killed was some deep dark secret.

She hadn't even wanted to keep it a secret, he reasoned. That weekend she came up to see him, she had tried to tell him, but he wasn't interested in listening. He had been too busy wallowing in his own sad misery to give two shits about anyone else, even his own sister, and maybe if he had just listened to her, she would still be here.

He reached his car and slammed his fist hard into the metal panel between the back and front doors. His hand stung, and bright red spots of blood appeared on his knuckles where the skin had broken. Belatedly he looked up at the light post two spaces away and the security camera mounted there. Well, it wasn't like he had committed a crime. They couldn't even get him on destruction of police property. The car was fine, only his hand had suffered any damage.

He let himself into the vehicle and sat there in the parking lot with Bud Ivan's scratchy voice still echoing in his head. Ivan had been aiming for his stepbrother. Who had Melodie's killer been gunning for?

Bud Ivan was busy drinking himself into oblivion the night Lily Esposito was killed, and Sage would wager he had been equally drunk the fateful day he shot his girlfriend instead of his shit-weasel stepbrother. And in that way they were alike, because when his sister had needed him the most, he was drunk and useless.

Sage hadn't needed a twelve-step program. He hadn't touched alcohol since his sister was murdered, but even a lifetime of sobriety wouldn't bring her back.

16

CAITLIN THOUGHT she was looking at a used maxi pad. It didn't make any sense. How would one of her pads wind up on the floor in the corner of the linen closet? Could Adam have come into their bathroom, taken it out of the trash, and stuck it in the closet? That seemed pretty gross, but then kids could be gross. There was that time she had caught him playing with some of his bath toys in the toilet, so who knows.

She wasn't supposed to be in the linen closet, but she was desperate and held out hope that somehow some of her stash had escaped Lance's mad purging. Unfortunately, her search hadn't turned up any more boxes of sleeping pills.

She kicked the used pad out of the dark reaches of the closet. Once it was out in the light, she saw it wasn't a pad at all. It was a sock, one of Lance's socks, and it was soaked with blood. Had he cut his foot? Maybe he had a blister that started bleeding.

Two things occurred to her. First, just days ago her husband had cleaned this entire bathroom top to bottom, and second, when she had done the laundry the other day, his white athletic sock with the blue stripe had turned up mateless. She toed at the bloody sock on the floor and saw the blue stripe on it.

In the past few days, Lance hadn't mentioned any cuts or blisters on his feet. She certainly hadn't noticed anything, but truthfully, she didn't spend all that much time looking at her husband's feet. Still, it wasn't just a spot of blood on this sock. This thing was pretty soaked.

Now she came back to that first thing. Her husband had randomly, out of the blue, cleaned their bathroom top to bottom. Why? What was he hiding? What besides her stash of sleeping pills had he thrown in the trash? Clearly he had meant to throw out this sock too but had missed it.

"Daddy is a bad man," she heard Adam say.

Caitlin's blood went cold. When had Adam said that? It was after waking up from one of his nightmares, wasn't it? What if she had it all wrong? What if Adam's dreams weren't a rerun of her own childhood nightmares? Adam might have been dreaming about something that hadn't happened yet, something Lance was going to do.

Caitlin shook her head. No, she was being ridiculous. This was Lance. He wouldn't do anything bad. She looked back down at that blood-soaked sock.

Where did he and Adam go today? Had Lance actually said where they were going? She ran out of the bathroom and retrieved her phone.

She ended the call when Lance's voicemail picked up. Should she be concerned that he didn't answer? Maybe he was driving and couldn't get to his phone, but didn't he always use that hands-free thing in the car? She tried again. Then, just to be sure, two more times. Voicemail, voicemail, voicemail.

She told herself there was no need to panic. But telling herself there was no need to panic and not panicking were two different things. Of course there had to be a perfectly reasonable explanation for the blood-soaked sock, and it was weird that Lance took Adam for some boys' day out, but it wasn't necessarily suspicious.

What she needed to do was talk to someone who would be calm and reasonable and who would allay all her fears. So probably her mother was the last person she should have called, but all the same, that was the contact she selected on her phone.

Unlike Lance, her mother picked up right away. There was so much background noise, she could barely hear Luanne's voice. It sounded like a carnival.

"Where are you?" Caitlin asked.

"Vegas," Luanne said. "You really are gifted, I was just about to call you. You must have known."

"I didn't," Caitlin insisted. "Wait, Vegas as in Las Vegas."

"Yes!" Luanne yelled over the background noise. "Guess what? Stu and I got hitched!"

"Wait, who's Stu? Is he the one who works at the supermarket?"

"No," Luanne said. "Stu has the insurance agency."

Caitlin had a hard time keeping track of all her mother's beaus. Then the full import of her mother's words hit her.

"Wait a minute, when you say hitched . . ."

"That's right," Luanne said. "Stu made an honest woman of me."

"Oh God, Mom," Caitlin said.

"I think the traditional response is 'Congratulations,'" Luanne said, snippy. She had moved into a quieter area, because the background noise died down.

"Yes, congratulations, I guess," Caitlin said. "Do you even know this guy?"

"Caitlin, we're in love!" Luanne shouted.

Caitlin tried her best to feel happy for her mother. It wasn't easy to do when she was worried about her own husband and the safety of her son, which was all she could think about as her mother described some show she and Stu had gone to and the restaurant where they had eaten the night before.

When she could finally get a word in edgewise, Caitlin told her mother an abbreviated version of the bloody sock story. She left out the part about her sleeping pills and Adam's pronouncement that Lance was a bad man. When she spoke everything out loud, it didn't really sound that bad at all. She had found a sock with blood on it, and her husband had taken Adam out for the day so she could have some peace and quiet to get some work done. And here she was wasting her time looking for sleeping pills and freaking out over a sock instead of using this time to work. She felt like such an idiot. Well, maybe she still had some time to accomplish something before Lance and Adam returned.

"Mom, I've got to go," Caitlin said.

"You know, I never really liked him," Luanne said.

"What? Who?" Caitlin said. She thought—hoped—her mother must be talking about one of her other beaus, the supermarket one perhaps.

"Lance," Luanne said. "There was always something about him. I could never really put my finger on it, but he just looks like someone who can't be trusted."

"Mother, honestly, I don't know what you're talking about. I'm going now."

"Intuition," Luanne continued. "That's something you were never really good at, listening to your intuition."

"Did intuition tell you to marry a man you barely even know?" Caitlin asked, but she hung up before her mother could reply.

~

Caitlin held herself responsible for her parents' divorce. She knew this was typical, misguided thinking for kids from broken homes, but her case was an exception. Sure, maybe she wasn't entirely responsible, but if she hadn't had that dream about the murdered little girl, they never would have gone to Culver Creek and her mom would never have met Bill Brighton.

Luanne had always been one for flirting. Even as a kid Caitlin had been embarrassed by her mother's antics at stores, mechanic shops, or anywhere she might have the chance to chat with men. But loud, brash Luanne was always doing something that embarrassed her daughter. The flirting was just one more thing in a long line of cringe-worthy behaviors.

Culver Creek was different. For starters, she and her mother were on their own, away from home. When Luanne read that news story, she packed a suitcase for each of them, and they hopped in the car and drove to the small Pennsylvania town over two hours away.

Caitlin recalled her father standing in the driveway beside Luanne's rolled-down window asking how long they would be gone.

"As long as it takes," Luanne snapped at him. He made his usual vague noises about this being a bad idea, but Luanne had shamed him into silence. "A little girl has been killed, and Caitlin may be the only one who knows how to find her murderer."

"But couldn't you just handle this over the phone?" he asked.

It was a question Caitlin had asked her mother as well, but Luanne was insistent. They needed to go out there. Her mother claimed that this was too important to handle over the phone and that right now the phone lines were flooded with tips from would-be sleuths from across the country. If they wanted to be taken seriously, they needed to show up in person.

There was probably some truth in her mother's words, but as she got a little older and wiser, Caitlin came to better understand her mother's decision to drive out to Culver Creek.

Her mother craved attention and loved the idea of being in the limelight, which were both things that assisting in solving a high-profile murder offered, but not if they simply made a phone call. If Luanne wanted to be in the spotlight, she needed to go to where the action was. So she and her psychic daughter trekked out to Culver Creek.

The swamped police department didn't have time for dealing with some crazy lady from New Jersey whose daughter had experienced a nightmare. They passed them off to some junior officer who made it very clear that he had better things to do than to write down a statement. It all might have ended right there, a scant hour after their arrival in the small town.

But Luanne decided it had been a long day for both of them, and they should treat themselves to ice cream. She had managed to book them a room at a motel a few miles outside of town that was filled with members of the news media still covering the hot story.

"We'll stay overnight," Luanne announced as they sat in

the ice cream parlor licking their cones. "It's too far to go back tonight, and maybe we can get one of the reporters interested in your story." Luanne frowned across the table at Caitlin. "I'll have to fix up your hair so it looks more photogenic. What do you think? Do you want to be on television? Wouldn't that be exciting?"

"I guess so," Caitlin said, though she was not at all enthusiastic about the idea of going on television. On the one hand, it would be a cool story to tell at school, but on the other, the reporters were going to have so many questions about her dreams, and that would be even worse than her mother quizzing her about her dreams.

As they sat there eating their ice cream cones, a police officer walked into the shop and walked up to the counter. Caitlin found herself staring at the Culver Creek patch sewn onto his uniform's sleeve. Her mother, too, seemed mesmerized by the cop.

Luanne instructed Caitlin to wait at the table, and she sauntered up to the counter beside the police officer. Even from a few feet away, Caitlin could see her mother's shameless flirting. She shrank into her seat as Luanne all but threw herself at the helpless cop.

It shouldn't have worked, but a few seconds later, Luanne returned to the table with the police officer in tow. Officer Brighton was a big, beefy man with a bristly mustache that became frosted with mint chocolate chip ice cream as he ate.

Luanne and Caitlin made a second trip to the Culver Creek police station that afternoon, but this time they were treated like expert witnesses as an enraptured Brighton took down a fresh statement and plied Caitlin with questions. He asked if they could return the next day because he wanted to bring in a sketch artist to talk to Caitlin about the man she had seen in her dream.

~

"I missed you today," Lance said as they came downstairs after putting Adam to bed.

By the time he and Adam had returned home, both looking exhausted from their boys' day out, she had realized how crazy her runaway thoughts had been. Maybe she had more of her mother in her than she realized. She didn't think she would ever marry someone on a whim, but there was a touch of her mother's penchant for being overly dramatic.

"Oh God, I almost forgot to tell you," Caitlin said as they went into the living room and sat on the couch. "My mother got married."

"What?" Lance said. "When? To who?"

"Stu," Caitlin said. "They went out to Vegas."

"Is Stu the retired postal worker?" Lance asked.

"No, he's the one who has an insurance agency. She's unbelievable."

"Maybe she just wanted to be a little more financially secure," Lance said.

Well, of course Lance would say something like that. Just because Raquel married for money didn't mean that was what was going on with Luanne, and Caitlin almost said it aloud, but then she realized she couldn't really pick on Raquel, not today anyway. Much as her mother-in-law annoyed her, Luanne's latest antics were making Raquel look like the normal one.

She was trying to work out how to casually bring the bloody sock into the conversation when Lance slipped his hand beneath her shirt. His touch sent a current of excitement coursing through her body. He leaned in and pressed his lips to the side of her neck before delicately teasing her earlobe with his tongue. She turned to him and gently pulled his lips to her own, and as she shifted position, pressing his body firmly against hers, she forgot entirely about socks, bloody or otherwise.

17

LANCE PECKED AWAY at his keyboard doing his best to draft the monthly progress report Doug insisted he file. Writing these things always reminded him of being back at Ryerson and trying to type up an essay or term paper. One thing about going to boarding school was it meant you learned how to work through any manner of distractions. A soccer game going on in the hallway? No problem. Half a dozen boys in your dorm room shooting the shit about whatever movie or band was the *in* thing at that moment? Nothing but background noise. And a cell phone that wouldn't stop ringing? Lance told himself he barely heard the thing, but he did slip open the drawer where he had stashed it to take a look at the display.

It was the damn dream whisperer again. He had been dodging her calls for days. Well, he had himself to blame for that. He'd actually answered the first time she called. It had been his intention to apologize and try to set things right with her. She responded by suggesting that he should bring Adam back in for a follow-up visit, at no charge. He assured her that was generous, but used the excuse that he was busy with work. She had countered that with suggesting that Adam's mom perhaps could bring him in. So he had to lamely say that his wife was busy too. It should have been enough, but for all her mystical intuition, Phelicity Green seemed to not be able to take a hint.

He didn't answer any more of her calls, but that didn't seem to deter her. She left one voicemail message after another. There was a lot of new-age mumbo jumbo interspersed with her assurance that she wasn't after his money, an assurance that to Lance's trained ears meant most assuredly she was after his money. She had no doubt taken note of his watch, his shoes. Maybe she had even spied his Audi parked on the street. She knew he had some dough, and now she just needed to figure out her best strategy for parting him from it.

His phone chimed to let him know he had a new voicemail message. He should ignore it and get the damn progress report done, but curiosity got the better of him. The dream whisperer's voicemail messages had been growing increasingly more bizarre, and he wanted to hear what she had to say this time around.

He set the phone on the desk and switched it to speaker. Her tinny voice spilled out of the device. "Mr. Walker, I'm sorry I missed you."

"Yeah, I bet you are," he muttered to his empty office.

"I can't stress enough how imperative it is that you and Adam come back to meet with me," she said. "As I've explained previously, there would be no charge for the visit. I detected a certain psychic energy when I spoke with Adam, and I think it's very important for me to see you and him again so that we can explore this further. I must emphasize that there could be grave consequences if we do not address this issue at once."

There was a rap on his door, and when he looked up, Corey was standing in the open doorway. Lance quickly silenced his phone.

"What's that all about?" Corey asked and nodded toward the phone. "Sounds serious."

"Just some nutter," Lance assured him.

"You're not sick or something are you?" Corey glanced back out into the hall to see if the coast was clear, then stepped into Lance's office, closing the door behind him.

"Trust me, I'm fit as a fiddle." Lance looked hopelessly at his computer screen where the two lackluster sentences of his unfinished progress report seemed to taunt him.

"Yeah, well, check this," Corey said. "I go into the doctor a few weeks ago because I feel like the old ticker's maybe not working like it used to, right? Honestly, it was Evelyn who made me go, you know what with my dad having his heart trouble and all. So Doc goes and gives me a prescription for these pills. Well, next thing you know, I can't get it up."

Lance abandoned any pretense of trying to work on the progress report.

"Probably just an off night," Lance said.

"Yeah, that's what I was thinking, too, I mean, it was Evelyn, who, let's face it, could probably shrivel up the testicles of even a sex-starved prison inmate with just one glance, but then the other night I'm with this fucking model, and it was just not happening, man."

"Maybe you should talk to your doctor," Lance said.

"I did one better. I took a look at that little paper they give you with the pills. You should see all the side effects this thing has. I mean, it's like a mile long in microscopic

type, and right there in black and white: impotence. I threw
the whole goddamn bottle in the trash."

"Is that such a good idea?" Lance asked.

"Look, I'd rather get felled by a heart attack than be
some limpdick loser," Corey said. "So all I'm saying is you
watch out for these doctors. Who knows what the hell shit
they're trying to shove down your throat." Corey nodded at
the phone still sitting on Lance's desk.

L ance stared, transfixed by the words on his computer
screen. After Corey had shared his story about the
heart pills, Lance was reminded of something he wanted to
look up. He had meant only to track down the sleeping pills
Caitlin claimed couldn't be picked up in the local drug
store. He thought he might be able to track some down
online. Instead he found an article about the pills having
been discontinued and a statement about the host of side
effects that had prompted this.

Like Corey's heart medication, the side effects list was
lengthy, but there were some particular symptoms that
jumped out at him. Prolonged use could lead to cognitive
dysfunction, memory issues, mental fog and periods of
confusion. Right away he saw their oven in flames. He
heard Caitlin's panicked voice on the other end of the
phone when she called to tell him about her car accident.
He had chalked up her recent mishaps to work stress and
trying to balance her career with the equally demanding
task of being a mother, but what if it was all side effects
from those damn sleeping pills?

He blamed himself. It had been clear to him for some
time that she was addicted to the pills, and a part of him was

troubled about her overuse of the drugs, though not troubled enough to try to help her. It had been pure selfishness on his part, because having a wife who slept soundly through the night was a huge benefit to him. There were a million things he loved about Caitlin, but the fact was he never would have considered the two of them moving in together and then later marrying if he had learned that she was a light sleeper or someone who woke often during the night.

Now Caitlin was suffering from the cognitive dysfunction that was listed in the side effects, and it might have all been due to his own selfishness. He might have saved her from herself without realizing it with his mad bathroom cleaning, but he also wondered, if the drugs were that habit-forming, if quitting them cold turkey might have serious repercussions.

There were other sleeping pills out there, ones that were still sold legally. Certainly their side effects couldn't have been anywhere near as severe as the Pacifcleon list. Weren't there even some herbal sleep remedies? If all else failed, maybe he could purchase some sort of magic sleep amulet from Phelicity Green.

That last idea made him laugh out loud in his empty office.

~

"I need to head out a little bit early," Lance said, peeking his head into Doug's office. "Have an errand I need to run."

"Did you have that monthly progress report?" Doug asked.

"I'm gonna finish it up tonight," Lance promised as he

started backing out of the doorway. "I'll email it to you first thing tomorrow morning."

Doug might have protested, but Lance had already made it so far down the hallway that his friend and boss would have needed to physically get up and intercede, which Lance knew wasn't going to happen.

L ance picked up one of those little baskets on his way into the drug store and navigated to the sleep aids aisle. Insomnia was clearly big business, judging by all the competing products that promised a good night's sleep. And this was only the over-the-counter junk. There was a whole market of prescription-strength stuff as well.

Lance started off reading the fine print on the back of each package, trying to compare them to each other, but there were too many different products, and he found he was losing track of which box had said what. He had a better solution. None of the packages were overly expensive, and since the ultimate decision would come down to Caitlin anyway, he would just buy one of each and let her decide what she wanted to use. She could even experiment with the different pills to see which worked best for her— well, if that was advised.

A woman stepped into the aisle as Lance was filling his basket up with sleeping aids.

"Wow, you must really have trouble sleeping," she said.

Lance chuckled politely. He waited for the woman to move on to the next aisle before he finished his sleeping aid shopping spree as quickly as he could. He didn't want to attract any more attention to himself.

When his phone rang, he thought it would be Caitlin

wanting to know where he was, but when he looked at the display, he saw it was Phelicity Green calling again. He went into his phone's settings and did something he should have done about five phone calls ago. He blocked the dream whisperer's number.

18

IT WASN'T Lance's fault. He didn't understand why none of the sleeping pills he had bought for her weren't what she was looking for. It was her own fault for not explaining that it wasn't sleep that she craved so much as sleep that was uninterrupted by dreams. In fact, from what she had gleaned from online forums, some of the pills Lance had purchased were all but guaranteed to give her all manner of crazy dreams. She would have gladly gone without sleep entirely rather than put herself through that torture, which was why, out of desperation, she was spending her day schlepping all the way out to some godforsaken place called Mudmound Township, Pennsylvania.

Caitlin glanced in the rearview mirror and saw Adam strapped into his car seat happily playing with his stuffed kangaroo. At least for now he was occupied, but their journey had only just begun, and they had a long way to go. She feared he would get restless long before they reached their destination. When she had done a quick calculation of how long it would take them to get to Mudmound Township and back—nearly four hours round trip—she realized she had no option but to take Adam with her today instead of dropping him off at school. She wouldn't be able to make it back in time to pick him up.

Should the issue come up, she would tell Lance that she kept Adam home from school because he was complaining of a tummy ache, but she didn't plan on telling him about driving all the way out to Pennsylvania and back, mainly because the reason seemed borderline insane, and because when he was showering her with his treasure trove of sleep aids last night, he kept stressing over and over again that Pacifcleon was too dangerous and that she needed to stop taking it at once, blathering on and on about cognitive dysfunction and such. The problem was that he couldn't begin to understand the cognitive dysfunction that would most certainly ensue when she started having her awful, terrible psychic dreams again.

When she failed to find any new online listings for Pacifcleon, she had decided to go more guerilla in her shopping methods. The media was always full of stories about the retail apocalypse. So she reasoned there had to be more than one drugstore out there that had closed up shop but still had some unsold inventory. There wasn't actually a database of closed pharmacies, so tracking them down took some serious internet searching, but her hard work had paid off.

After contacting a pharmacy in Connecticut that had liquidated all their remaining inventory in an auction and another in Maryland that said they had no more Pacifcleon in their inventory, she finally got ahold of Wright's Pharmacy in Mudmound Township, PA. The woman who answered the phone said the pharmacy had closed its doors after her husband, the proprietor, passed away, but while Caitlin was on the phone, the woman had gone into the storeroom to check and assured Caitlin they still had a case of Pacifcleon in stock. They made arrangements to meet at the shuttered pharmacy to pay cash for the expired old pills. Perhaps sensing the note of desperation in Caitlin's voice, she quoted a price that was the equivalent of highway robbery, but Caitlin didn't care. She considered it a miracle that the store even had the drug, because as of the previous evening she had officially exhausted her supply.

As she watched her estimated arrival time nearing, Caitlin began to get a prickly sense of déjà vu. Things looked vaguely familiar. She was pretty sure she had never been to Mudmound Township, but maybe on one of their road trips they had passed through this way.

What surprised her was that things looked even more familiar once she took the exit off the highway. Why did that gas station look so familiar? What was it about that intersection that felt like something buried at the back of her head?

Then she saw two words on one of those mileage signs that made her suddenly dizzy: Culver Creek. They were only two miles from that awful town, and from what she could tell, they were going to drive straight through the town she had planned on never setting foot in again. How was it possible that Mudmound Township was so close to Culver Creek, and how had she missed it?

∽

Time had not been kind to Culver Creek. It certainly looked more vacant and run down than Caitlin remembered, but it was also instantly recognizable. Her palms grew damp with sweat, and she gripped the steering wheel a little tighter.

"Mommy, can we have ice cream cones?" Adam asked from the backseat.

She almost let out a yelp. Instead she said, "Later, honey. First Mommy has to run an errand."

She saw where he was looking—that ice cream parlor where her mother had first met Bill Brighton. Something unnerved her about it, and it wasn't just the bad memories. The sign had pretty pastel lettering but no ice cream cone graphics. Adam had mastered writing out the four letters of his first name, but he hadn't learned to read yet. So how did he know the little building was an ice cream parlor? Some sort of childhood intuition? Or were darker forces at play?

She sped up despite the posted twenty-five miles per hour speed limit in town. More than ever she wanted to get out of this place.

Mudmound Township was further than she realized, and it didn't help that Caitlin had made more than one wrong turn along the way. By the time she pulled into the small parking lot in front of the closed-up shop, Adam had fallen asleep in his car seat. He looked so cozy and serene with his fleece blanket tucked around him. She hated the idea of waking him, and she hated herself for thinking that if she didn't bring Adam in with her, he wouldn't be able to rat her out to Lance, but her thoughts went there.

The shop was tiny, and there was a big picture window in the front. Plus, there didn't seem to be a soul around in this desolate town. She would just run inside quickly. She could keep watch on the car through the window. No, she couldn't do that. She would wake him up. He would be tired and cranky. He would be hungry. It was way past lunchtime. She was hungry too.

She would be inside the store for what? Two minutes? She had already arranged everything over the phone. Mrs. Wright said she had set the case aside for Caitlin, and Caitlin reached into her purse and slipped out the envelope filled with the agreed-upon cash amount. She would be in and out lickety-split, and she would watch the car the whole time.

The front door of the pharmacy was locked. Well, of course it was. The place was closed for business. Caitlin knocked on it, while watching the car for signs of movement. Adam didn't stir in the backseat. Maybe he would keep sleeping on the ride home. That would be good. It meant he wouldn't wake up looking to eat lunch.

Thanks to her wrong turns, they didn't really have time to stop, plus she didn't want to stop anywhere around here. The last restaurants she had seen were back in Culver Creek, and despite her ice cream promise, there was no way they were stopping to eat in that town. What she wanted was to get home. They could eat when they were safe and sound at home.

A white-haired woman came to the door and smiled at Caitlin before fumbling with the door lock. It took her nearly a minute to figure the thing out.

"You must be Katy," the woman said.

Caitlin considered correcting her but decided it didn't matter. She followed the woman into the store, still keeping her eye on the car outside.

"I put the box on the counter." The woman led Caitlin over to the desk that held a covered-up cash register. Beside it was a cardboard box printed with the familiar Pacifcleon logo. Caitlin's heart skipped a beat. Everything was going to be okay.

Caitlin thrust the envelope at Mrs. Wright and grabbed the box, but of course the older woman wanted to count the money and make sure it was all there. She did her money counting with the same speed at which she had opened the door, lost track, and had to start over from scratch. Caitlin shifted her feet restlessly. She looked back at the car. The way the sun was reflecting off the windshield, she couldn't really see into the backseat from here.

Well, if Mrs. Wright was going to check the money, then Caitlin could at least check her goods, make sure she wasn't getting short-changed. She set the box back down and lifted the flap on top. The box wasn't sealed, so it was possible she wasn't getting the promised full case.

Something was wrong. Caitlin stared at the contents of the box. It was filled to the top, but the boxes were unrecognizable. It wasn't Pacifcleon. It was some other sleep remedy. Maybe it was just the ones on top. Caitlin began to frantically dig through the box, but the whole thing was filled with boxes of the other stuff.

"Well, looks like it's all here," Mrs. Wright said.

"This isn't the right stuff," Caitlin said. "It's not Pacifcleon."

Mrs. Wright pushed her glasses up her nose and squinted at the side of the box.

"No, that's what it says," she said, pointing at the printing.

"It's different stuff inside." Caitlin pulled out one of the boxes and waved it in the air.

"Well, it must be in the back storeroom," Mrs. Wright said. "There's so much back there. Do you know what it looks like?"

"The package is green, and . . ." Caitlin searched her brain for a description that would make it jump out at the old lady. Caitlin would have recognized it in a second, if it was even back there.

"Perhaps you should come back and take a look," Mrs. Wright suggested.

Caitlin glanced back at the car. She would just be a moment. How big could the storeroom be in this little shop? If it was there, she would spot it right away.

Caitlin hadn't expected the disarray that greeted her when she stepped into the back storeroom. Stuff was piled up every which way, half-filled boxes scattered on the floor.

"I keep meaning to get this all cleaned up," Mrs. Wright said.

Caitlin scanned the room quickly, but nothing caught her eye. That didn't mean the Pacifcleon wasn't here, though. It could be anywhere in this mess. She began digging through the boxes on one of the shelves, adding to the disarray in her desperation. Mrs. Wright made some murmurs of disapproval, but Caitlin was long past caring. She had driven all the way out here. She was going to find the pills she needed. There seemed to be no rhyme or reason to the boxes and shelves that crowded the little room. Caitlin moved quickly but left no area uncovered, and by the time she reached the farthest corner, the ugly truth began to sink in. There was no Pacifcleon here.

Caitlin wanted to scream or cry in frustration. It wasn't fair. She had taken her son out of school and driven all the way out here, and for what? Adam! She needed to get back to the car.

"I have to go." Caitlin blinked back tears as she made her way out of the storeroom and then back to the shop's front door. Back outside, she could make out Adam's form still perfectly safe in his car seat. She heard the shop door open behind her.

Mrs. Wright came running out of the store, carrying Caitlin's envelope of cash.

"I have your number written down," Mrs. Wright said. "My son's supposed to come over this weekend and help me clean up the shop. I'll call you if we find those pills."

But Caitlin had searched that little room, and she knew there was no Pacifcleon. She thanked Mrs. Wright and shoved the envelope into her jacket pocket.

She was as quiet as she could be when she got in the car, even though she wanted to scream with rage. She fought the desire to speed out of the parking lot in the interest of not waking her napping son.

~

The day after she and her mother had ice cream with Officer Brighton, Caitlin sat in a room at the police station. She was nervous. She wished she had never told her mother about her nightmare. All she wanted was to go home. In the hall outside she heard her mother giggling in a high-pitched voice at something Officer Brighton said. It was like her mother was going out of her way to be extra annoying.

When Officer Brighton and her mother stepped into the room, there was a third person with them, a woman with a large drawing pad in her hand—the police sketch artist.

"Caitlin, I want you to close your eyes and try to remember what the man you saw looked like," Officer Brighton said. "Do your best to see every detail you can. Can you remember if he had any scars or distinctive marks? That will help us a lot."

The sketch artist set up her stuff on the table in the room, and Caitlin did as she was instructed. She closed her eyes and took a deep breath before returning to her memory of that horrible dream. She didn't want to go back there. She didn't want to see what happened to the little girl in her dream. Most of all, she didn't want to see the face of the man who had done it.

She was silent, and when she opened her eyes, the three adults in the room were looking at her expectantly.

Brighton squatted down on the floor in front of her so that he was looking at her at eye level.

"Caitlin, can you please tell this lady what the man you saw looks like?"

Caitlin didn't say anything. Tears started to form at the corners of her eyes. Why had she ever told her mother about her bad dream?

"Caitlin," Luanne said, "remember, this is the only way they are going to find that bad man so that he can't hurt anyone else. You don't want him to hurt anyone else, do you?"

Caitlin shook her head and wiped at her damp eyes with the back of her hand.

She closed her eyes again, and this time she described the man she saw—the way he loomed over little Lily. She described his short, dark hair, his pale skin and his dark eyes. Brighton asked her if there were any scars or marks on his face, but she didn't see any. She described the faint stubble on his face, how his hair was maybe a bit thinner on the top than on the sides. She answered the questions Brighton and the artist asked.

The whole ordeal felt like it lasted forever. When she was finally done, she felt exhausted, like she was ready for bed, even though it wasn't even lunchtime yet. Brighton held up the sketch so she could see it and confirm whether or not it looked like the man she had seen. She nodded. It was a face she never wanted to see again, and she vowed to do everything she could to erase it from her memory.

"We can go home now, right?" Caitlin asked as she and Luanne left the police station. There were a few news crews outside the police station, and Caitlin saw her mother eyeing them with interest.

"You did a very good job in there," Luanne told her, which Caitlin noted was not an answer to her question.

"Can we go home?" Caitlin repeated.

"Well, first, how about we go get some lunch. Then after lunch, that nice Officer Brighton has some pictures he would like you to take a look at."

Her mother neglected to tell her that Officer Brighton would be joining them for lunch. Caitlin picked moodily at her sandwich, unable to avoid seeing the way her mother repeatedly patted and touched the police officer's hand and arm. She was disgusted when she returned from using the bathroom to find the two of them blushing and her mother giggling like a little girl.

She could barely contain her annoyance as she spent the afternoon paging through what seemed to be hundreds of photos to determine if any of the unhappy-looking men in them could have been the man she had seen in her dream. After a while their features seemed blur together, but none of them jumped out at her as looking familiar. The afternoon spent looking at photos did have one small upside. By the time she left the police station late in the afternoon with an aching head, she found that she no longer saw the face she had spent the morning trying to recall. She supposed if she tried hard enough she could conjure it back up from the depths of her memory, but she had no desire to do that.

～

Caitlin spent the drive back stressing. What was she going to do? She was officially out of Pacifcleon. She could try sleeping without it, but maybe her body was so dependent on the stuff that she wouldn't even be able to. Well, that wouldn't be such a bad thing—staying awake. Maybe that was the solution.

She was a few miles from the house when she decided to make an emergency stop at a convenience store. Energy drinks were the answer. Caitlin made a beeline for the refrigerated case at the back of the store and grabbed an assortment of energy drinks. As she juggled the five cans in her arms, her stomach growled. She had forgotten all about eating lunch, and that was when she remembered Adam.

He had been so silent sleeping in the backseat, she had forgotten all about him. She dropped the armful of energy drinks on the ground and sprinted toward the door. One of the cans must have punctured when it fell because she heard a spraying sound behind her, and the clerk shouted at her, "Ma'am, you have to pay for that. Ma'am?"

Caitlin ran out to the parking lot and yanked open the back door. She pulled off the fleece blanket and went to scoop Adam up, but she got only a handful of stuffed kangaroo. She shoved the toy away, as if Adam could somehow be hiding beneath it, but his car seat was empty. She let out a strangled cry and spun around.

She scanned the small parking lot. She squatted down to peer under the parked vehicles, but Adam wasn't there.

"Did you lose something?" a man coming out of the store asked.

"My son!" Caitlin said.

"Did he run off?" the man asked.

"My son!" Caitlin repeated as she looked uselessly around the parking lot. "Adam!"

19

SAGE SAT at his desk flipping through the pages of the Lily Esposito file. The car Raquel Walker described hadn't belonged to Bud Ivan, but could it have belonged to Lily's murderer? Culver Creek was a small town, and the neighborhood down near the creek was even smaller; a strange car would have been noticed, and likely by more than one resident. Yet as he flipped through the pages of the report, there didn't seem to be any follow-up investigation on the car. It was yet another example of the shoddy work that had been done on the case.

Sage went back and reread the statement from Raquel Walker, and that was when he noticed something he had missed before. There had been two officers there when she made her statement, and one of them was Steve Arlo.

Sage jumped up from his desk and went over to where Rod was regaling a couple of junior officers with some tale of heroic derring-do.

"You know where Steve is?" Sage asked.

Rod looked pissed that Sage had interrupted his story, but Rod had a gift for gab. Once he got going on one of his stories, he might end up talking for a quarter of an hour or more.

"Why?" Rod asked. "You going to arrest his son again?"

This earned him a laugh from the two other officers. Sage kept his expression impassive. He wasn't going to take the bait. Kevin Arlo was never formally charged, but that decision had not been Sage's. Nor had it been Steve's. He wisely kept himself out of the whole affair. It was Rayanne who made the final decision. Sage hadn't agreed with her. Kevin needed a wakeup call. Sage hadn't shared this opinion with Steve or any of the other officers, but maybe Kevin had shot his mouth off, or maybe Rod was just trying to get him riled up.

"I need to ask him a question about the Lily Esposito case." Sage started to return to his desk, but Rod wasn't done with him.

"Here's what I don't get, why in the hell are they paying you all that money to stick your nose into some dusty old files and chase after some murderer who's long gone?"

"Because maybe he's not long gone," Sage said. "And either way, that little girl deserves justice."

At this Rod rolled his eyes, and the two junior officers laughed like he was a comedian. Sage might have delivered a longer explanation about closure for Lily's relatives and the importance of a fresh perspective and the benefits of modern technology, but Steve walked in the door and Sage decided he had wasted enough time talking to Rod and his cronies.

∼

S teve didn't remember the car.

"We talked to a lot of people that day," Steve said. "We canvassed the whole neighborhood. It was a hot summer day, up in the nineties I think."

They stood at the far corner of the squad room.

"This was at the Walker house," Sage said, and he thought he saw a flash of recognition. Sage double-checked the notes. "It was a single mom and her son, a few years older than Lily."

"A widow," Steve said.

"What?"

"She was a widow," Steve said. "I was there the night her husband died."

Sage's cop instincts tingled.

"Natural causes?" Sage asked.

"A bad fall down the stairs," Steve said. "Fell at an awkward angle and broke his neck. It was an awful thing."

"Did you suspect the wife at all?"

"She was out of town," Steve said. "Poor bastard was home babysitting the boy."

"Parenting," Sage corrected automatically.

"What?" Steve asked.

"He wasn't babysitting because it was his own kid. He was just performing his parental duties."

"Okay," Steve said.

He started to walk away.

"But what about the car? Do you know if you ever followed up on it? It seems like it could be significant."

Steve wasn't facing him when he said, "I think we worked out that it belonged to a friend or a relative of one of the other neighbors. Just someone who came in for a visit or something."

Sage stared at the retreating back of his colleague. A minute ago, he couldn't remember anything about the car, and now suddenly he knew it belonged to a friend or relative of one of the neighbors?

"You sure about that?" Sage asked. "There's nothing in the file."

"There were a lot of notes, not everything got saved. That was back before we digitized everything, so some stuff might have been lost in one of the floods."

This was the first Sage heard about records being lost in a flood. Was it possible he didn't have the complete file?

"Hey, Sage, can I talk to you a second?" Rayanne said, poking her head out of her office.

He had a feeling this was going to be a dressing down for how he had handled the Kevin Arlo thing.

It wasn't about the Kevin Arlo thing. Rayanne returned to her desk chair, while Sage sat down in one of the chairs facing her desk.

"How's everything been going?" Rayanne asked.

"No complaints," Sage said.

"You making any headway with that old murder case?"

"Not as much as I would like," Sage said, which felt like a gigantic understatement.

Rayanne nodded absently. "I've got a favor to ask of you," she said, and Sage wondered if the son of another officer had run afoul of the law. But then she said, "Mick Hillman is visiting the Rixby plant tomorrow."

The politician's face appeared in Sage's head as one of his recent campaign videos played out. Family values and hardworking Pennsylvanians and other vague, meaningless catchphrases swirled around in his head.

"Is he under investigation?" Sage asked hopefully.

Rayanne shook her head. Sage didn't have anything against Hillman personally. It was more of an aversion to all politicians.

"After touring the plant," Rayanne said, "he's scheduled to make a speech on the lawn outside. Hillman has his own security detail, but we've been tasked with providing crowd control."

"Are we really expecting the masses to turn out?" Sage asked.

"Apparently there's some sort of bonus being offered to Rixby employees and their families who attend the speech," Rayanne said.

"Bribery," Sage mused.

"I know it's not in your job description," Rayanne said, "but would you be willing to put on a uniform and pitch in?"

Sage could have come up with a thousand better ways to spend his time, but Rayanne wouldn't have asked him if she didn't really need him. Besides, it might be a good opportunity for him to show some solidarity with the rest of the Culver Creek police force.

"You can count on me."

20

LANCE HAD JUST STEPPED out of the men's room when Corey shouted, "Think fast, Walker!" Lance looked up to see a black and neon-pink nerf football sailing toward his head. Reflexes took over, and he reached up and plucked the ball from the air.

"What's going on out here?" Doug called from his office. He stepped out into the hallway and saw Lance with the football in his hands. For a moment Lance expected a dressing down from Doug, but instead a big grin appeared on Doug's face and he shouted, "I'm open!" as he took a running start down the hallway.

Lance sent the ball sailing over Corey's head and into Doug's waiting arms.

"Looks like somebody's a monkey in the middle," Doug said with a laugh, and as Corey started to charge in his direction, he hurled the ball back down the hallway to Lance.

The impromptu game continued, and at least for a few seconds, Lance felt like he was still a kid back at Ryerson and not a grown man playing catch at work. Frustrated with his monkey in the middle status, Corey charged at him, and Lance wasn't quick enough. The two of them toppled to the ground as the ball rolled harmlessly away. Someone cleared their throat, and when Lance looked up, he saw their receptionist Sheryl standing just behind Doug.

"Lance, there's someone here to see you," Dana said.

"Oh," Lance said. He was confused. He didn't have any appointments scheduled. Corey stretched to retrieve the dropped ball, and Lance couldn't resist kicking it just out of reach before he went down the hall to see who was here to meet with him. It wasn't until he stepped out into the reception area that he realized the quick game of catch and Corey's tackle had left him looking a bit disheveled. His shirt was untucked, his hair was askew, and he felt a bit flushed. If it was an important client, he would have to come up with a quick excuse on the fly, but his stomach dropped when he saw that the only people in the waiting area were two uniformed police officers.

Could this be about Caitlin's accident last week? Maybe they had something they needed to go over with him—a form he needed to sign, perhaps. He tried to reassure himself that there was probably a perfectly harmless reason they were here, but his voice still cracked when he asked, "Can I help you?"

"Mr. Walker?" the heavier police officer asked. Lance nodded. "Is there somewhere we can speak privately?" the cop continued.

Lance showed the two of them into his office. The doorknob rattled in his shaking hand as he shut the door.

"Is this about Caitlin's accident?" Lance asked as he sat at his desk. On the other side, the two officers exchanged surprised looks.

"Accident?" the heavier one repeated. Officer Young,

his name tag read, even though he was at least a decade older than his partner.

"Last week," Lance said, "the fender bender." But his voice trailed off at the end, because clearly that wasn't what they were doing here, which meant this was something more serious.

"Mr. Walker, when was the last time you saw your son?" Young asked.

"This morning," Lance said. "Why?"

"And he wasn't feeling well? That's why he didn't go to preschool?"

Adam? Lance felt dizzy. He placed a hand on the desk to steady himself.

"What's happened?" Lance asked. "Is he in the hospital?"

"Why would your son be in the hospital?" said the other cop—Marley, his name badge read.

"I don't know. You're the ones who came in here talking about him being sick." Lance's panic and dizziness were quickly giving way to impatience and anger. What right did these cops have to come in here asking questions without telling him what the hell was going on?

"Mr. Walker," Young said in a slow deliberate way, "was your son sick when you saw him this morning?"

"I don't know," Lance said. "I had to leave early. I had a meeting this morning. He was just waking up. Can you please tell me what the hell is going on?"

"Mr. Walker, your son disappeared this afternoon from a Quick Chek parking lot," Young said. Lance jumped up from his desk. "Please," Young continued, "we're just trying to piece together a timeline of events."

"Where's Caitlin?" Lance demanded. He yanked open his desk drawer and removed his phone and his keys.

"She's been cooperating with the police," Young said. "There's just some things we're trying to get straight."

"For God's sake," Lance said. "My son's missing, and you're sitting here asking me stupid questions? You should be out there looking for him!" Lance shoved his keys into his pocket and started dialing Caitlin's number as he stepped out of his office.

Doug and Corey were still in the hallway, Corey tossing the football up in the air and catching it again.

"I've got to go," Lance told them.

"Sore loser," Corey said with a laugh, but he shut up when he saw the two police officers follow Lance out of his office.

"Is everything okay?" Doug asked.

"It's Adam," Lance said. "I'll text you when I know more."

~

Of course Lily Esposito's murder had shocked Lance, as it did everyone in their small town. It didn't frighten him the way it did his mother, and he didn't feel sadness, exactly, but it left him with a funny hollow sort of feeling inside.

The day after it happened, or maybe it was two days after—time seemed to move at a different rate of speed that summer—police visited each house in the neighborhood. Lance remembered kneeling on the couch and watching them from the living room window as his mother paced and fidgeted in their small house. When the knock at their door came, she nearly jumped out of her skin. He was still kneeling on the couch but spun around to look at the door.

"I'll get it," she said in an unnaturally high voice. "You stay there."

She opened the door just enough to wedge her body into the opening. Sometimes his mother didn't like for someone to come inside if she feared the house wasn't clean enough, but the place was immaculate. Since the news of the murder, she had been trying to ease her nerves by cleaning the place obsessively.

Lance strained to hear what was being said at the door, but he caught only stray words, then he heard one of the police officers say his name. There was more mumbling, and then he heard the officer say in a louder voice, "May we speak with him, ma'am?"

He watched as his mother reluctantly moved out of the doorway and led the two officers into the living room. From where Lance sat on the couch, the two cops seemed to tower over him like giants. His mother stood beside them, her hands endlessly fiddling with a ribbon on her blouse.

"Hi, Lance," one cop said to him. "I'm Officer Goyle and this is Officer Arlo. Is it okay if we ask you a few questions?"

Lance nodded. His mouth suddenly felt too dry to form any words.

"He's not going to know anything," his mother said. Her voice still sounded unnaturally high. "He didn't know that girl."

"Is that true?" Officer Barnes asked him. "You didn't know Lily?"

Lance shrugged and looked to his mother for guidance. "No," he said at last, but it seemed to come out like a question.

"You never saw her before?" Barnes squatted down so he was at eye level with Lance.

"Sometimes," Lance mumbled.

"When was the last time you saw her?" Barnes asked.

Lance shrugged again. He honestly didn't know.

"Last week?" he said, but he really wasn't sure.

"Lance, can you remember seeing anyone around? Anyone who didn't seem to belong here? Anyone who might have been watching Lily?"

Lance shook his head.

"Are you sure?" Officer Barnes asked. "Think about it."

Lance tried to remember if he had seen anyone around. Nothing came to mind, but then his mother made a high-pitched squeaking noise, and the three of them turned to look her way.

"There was something I saw the other day." She bounced on her heels in excitement. "I forgot all about it until just now, but there was a car one afternoon driving very slowly down the road. I'd never seen it before, and it was older, kind of beat up."

Officer Arlo whipped out a notepad and began to scribble on it. He asked for more details about the car, and Raquel provided a vague description. It was dark blue or maybe green, and it had some rust on it. It looked like a man wearing a baseball cap driving the car.

It was the first time Lance heard his mother say anything about this car. Had that really been the murderer? Could she have seen him? He felt a little thrill of excitement at the idea, and then felt guilty about it. What if her description helped them find the murderer? Would she have to go to court to testify at the trial? His mind went off on a tangent as he considered this. Maybe he would get to go to court, too, but judging by the way both police officers had lost interest in him when she mentioned the car, he highly doubted it.

When Lance stepped into the police station, he saw Caitlin right away.

"What's going on?" he asked her.

She ran to him and threw herself into his arms. A jumbled stream of words flowed out of her mouth, and he struggled to understand what she was saying.

"Slow down," he said. "Take a deep breath."

She stepped back and took a gasping breath.

"He's missing," she said. Then the stream of words started back up, but this time Lance worked harder to make sense of it. What he gathered was that Caitlin had stopped off at Quick Chek but had left Adam alone in the car, and when she came back out, he was gone.

Lance thought of the exploded stove and Caitlin's car accident, and he had a sudden spark of inspiration.

"Are you sure he was with you?" Lance asked. "Could you have forgotten him at home?"

Caitlin shook her head, and one of the police officers, Marley, stepped in to say, "We went back to the house with Mrs. Walker and looked around, but Adam wasn't there."

"And you're sure he didn't go to school?" Lance asked.

"I kept him home," Caitlin said, "because he wasn't feeling well. It's all my fault."

"Mr. Walker," the other cop, Young, said. "If you could please step in here with us, there are some questions we need to ask you."

"Shouldn't you be out there looking for Adam?" Lance asked.

"We have officers searching for the boy," Young assured him. "If you could help us by answering some questions, we might be able to find him sooner."

Lance didn't see what he could tell the cops that would be of any help, but he relented. The sooner he answered their questions, the sooner they might actually get to work and try to find Adam.

Lance stepped into a small room, and Young and Marley followed. Young waved at a chair at the table, and Lance sat down. Young took the seat opposite him, but Marley remained standing.

"When did you last see your son?" Young asked.

"I already told you, this morning before I went to work," Lance said.

"But you didn't go to work first thing, right? You had a meeting?" Young asked.

"A work meeting," Lance explained.

"A meeting at your office?" Young asked.

"No, this was off campus, at a client's office," Lance said. "Or I was supposed to anyway."

"Supposed to?" Young asked, he leaned over the table just a bit, as if he was readying himself to listen to some fascinating story.

Lance sighed.

"I was nearly all the way there when I got a message that the meeting had been cancelled."

"So what you're saying is that no one can vouch for your movements this morning?" Young said. "About how long of a span of time are we talking about here?"

"I don't know," Lance said. "Maybe an hour and a half or so. I don't see how any of this is relevant. Caitlin had Adam with her when she went to the convenience store this afternoon. He was taken from the parking lot."

Young and Marley exchanged a glance, and Lance tried desperately to see what unspoken things were being said between the two police officers.

"What?" Lance asked. "What was that?"

"We have the security camera footage from the Quick Chek parking lot," Marley said. "Your wife's vehicle is in view the entire time. At no time did we see anyone other than her open any of the doors of the vehicle."

Lance slouched back in the seat. This was all his fault. There had been clear warning signs that Caitlin was not thinking clearly, and he hadn't done anything. She had been confused about taking Adam with her to the convenience store, but if he hadn't gone with her and he wasn't at home, then where was he? Wait, Caitlin probably wouldn't have made a whole trip out just to go to Quick Chek. She must have been running other errands too. She could have simply left Adam at the post office or the bank or something.

"We need to retrace her route," Lance said, sitting back up. "We need to find out all the places she went."

"Actually, Mr. Walker," Marley said, "there is some security camera footage we would like you to take a look at."

Lance shifted uncomfortably in his seat as Marley brought a laptop over to the table. He wasn't sure what to expect. Did they have footage of whoever had taken Adam? Did they think it was someone he would recognize?

Marley opened the computer and clicked a few buttons on the keyboard to bring up a video. "Can you tell us what exactly is going on here?"

The video was from a ceiling-mounted security camera that showed part of the interior of the convenience store. Lance watched as the front door of the store opened and Caitlin stepped inside. She walked toward the beverage case at the furthest edge of the video screen. He saw a couple of other shoppers in the store. Were they who he was supposed to be watching? Was it Caitlin he needed to keep his focus on? Caitlin had picked up a soda from the beverage case, but then she pulled out more. No, the cans looked taller than soda cans. Beer? But they wouldn't have that at Quick Chek. No, it looked like different cans of energy drinks. What the hell? Did Caitlin even drink that stuff?

He watched as his wife struggled with an armful of the cans, walking toward what he assumed was a register, but then she froze in the middle of the aisle. She dropped all the cans on the ground and bolted. He watched her run back out the front door and disappear from view. Something about the whole thing made him inescapably sad. It was like the stove all over again.

Marley took back over at the computer keyboard and backed up the video to where Caitlin was walking toward the register with the energy drink cans.

"See, what happened right here?" Marley asked at the point where Caitlin froze. "Something spooked her, but what?"

"There's no audio on the camera," Young added, "so we don't know if someone shouted something at her, if it was a song on the radio, or what."

On the computer screen Caitlin ran out the door again, and Marley rewound it to the same point and let it start playing. Lance turned away from the screen.

"Turn it off," Lance said. The cops both stared at him, but neither one said anything or made any move to stop the video. "I said turn it off!" Lance repeated, and this time he took matters into his own hands and slapped the laptop closed.

"Whoa," Marley said.

"Right now, my son is missing, and you're sitting here wasting your time with some stupid video," Lance said.

21

CAITLIN SAT in the stiff chair in the police station waiting area. Lance had been in the little meeting room with the police for what felt like forever, but when she pulled out her phone to check it, she saw it hadn't yet been ten minutes. Time no longer had any meaning.

Caitlin tried to deal with her racing heart and the all-over ache of her body by exhaling loudly through her mouth. She had a memory of watching breathing exercise videos on YouTube when she was pregnant with Adam. Thinking about her pregnancy sent a fresh wave of pain through her. Where was her baby? Where was her baby boy?

She had told the police everything she could remember about her stupid convenience store stop. Well, almost everything. The stuff that was relevant, she reasoned.

What she said was that she had to go out and run some errands, that Adam had fallen asleep in the car, and she had forgotten him when she made a quick stop at the convenience store. When she realized her error, she ran outside, but it was too late. He was already gone.

"I couldn't have been in the store more than a minute," she said.

"Two minutes, twenty-five seconds," that smartass Marley had said. They had security camera footage of her in the store, but how stupid was this? They could see her plain as day shopping, but those cameras hadn't picked up the sick psycho who had kidnapped Adam from the back of the car.

"What's the point of the cameras?" Caitlin asked in frustration. "How is that even legal?"

Her question did not get an answer. Instead Officer Young said, "Tell me about the energy drinks, Ms. Walker."

"What?" She couldn't believe that was what he was going to focus on. "I have a big project I'm working on," she said. It wasn't entirely a lie. "I needed to stay up late to work on it."

As she sat in the waiting area chair, Caitlin played back over the whole exchange in her head. They suspected her, she was sure of it. Well, that was how it was a lot of times in these cases. She had seen the news stories.

It convinced her that she had done the right thing in not telling them about driving out to Pennsylvania. That would have looked weird and suspicious, and how would she have explained it? She imagined herself saying she drove out there to pick up some discontinued sleeping pills, what were technically illegal drugs. As if that wasn't bad enough, there was the fact that she had nothing to show for her travels. How suspicious would it have been to tell them she went out there to buy some discontinued medication but had come back empty-handed? Plus, they would have relayed all that to Lance, and he would have lost his shit for sure. As it was, what were they telling Lance in that little meeting room? She pulled out her phone again to check, astounded to see that only two more minutes had elapsed.

She stood up, surprised at how wobbly and unsteady her legs felt. She steadied herself against the wall before walking in the direction of that little meeting room. She wasn't going in, but maybe if she stood close enough to the door, she would be able to overhear.

"You can't be back here," a female employee in plain clothes said as she approached and steered Caitlin back toward the waiting area.

"I need to talk to my husband," Caitlin said, nodding toward the door. "Can you interrupt them for a moment."

The secretary or whoever she was glanced toward the closed door.

"I can take a message down." She grabbed a pad and pen from one of the desks and looked at Caitlin expectantly.

Caitlin didn't actually have a message planned out, so she said, "Just tell him I went back to the house to wait for any calls."

It was a lame excuse. They had discontinued their landline two years ago, but it wasn't as if this secretary was going to know this. If it came to it, Caitlin figured she could always use the excuse that she had left her charger at home, and her phone's battery was dying. At last check, it had been at about thirty percent, so this wasn't really a lie.

❧

Caitlin stepped outside into the cool, late afternoon air, and for a moment she remembered how to breathe. She was relieved to be outside that awful building. It was only the second police station she had ever been in. She would be happy if she never visited another one for as long as she lived.

Memories of the interview room at the Culver Creek police station flooded back. How strange that twice in one day that awful place would be so present in her mind. She felt that cursed town looming over her as she walked to her car, and of course, she remembered that night in the motel room.

She had been asleep, but the unfamiliar bed and her mother's insistence on keeping the television on meant Caitlin didn't sleep well. That, and a part of her was afraid she would have that dream about little Lily again. That wasn't usually how it worked, but she had spent the whole day trying to recall the details of the dream, so she feared it would repeat itself in her head that night.

Caitlin had awoken with a start, her heart racing as she tried to figure out where she was, then the slightly musty odor and the sound of the television reminded her that she was still in the Culver Creek motel room. Would they finally go home tomorrow? Her mother hadn't given her a definitive answer, but they had talked to the police and told them everything, so why would they need to stay here anymore? Maybe it already was tomorrow. Caitlin rolled over to get a look at the room's window, but she saw only darkness beyond the heavy plaid curtains.

She saw her mother's body squirming around beneath the covers on her bed. Apparently, Caitlin wasn't the only one who couldn't sleep. Her mother said something, and Caitlin quickly shut her eyes and rolled over, feigning sleep. The last thing she wanted was for Luanne to start pestering her about her dreams. Caitlin did her best to mimic sleep, breathing as she lay there listening to the voices on the television show her mother wasn't watching. She heard her mother giggle, and then a man on the TV said, "You've been a bad girl. Don't make me use my handcuffs."

The voice was louder than the others and vaguely familiar, and Caitlin risked getting caught awake to take a look at the show on the television. She was staring at the screen when she heard the man's voice again, only this time she realized it hadn't come from the TV at all. She looked over at her mother's bed and saw the covers slip off to reveal a man's broad, bare back. In the dim light she recognized Officer Brighton's haircut, and before she could look away, she saw her mother pull the police officer's face toward hers, pressing her lips to his. From what Caitlin could see, her mother didn't have any clothes on either.

She had seen more than enough. She was old enough to know exactly what was going on between her mother and the policeman, and it disgusted her. She burrowed beneath her covers, even though she was too warm, and tried to shut out the noises coming from the bed beside hers, to no avail.

Caitlin blinked away the awful memory as she sat behind the wheel of her SUV. Out of habit, she glanced at the rearview mirror, and her heart leapt. Adam was here! He had been here all along, it was all some terrible mistake. She spun around, but even before she grabbed hold of the blanket, she realized her mistake. The car seat was empty. Her mind was playing tricks on her.

Still clutching the blanket, she turned back around. She buried her face in the folds of the soft cloth and inhaled deeply. The blanket smelled of juice, Cheerios, slightly sour yogurt and fabric softener. It smelled like Adam. Tears ran down her face, and she mopped at them with the blanket.

She thought of the first time she laid eyes on her infant son. His tiny body looked so fragile. She remembered holding him to her chest, silently promising to take care of him and keep him safe, but now she had broken that promise. How many times had she read of some tragic news story about a young child and wondered how the parents could have ever let such a thing happen? How many times had she faulted her own mother for being horrible and selfish? A vision of her naked mother locking lips with Officer Brighton in a motel bed flashed into her head before she could stop it.

The thing about that night in the motel room that had always bothered Caitlin was not that her mother cared so little for her father that she would break her marriage vows and have sex with some man she barely knew, but that her mother was so self-centered that she didn't even think of her daughter sleeping in the next bed. Certainly Luanne and Officer Brighton had not worried much about keeping the noise levels of their lovemaking in check. Her mother had forgotten all about her daughter during her night of passion. Had she even spared a passing thought for Caitlin's safety? What if Brighton had turned out to be some dangerous psycho?

Maybe Caitlin wasn't shacking up with random men in seedy motel rooms, but she knew she was to blame for her son's disappearance. It was her self-centered actions that had led to this. She had been so worried about her own nightmares and so desperate to avoid them that she had forgotten entirely about Adam as she ran into the convenience store for her energy drink shopping spree. The truth was, she was no better than Luanne.

Luanne. Shit. She had to call her mother. She set Adam's blanket on the seat beside her and pulled out her phone. Luanne sounded giddy, though she was hard to hear over the sound of slot machines and music in the background.

"Mom, something's happened," Caitlin managed to get out before she broke down sobbing.

Luanne's voice turned suddenly serious. Through sobs Caitlin told the whole, ugly story. The same one she had told the police, anyway.

"I'm on my way," Luanne said. "We'll be on the next flight."

22

"DID YOUR WIFE EVER HURT ADAM?" Officer Young asked Lance.

"Caitlin?" he said, incredulous. "No, of course not." He was beyond frustrated. They weren't getting anywhere asking him all these ridiculous questions. Meanwhile his son was out there with god-knew-who, and these two nitwits did not seem to be in any hurry to track him down. It was maddening. And Caitlin. He needed to see Caitlin. She must be going out of her mind with worry.

"Did *you* hurt your son?" Marley asked.

Lance was trying to keep his cool, but it was getting increasingly difficult.

"No, it's not like that, you have it all wrong."

"Do we?" Marley asked. "Because we spoke to your son's teacher. She confirmed that Adam was not in school today, but she also told us something else. She said last week she noticed some bruises on his neck."

Lance felt like all the air had been sucked out of the room. He tried to remain passive, but he felt Young's eyes boring into him.

"You know anything about that, Mr. Walker?" Young asked. "The bruises on Adam's neck?"

"No, nothing," Lance said, forcing his voice to remain neutral, even as a storm raged in his head. "Maybe his teacher is mistaken."

"Yeah, maybe," Young said. He didn't sound convinced.

Lance couldn't believe he was such an idiot. He had been raised better than this. You never talked to the cops without a lawyer. That was the rule, but he had been in such a desperate rush to find out what was going on with Adam, he had forgotten all about that rule. He hadn't stopped to realize that the cops would consider him a suspect, but of course they did. Hell, they might not even be out there looking for Adam or his kidnapper because they thought they already had their man.

In his head he caught a glimpse of a memory. His mother saying, "The police won't understand." He thought of the day they showed up to ask about who might have murdered little Lily. He pictured the four of them in the living room, his mother telling them about the car she had seen as they jotted down notes. Had she said that about the police not understanding before they showed up, or was it after? But no, that was all wrong.

The vague memory resolved itself slightly. He saw his mother saying the words while wearing her terry cloth bathrobe. They were in the bathroom. He saw the hideous baby blue tile that she despised in the sad, outdated room. She was always cutting out pictures of bathrooms that she liked from magazines and taping them to the mirror, dreaming about the remodeling project she could never afford. Well, that was until she married Tucker Rixby and got her whole life remodeled.

Yes, he could see it plain as day. His mother was at the

sink washing her hands, washing something, as she told him, "The police won't understand."

The memory was so vague and indistinct that it occurred to him it probably didn't have anything at all to do with Lily. It was likely much earlier than that. Did it have something to do with his father's heart attack? Yes, this felt right. Lance had only hazy memories of his father, who had suffered a fatal heart attack when Lance was just five years old. Whatever his mother had been talking about that night in the bathroom had something to do with his dad, but what? Lance couldn't say. He might not even have her words right. He wondered if the police had questioned her after his dad died. Surely they couldn't have blamed her for his heart attack, but maybe that was how it always was.

They always suspected next of kin—wives, husbands, parents. A child goes missing, and they immediately suspected the parents had something to do with it, and when that same boy showed up at school the previous week with bruises, well, it did kind of make one wonder, didn't it? Of course, he couldn't tell them what had really happened, because like his mother said all those years ago, they wouldn't understand.

"I would never lay a hand on my son," Lance said, "and I'm offended that you would even suggest such a thing."

He realized the last bit was too much. It made him sound guilty. He had no business talking to the police on his own. This was why you always had a lawyer with you, but here was the dilemma: If he asked to call his lawyer now, he would succeed in looking even more guilty. The cops would stop any pretense of a search for Adam. So he couldn't call his lawyer, but he had to get the hell out of there.

"Look, unless you plan on arresting me," Lance said, "I need to go see my wife."

"We're not arresting you," Marley said. He didn't actually say the word *yet*, but Lance heard it in the tone of his voice. "But it will be much easier to find Adam if we know the truth."

"I've told you everything there is to tell," Lance said, and he stood up. Neither officer made a move to stop him, so he walked out the door, his heart racing.

He scanned the police station, but he didn't see Caitlin anywhere.

"Mr. Walker!"

Lance looked over at the woman who jumped up from a desk and walked to where he stood.

"Your wife asked me to tell you she went back to the house."

Still worried that Young and Marley would change their minds and call him back in for more questioning, Lance left the station, got in his car, and drove down the road. He pulled into the parking lot of the dry cleaners, and with the car still running, he pulled out his phone. His first impulse was to call Caitlin and make sure she was all right, but the police interview was still fresh in his mind. He needed to talk to his stepfather.

He didn't have anything against the local attorney who had represented them when they bought their house and who had prepared their wills, but Lance figured a criminal case was probably above his skillset. This wasn't the sort of thing where you wanted to mess around. His stepfather was the kind of man who knew a lot of people. Even if he didn't personally know a good criminal lawyer in New Jersey, he would know someone who did.

Lance dialed the house number. His mother picked up on the third ring.

"Hi, Mom," Lance said. "I need to talk to Tucker. Is he around?"

Then he realized he had to tell Raquel what was going on.

"I think he's in his study. Let me grab him," Raquel said.

"Wait, Mom, I actually need to talk to both of you," Lance said.

"Is everything okay?" Raquel asked.

"If you can just get Tucker, I'll explain everything to both of you," Lance said.

He was surprised at how steady and calm his voice was as he explained the day's events to his mother and stepfather. Maybe it was genetics, because after hearing the story, Raquel seemed to remain composed, while Tucker Rixby had a bit of a freak out.

Tucker's voice cracked as he asked, "Just tell me what I can do."

"Well," Lance said, "do you know of any attorneys who have experience with this sort of thing?"

"Of course, there's—" Tucker began, but Raquel cut him off.

"No, we're wasting time. We'll talk about that in person. We're on our way now."

"Mom, wait—" Lance said, but he, too, was overruled by his mother's decree.

"We'll throw some stuff into a suitcase and head right out," she said.

Lance hadn't counted on this, but he didn't see how he could stop the two of them. He reasoned it might be for the best. They would be able to help, and though Caitlin and Raquel weren't exactly the best of friends, he thought it would be good for Caitlin to have a sort of mother figure around. Then he remembered he needed to get back home to comfort his distraught wife.

"I've got to go," Lance said.

"So do we," Raquel said.

As he drove up to the house, Lance spotted the dark car parked on the road out front. In this upscale suburban neighborhood of garages and long driveways, no one parked on the road. Lance had a moment of panic. It was the kidnappers. They had shown up at the house. What if they were holding Caitlin hostage? But the panic melted in an instant as he recognized the dark car for what it was, an unmarked police car. Had they posted the police detail outside to keep an eye out for kidnappers or because they wanted to keep Lance and Caitlin under surveillance? Lance guessed it was probably the latter, though no doubt, if asked, the police would say they were hoping to catch the kidnappers.

Caitlin was in the living room when Lance stepped inside. She was holding the blanket they kept in the car for Adam. She twisted it in her hands as if she were trying to wring out damp laundry. Her hair was a tangled mess, and her eyes, surrounded by puffiness, looked wild and glassy.

He went to her and embraced her. Holding her, he could feel his blood pressure drop, but she went stiff in his arms and pushed him away. She shook her head and resumed her wringing of the blanket.

"I should have seen this coming," Caitlin said.

"What are you talking about?" Lance said. "How could anyone have seen this coming?"

"I should have seen it coming," she repeated.

But he knew the truth. If anyone should have seen this coming, it was him. He knew Caitlin was in trouble. He had seen the evidence of it, but he had ignored the warning signs. What had he done? He went and bought her sleeping pills. His wife needed medical attention, and his method of dealing with it had been to buy her sleep aids. He couldn't believe he was such a colossal idiot.

He saw that video of Caitlin in the convenience store, trying to carry all the energy drink cans in her arms. Just the memory of it made him shudder. She had seemed so crazy and deranged, he had barely recognized her. And now, pacing around while obsessively twisting a blanket in her hands, she did look a lot like a seriously disturbed mental patient.

What if, in her altered mental state, she had done something to Adam? Maybe she had made up the whole story of him disappearing in the Quick Chek parking lot to cover for whatever she had done earlier. The police certainly suspected she was lying about him disappearing from the parking lot.

Had she told them about the sleeping pills? he wondered. The thought had crossed his mind while he was in the police station, but he was smart enough to not say anything to implicate his wife. The more and more he and Caitlin looked like culprits, the less attention the police would devote to tracking down the real evildoer.

"I should have seen this coming," Caitlin said again. "Stupid, stupid. Those goddamn pills."

"What happened?" Lance asked. "I need you to tell me exactly what happened."

She stopped twisting the blanket and turned to stare at him.

"Don't you know?" she asked, confused. "I stopped at

the convenience store, and Adam was taken out of the back-seat while I was inside the store."

It was the same story she had told the police, but he had seen the security camera footage from the parking lot. No one but Caitlin had entered the car.

"I need you to retrace your steps," Lance said. "Think carefully about everywhere you went."

"He was in the car when I pulled into the parking lot," she said.

"I looked into those pills you were taking," Lance said. "They had some pretty serious side effects. They can cause disorientation and confusion. There was a class action lawsuit."

"If I hadn't been taking those pills, this never would have happened," Caitlin said. Her voice had gone quiet as she stared down at the floor.

Lance felt the tears well up in his eyes.

He had failed her. For years she had taken those things. Why hadn't he ever looked into them before? The least he could have done was look up their side effects, but he hadn't done that, and why? Well, he knew why—because Caitlin's sleeping pills made everything perfect for him. Caitlin was perfect in so many ways, and her dead-to-the-world sleep was like the cherry on top. He hadn't wanted to screw things up for himself, but all the while Caitlin was in trouble, and he had been too self-absorbed to realize it.

"I'm sorry," he said as the tears rolled down his face.

She took a step away from him, confused. Was it his imagination, or did she look afraid?

"Caitlin?" he asked. "What happened? You need to tell me what happened. Whatever you can remember. I know the pills have made you confused, but I need you to think. Try to remember, please."

"If I hadn't been taking the pills, I would have seen all this coming," Caitlin said. "It's all my fault."

Lance didn't know what she was talking about. She wasn't making sense, but that was probably because of those pills.

He reached out and placed his hands lightly on each of her shoulders. "I need you to think carefully. Are you positive Adam was in your car when you pulled into the Quick Chek parking lot?"

"Yes," she said. "I didn't go anywhere else."

"You went straight to the convenience store from the house?" he asked.

"He was asleep in the car seat," Caitlin said, but that didn't make any sense. It was a two-minute drive to the convenience store, maybe three. Adam wouldn't have fallen asleep that quickly.

"Are you sure?" Lance asked.

Caitlin started to nod her head, but then she froze.

"Caitlin?" Lance asked. "What is it?"

She didn't answer.

23

A MOSTLY ORDERLY crowd filled the folding chairs set up on the lawn outside the Rixby plant, but Sage supposed that was what one could expect from paid attendees. Behind this area on the grass and the paved parking area beyond was where the problem was. Uninvited attendees equipped with signs and posters were there to protest Mick Hillman.

"They demote you already?" Rod Smith asked. As luck would have it, Sage had been paired with him to handle the crowd control duty.

"Just pitching in." Sage expected some wiseass remark from Rod, but the other police officer just gave him a nod before turning to look at the beefy man dressed in a suit and wearing an earpiece who strode purposely toward them. He was a member of Hillman's security detail.

"We need to do something about this mess," the security guard said to Rod and Sage. The guard waved his arm in the direction of the protesters beyond the perimeter.

"It's a free country," Rod said.

"This is private property," the guard said. "They're trespassing. You can have them arrested."

"With all due respect," Sage said, "they're not being disruptive, but if we try to remove them, things could get ugly. Tell your guy to give his speech, and we'll keep things under control."

"Yeah," Rod agreed, leering at the guard. "If Hillman don't start saying his pretty words soon, even the natives will get restless." He indicated the attendees in the folding chairs as they shifted around in their seats waiting for the event to begin, which was already ten minutes behind schedule.

"If there's any type of problem at all, you two will be looking for new jobs," the guard said. "Mr. Hillman has some powerful friends." He turned and walked back toward the stage, pressing his earpiece to his ear as he went.

"Mr. Hillman has some powerful friends," Rod mimicked. "Unbelievable."

"I assume the Rixbys must be some of them," Sage said.

"The Rixbys," Rod said as if the word was a euphemism for excrement.

"Aren't they the bigwigs in this town?" Sage asked.

"They don't even live in this town," Rod said. "They're too good for Culver Creek. They live in Atkins, and their potato chips taste like ass."

"I haven't tried them," Sage said.

"You're not missing anything. Trust me."

A ripple went through the assembled crowd, and Sage looked toward the stage. There was movement there, and Sage caught a glimpse of Mick Hillman with his slicked-back hair on the steps leading up to the stage.

"Looks like showtime," Sage said.

"Do you think someone grows up thinking, What I'd

really like to be is a political blowhard?" Rod asked as Hillman dashed out onto the stage to applause and cheers, as well as some boos from the area behind the fence.

"You never wanted to be president when you were a kid?" Sage asked.

"I guess I always knew I would be a cop," Rod said. "My dad was on the force, and his father was before him."

"Smith," Sage said, remembering something he had read recently. He couldn't quite place where it had been. The Lily Esposito file was the most obvious answer, but that didn't feel right. As Hillman extolled the virtues of some hardworking single mom he had met on the campaign trail, it came to him. It was something he had read yesterday, the police report on the death of Craig Walker. An Officer Smith had been working with Arlo when they were called to the scene of a young father who had taken a bad tumble down the basement stairs.

"Your father ever mention Craig Walker?" Sage had to raise his voice to be heard over the amplified words of Mick Hillman.

"Name doesn't ring a bell to me," Rod said.

"He died after falling down his stairs," Sage said.

"Oh that," Rod said. "Yeah, I got my ass whooped one time over that goddamn thing."

"How?" Sage asked.

"My brother and I were horsing around near the top of the stairs, and my father exploded at me, started screaming about some guy who had broken his neck and died after getting pushed down his stairs and how would I like it if I died that way or if I had to live the rest of my life in a state of guilt for causing my brother's death. My father could be dramatic at times, and unreasonable."

"Yeah, except no one pushed that guy down the stairs. He just fell," Sage said.

"Really?" Rod said. "Why did I always think the guy had been pushed?"

"I don't know," Sage said.

Hillman's speech clocked in at twenty-eight minutes, but to Sage it felt interminable. There were a few times his words and empty promises were drowned out by the small but orderly group of protestors, but in general, things went smoothly and Sage figured he and Rod probably wouldn't be collecting unemployment anytime soon.

24

CAITLIN LOOKED DOWN at the blanket in her hands. She remembered the dizzying moment when she had come out of the police station and sat down in her car, how for a second she looked into the rearview mirror and saw Adam asleep in the backseat. Of course, what she had seen was only his blanket draped over the empty car seat.

What if that was all she had been seeing on her drive back from Pennsylvania? No, she had seen him in the backseat. She had definitely seen him, hadn't she? She thought of Lance prattling on and on about Pacifcleon's side effects. No, she wasn't having hallucinations. She wasn't crazy.

She tried to play back what had happened in her mind, but her head was a jumbled mess and it was hard to focus on her memory. Mental confusion was a Pacifcleon side effect according to Lance, but she had a feeling her own mushy mind was a direct result of her child having been kidnapped.

She shut her eyes and tried to focus her thoughts. What she remembered was stepping out of the little drug store. Her Pacifcleon search had proved fruitless, and it had left her feeling frantic and desperate, but the first thing she had done when she got to the car was check on Adam, and not in the rearview mirror, either. She had gone straight to the back door. A memory of patting his little head, of pulling the blanket up to his chin, came back to her. But had that really happened? As she recalled events, she didn't think she had opened the back door. She hadn't wanted to wake him. Still, she had seen him through the back window. She wouldn't have made the mistake she made looking in the rearview mirror. In her head, she saw Adam sound asleep in his car seat.

"He was there," Caitlin said aloud, her voice barely more than a whisper. She felt like speaking the words would make it real, but she heard the uncertainty in her tone.

"What?" Lance asked.

Caitlin waved away his question.

Adam asked for ice cream. That proved he had been there. No, wait, he had asked for ice cream before they got to the pharmacy. He had been sound asleep the whole ride home. He hadn't said a word.

That had been strange, hadn't it? It was a long ride, and Adam barely napped anymore. Maybe if he had a cold or the flu or something, but despite what Caitlin had told Adam's teacher, her son was perfectly healthy. He might have dozed off for a couple of minutes here and there, but there was no way he would have been so sound asleep that he wouldn't have made a single noise on a ride that lasted nearly an hour and a half.

"No," Caitlin said as she realized her mistake. Adam hadn't gone missing here in New Jersey like she told the police. He had been kidnapped out in Pennsylvania, that wretched, awful Culver Creek.

"No, what?" Lance stared at her as if she was a lunatic, and she had to admit she was feeling a bit crazed right then.

She needed to call the police. She had to tell them to search for Adam out in Pennsylvania. But wait, was she sure of this? That memory of seeing Adam sleeping in the backseat was so real. She closed her eyes and saw him through the window resting peacefully, but even as she stared at him, the scene shifted. His shirt changed colors, then the blanket was draped over the whole seat so that she couldn't see his face. What had she actually seen? She realized she had no idea.

What would she tell the police? If she told them she thought Adam might have been kidnapped while she was out in Pennsylvania, they were going to want to know why she hadn't told them about being all the way out there. They would ask her how she could have driven the whole way back without realizing Adam was not in the backseat. She would have to tell them the truth, that she was a terrible mother—the worst.

She felt in her jeans' back pocket for her phone, but it wasn't there. It was upstairs plugged into the charger beside the bed. That was the first thing she had done when she came home. It was just as well, she couldn't make the call with Lance standing here. The police weren't going to understand why she hadn't told them about driving to Culver Creek, but Lance would flip out for sure.

"I have to get my phone," she told him, and ran up the stairs.

"Caitlin, what's going on?" Lance called after her. "Talk to me!"

She unplugged her phone from the charger and stood there staring at the bed. How stupid and selfish she had been. If she hadn't run away from her gift, Adam would be here with her right now. She would have had a dream about him being kidnapped, and she could have done everything in her power to make sure it didn't happen. But no, she had spent her entire adulthood running away from the inconvenience of a few bad dreams, and now she was paying the price.

What's worse was she had been telling Adam to ignore his dreams, teaching him they weren't real. What if he had a dream that warned him? Maybe he could have kept himself safe if Caitlin hadn't steered him in the wrong direction.

But he did have a dream, didn't he? Caitlin recalled listening with horror as Adam described a dream that seemed so much like the nightmare she had all those years ago. She had mistaken it for a repeat of her dream, but what if that wasn't what it was at all? Something else bubbled up from her jumbled thoughts. Adam asking for ice cream as they drove through Culver Creek. She hadn't understood how he could have known what the ice cream parlor was, but what if he recognized it from his dream?

She ran out the bedroom door and straight into Lance coming down the hallway. He attempted to hug her again, but she pushed him away. Couldn't he see she didn't have time for that?

She ran into Adam's room. The other day he had been drawing a picture of one of his nightmares. There might be a clue there. There might be other drawings. She flipped through a stack of papers on his little desk, discarding rockets, dinosaurs and octopi. Where was the nightmare drawing? There was another stack of papers on the floor, and she grabbed it and began to flip through it. The subjects were more realistic, and it was possible these were drawings based on his dreams.

"What are you doing?" Lance asked. "Maybe you should lie down for a few minutes."

"Our son is missing, and you want me to lie down?" she asked, as she shuffled frantically through the papers looking for vital clues.

"Well, it might make a little more sense than whatever the hell this is," he said, waving a hand at her and the room that now was in a serious state of disarray, crayon-colored pieces of paper littering the floor.

"Adam had a dream about this," Caitlin said. "He knew this was going to happen!"

Her voice had reached a frantic pitch. She still hadn't found the paper she was looking for, but she spotted Adam's school bag hung on his closet door and grabbed it, dumping the contents on the ground.

"Caitlin, please," Lance said.

"He wanted ice cream," Caitlin said, jabbing a finger in Lance's direction. "He recognized the ice cream place."

Lance shook his head because, of course, he didn't understand, but she didn't have time to explain things to him. She moved papers around on the floor until at last she found it. She recognized the familiar scene right away: the creek, the fallen body, the spurting blood.

Of course, she had assumed the injured child was Lily Esposito, but what if it wasn't at all? What if it was some new victim? What if the same man who had killed Lily was about to kill again? Then a sickening realization hit Caitlin. Her son had a dream about a child being killed in a vicious murder in Culver Creek, and now her son had been kidnapped near that same town. What if the child he had dreamed about was himself? Caitlin fell to her knees.

This was all her fault. She had silenced her dreams, and she had told Adam to ignore his own. She let out a yell that sounded like it came from an injured animal. Lance came over to her and rested a hand on her shoulder.

"Please," he said, "come lie down."

He gently removed the drawing from her hand. The nightmare vision floated harmlessly to the ground, but Caitlin noticed the way her husband's eyes flicked to the frightening illustration.

"We have to give that to the police," Caitlin said.

A moment later, Lance jerked his head away from Adam's artwork, his expression unreadable.

"They don't want that," he assured her. He helped her to her feet and began to lead her toward their bedroom. "Shh, let's go lay down. Everything's going to be okay."

"Is it?" she asked.

He didn't answer.

25

LANCE STOOD at the kitchen counter, looking at the peanut butter and jelly sandwich he had made for himself. He had eaten half of it but hadn't tasted a single bite. Would the police be calling him with updates? What was he going to do about Caitlin?

He had convinced her to lie down, but she needed more help than he could give her. Did you call 911 for that sort of thing, or could you just call a psychiatric hospital directly? Maybe she could just talk to someone, a therapist. He thought of her in Adam's bedroom, tearing the place apart as she went through all of Adam's drawings and babbled away, spewing nonsense. He feared her affliction may have been more than a therapist could handle. Plus, she would never go see one anyway.

She had been adamant that they weren't going to take Adam to any sort of psychiatrist or therapist for his nightmares, so he didn't see how he was going to convince her to seek professional help for herself. He slipped his phone out of his pocket and Googled "involuntary mental health treatment," watching as a page of links loaded. Before he could click on any of them, he heard a car door close outside and went to the window. His mother stepped out of the passenger seat of the Mercedes, brushing invisible lint off her cardigan and smoothing out her unwrinkled pants. His stepfather climbed out from the driver's seat, looking for all the world like he was about to play eighteen holes of golf. Lance went out to meet them.

"Have you heard anything?" his mother said.

Tucker had gone around to the trunk and was carrying out two overnight bags. Apparently, they were planning on staying here. Lance wondered what sort of state the guest bedroom was in and then decided that was the least of his worries.

"Nothing," he said, answering his mother. He gave her a perfunctory cheek kiss. They weren't huggers. "Let me help you with those," he said to Tucker, but his stepfather waved him off.

The three of them settled in the living room. Well, as settled as any of them could be. Lance found he was too restless to sit. He had asked them to keep their voices down since Caitlin was resting upstairs, which had earned him a sour look from his mother.

"I've already called Garvey," Tucker said. "Left a message for him. He's a top-notch criminal attorney. One of the best."

"Thank you," Lance said.

"He was kidnapped from your car?" Raquel asked. Lance had done his best to catch her up to speed, but maybe he hadn't been too clear about things.

"Caitlin's car," Lance said.

"You were with her?" Raquel asked.

"I was at work," Lance said. "She was out running

errands, stopped at the store, forgot Adam was in the backseat."

Raquel nodded as she took this information in. He waited for some dig to come, but surprisingly his mother kept her mouth shut.

"Well, do the police have suspects? Do they have any idea where he might be?" Raquel asked.

"They issued an Amber Alert," Lance said. "I got it on my phone."

"The police are incompetent," Tucker said. "I'm going to hire a private investigator."

"Thanks, but—" Lance began, but his stepfather cut him off.

"There's this fellow out in California who did a bang-up job with a kidnapping case out there. Got the kid returned safe and sound without a scratch on her and kept the whole ugly thing out of the papers. They're family friends. I've got a call in to them to get this guy's number."

Lance sighed. His stepfather just wanted to help, but it was bad enough he had the police breathing down his neck, he didn't look forward to some ace private investigator sticking his nose into things. Well, with any luck they would have this all sorted before Sherlock Holmes even stepped onto a plane. How far could Adam be? Even the incompetent local police must have picked up some sort of trail by now.

"Can I get you anything to eat or drink?" Lance asked.

"Who can think about food at a time like this," Raquel asked. Then she stood up and went into the kitchen.

Lance followed her and heard his stepfather making a phone call as soon as they left the room.

He went for the refrigerator, but his mother waved him away. She pulled out milk and eggs. She grabbed a frying pan from the cabinet and set it on the stove. Within minutes she was chopping a pepper and then a block of cheese.

"Mom, you don't have to," Lance said.

"Well, I have to do something," she said.

He remembered her obsessive cleaning after Lily's murder.

"You know, I'm mad at you," she said as she whisked the eggs and milk together.

"Join the club." He was angry at himself for not getting Caitlin the help she needed. He couldn't imagine what his mother was mad at him about. But maybe she knew Caitlin had been spiraling out of control and he had dropped the ball. His mother always seemed to know more than he realized.

"You were all the way out there last week, and you didn't come see us." Raquel tossed a pat of butter into the hot frying pan, and it sizzled and spat. Satisfied, she poured the egg mixture into the pan. "Pamela Duke said she saw you and Adam at the miniature golf course. She said she waved to you, but you didn't see her."

"I, uh," Lance stammered. She had caught him off guard. He didn't have any sort of explanation ready. "It's a long story," he finally said.

His mother pursed her lips as she poked at the eggs with a spatula.

"I don't know why you would go to that seedy old place," Raquel said. "You can play anytime you want with Tucker at the club. Anyway, I felt like a big old fool when Pamela told me that story."

"Yeah, Mom, maybe don't mention that to Caitlin, okay?" Lance said.

She turned to give him a look, then shrugged and returned her attention to the omelet.

"You really don't know what happened to Adam?" she asked quietly as she folded the chopped peppers and cheese into the eggs.

"What the hell kind of question is that?" Lance asked. Did his own mother suspect him? Jesus! She turned to look at him, expectant. "No, of course I don't know what happened to him."

Raquel pulled some dishes out of the cabinet and set them on the counter.

"Come on," she said. "You need to eat something."

"I need to check on my wife," Lance said, and on cue Caitlin stepped into the kitchen. Though it didn't seem possible, she looked more crazed and frazzled than she had before.

Raquel thrust a dish at each of them. The sunny yellow omelet steamed.

"You need to eat something," Raquel said. "Both of you."

They carried the plates over to the table, and Lance shoved forkfuls of the eggs into his mouth without tasting them. Caitlin sat beside him, but she looked like she was a million miles away.

"Uh, Lance," Tucker called from the living room. "There's an airport shuttle in your driveway."

"My mom!" Caitlin jumped up, and her fork fell onto the dish with a clatter. "I forgot!"

Lance followed her outside in time to see Luanne step out of the van dressed in cheetah-print leggings and an over-sized T-shirt that read "Gambling Grandma" and featured an illustration of a slot machine. She was followed out of the vehicle by a gray-haired man in an equally loud shirt, though his was of a Hawaiian style.

Luanne ran up the driveway to Caitlin and enveloped her daughter in a smothering hug.

"Oh, baby," Luanne said. "How are you holding up?"

If Caitlin replied, it was lost in the folds of Luanne's T-shirt.

"Hey," the guy in the Hawaiian shirt said to Lance.

"Oh, I almost forgot," Luanne said, releasing Caitlin from her embrace. "This is Stu." She waved a hand at the man with her, then waved toward Caitlin and Lance. "Stu, this is my daughter Caitlin and my son-in-law Lance."

Stu nodded at Caitlin, then shook Lance's hand as he muttered something about wishing it was under better circumstances. They went into the house, where more introductions followed, and Lance was surprised he didn't catch his mother roll her eyes even a single time.

When Tucker's phone rang, everyone turned to stare at it expectantly. Tucker slipped into the kitchen to take the call in private, but Lance strained to listen, hoping he could hear at least half the conversation. That proved fruitless. His mother-in-law decided histrionics were in order and began a loud, melodramatic tirade about the insanity and the injustice of the whole situation.

"I can't believe you didn't see this coming," she said to Caitlin, which seemed like a weird and completely insensitive thing to Lance, but that was Luanne for you.

When Tucker returned to the living room a few minutes later, he waved Lance over and in low tones explained that he had gotten ahold of the attorney, Garvey, and he was on his way.

"I'm famished," Luanne announced. "They didn't feed us anything but pretzels on the flight, and we missed lunch."

Lance followed his wife and mother-in-law into the kitchen, while Stu stayed behind in the living room, promising to show a video on his phone that would make Raquel and Tucker bust a gut laughing.

Since he had last seen her, Luanne had switched to a gluten-free diet, and after a quick survey of the kitchen pantry, half a bag of certified gluten-free tortilla chips was located. Luanne dragged one of the counter stools over to the too-low table and sat sideways on the stool while she ate the chips straight from the bag, crunching loudly.

"What happened?" she demanded as Caitlin stirred the now cold omelet around on her plate without really eating.

"I forgot he was in the car," Caitlin said. "I went into the store, and when I came out, he was gone."

Caitlin's voice was flat and expressionless as she spoke the words. It was like she was reading from a script. He hated how vulnerable she sounded. He hated himself for bringing this on her.

"But, I mean, how?" Luanne demanded, spraying tortilla chip crumbs on the table. "How could you not have seen this coming?"

It was the second time Luanne had asked that question, and Lance squirmed as he stood at the counter watching the two of them. He didn't think it was at all helpful that Luanne and Stu had shown up. Raquel at least had cooked them food, and Tucker had been busy working the phone, hiring an attorney. In what way were Luanne and Stu contributing?

"Do you think you could stop picking on her?" Lance asked.

Luanne gave him a surprised look. The slot machine graphic on the front of her shirt was littered with crumbs.

"I just don't understand how—" Luanne began.

"It's okay," Caitlin said. She offered Lance a weak smile as she shoved the unfinished omelet away from her.

"What you should do is go to sleep," Luanne said.

"I just took a nap," Caitlin said.

"No, a nap's not good enough. You need to go to sleep for the night, really get the old REM going."

Lance was surprised to see that the comment upset Caitlin more than her mother's how-could-you-not-have-seen-this-coming question. Well, maybe it was because of the reference to dreams. Didn't Luanne know her daughter didn't dream?

It made him think of Adam and his nightmares, and that stupid trip he made out to Culver Creek. What were the chances that one of his mother's friends would see him out there? It didn't matter. At least he didn't think it mattered, but what if Raquel let something slip to Caitlin. Well, that, like everything else, would be all his fault.

What had he been thinking? He never should have taken Adam to that dream whisperer, but at the very least he should have told Caitlin about it. If he had told her ahead of time, she would have stopped him from going and that would have been the best thing all around. But at the very least, he should have told her after the fact. She deserved that much. It didn't affect anything. Still, after all he had put her through, he needed to be completely honest with her. And he would start right now, this second. It came with the added benefit of getting Luanne out of Caitlin's hair.

"If you don't mind, I'd like to talk to Caitlin alone," Lance said. He approached the kitchen table.

"What, now?" Luanne had abandoned the tortilla chips on the table.

"Yes," Lance said. "We'll just be a few minutes." Lance

stopped short of pointing toward the living room, but he sort of nodded in that direction, and Luanne got the message.

She clambered off the stool and started toward the living room, but she stopped in the doorway.

"Don't you think it would make sense to get some sleep?" Luanne said to Caitlin. "You know what they say, the first twenty-four hours of a missing persons case are crucial."

Lance waited until he was sure Luanne was out of earshot before he asked, "What was that all about?"

"She's really into those police shows," Caitlin said. That hadn't been what he meant. He meant about Luanne's weird insistence that Caitlin get some sleep, but he wasn't going to get into that now.

Lance sat down at the kitchen table across from Caitlin. Despite the harrowing day, despite her frazzled state, she was still beautiful, and he was so completely in love with her. It was that love that gave him the courage to go on.

"Remember Saturday when Adam and I had our boys' day out?" he asked.

"There's something I need to tell you," Caitlin said.

"Okay," he said, "but me first."

She smiled at this, and his heart just about broke with how beautiful she was. How had he failed so horribly to protect her?

"The thing is," Lance began. He heard the chime noise from the living room, and even though it was familiar, he first thought it must be coming from somebody's phone. Maybe that private investigator was texting Tucker back. Maybe someone had commented on Luanne's latest Facebook post. He heard the movement and commotion in the living room, but it was a world away. In fact, he was grateful for it. It would make it that much more difficult for anyone to listen in on their private conversation. "I was worried about Adam and his nightmares," Lance said. "I only wanted to help. I didn't know what else to do."

He saw the stricken look that passed over his wife's face at the same time he heard Tucker call his name. He looked between Caitlin and the living room, which was when he realized the chime he heard hadn't been a phone alert at all. He knew the sound because it was their doorbell.

Raquel poked her head in the kitchen. "Lance, honey, the police are here. They've asked to speak with you."

A wounded animal sort of cry burst forth from Caitlin's mouth.

"It's probably nothing," he reassured her, and he gave her hand a little squeeze before standing up and walking to the door, his heart hammering away in his chest.

26

"WHERE WERE you on March nineteenth between the hours of midnight and one a.m.?" Young asked.

Lance was back in the same windowless police station room he had been in before. The officer who showed up at the house had said they had some important information they hoped Lance could review but that he would need to come back to the station.

Against his own better judgment, and against Tucker's warnings, Lance had agreed to go back to the police station. Wasn't there a chance they really did have some important information, and that it might be able to bring Adam home? How could he afford to take a risk when his son's life could be hanging on the line?

He told himself he wouldn't allow them to interrogate him, but here he was in this little room with these two police officers, and it felt an awful lot like an interrogation.

The question didn't even make any sense. March nineteenth? That had been more than two weeks ago. What could it possibly have to do with Adam's disappearance?

"Answer the question," Marley said.

The date meant nothing to him, but he felt pretty comfortable answering, "At home. In bed." After all, his partying days were well behind him. And it was a rare evening that he and Caitlin were out past ten, let alone past midnight. Certainly there hadn't been any nights in the recent past that he had been out late.

"Are you sure about that?" Marley asked.

They were trying to trap him, Lance could tell, but he didn't see how they possibly could. Still, he wondered if he should just wait for the lawyer Tucker had contacted to show up. Tucker had probably texted him about Lance going to the police station. In all likelihood, he would meet Lance here. He could show up at any minute. He could just say he wasn't answering any more questions without his lawyer present.

Still, whatever the police thought he had been up to after midnight, they were dead wrong. So he said, "Yeah, I'm sure."

"How do you know Jacob Pinochet?" Young asked.

The name meant nothing to Lance. It further confirmed that the police were way off track. Tucker had said they were incompetent, and this proved it.

"I have no idea who you're talking about," Lance said.

"I mean, I don't blame you one bit," Young said. "The man's a total scumbag, but I'm just wondering how someone like you ever got involved with someone like Pinochet."

"Do you have money troubles?" Marley asked. "They not paying you enough at that, what is it, the pillow factory?"

"Mattresses," Lance said, "and they pay me plenty. Who's Jacob Pinochet?"

Young raised one eyebrow at him, like he was sizing him up.

"Jacob Pinochet is the man you beat the ever-loving crap out of on March nineteenth, oh around 12:42 a.m. outside the Wild Boar Tavern," Young said matter-of-factly. "You know, there was something so familiar about you when we were talking to you earlier. It was nagging at me, but I thought maybe I had seen you around town some-where, and then I remembered those stills we pulled from the security camera outside the Wild Boar."

A chill passed over Lance. It began with Young saying the words *the man you beat the ever-loving crap out of* and led him down a dizzying spiral of realization. It wasn't the first time Lance had beaten the ever-loving crap out of someone, and that combined with the haunting memory of that day he had woken up in the bathroom in bloodstained clothing with no recollection of how he had gotten there or what had happened. He couldn't be sure about the date, but now he was 99 percent positive that March nineteenth was the same day he had gone on his bathroom cleaning spree and inadvertently thrown out his wife's stash of expired sleeping pills. That was what made what happened next all the more dizzying.

Marley threw a plastic shopping bag on the table. Lance flinched.

"Did you drug your son, Mr. Walker?" Marley asked. The question caught Lance off guard.

"No! No, of course not," he said.

"No? Then how the hell do you explain this?" Marley asked. The cop picked the bag back up and this time spilled the contents out onto the table.

Lance watched as assorted boxes of sleeping aids fell onto the table.

"Because according to this receipt," Marley said, pulling the strip of paper out of the bag, "you purchased all these last night. That's your signature at the bottom, isn't it?"

"Yes, but these were for Caitlin," Lance explained calmly.

"You drugged your wife?" Young asked.

"I didn't drug anyone!" Lance shouted. His voice broke on the word *anyone*.

The door to the room burst open, and the three men turned to stare. In the doorway stood a large man with a florid complexion and a crazed expression in his eye. That coupled with his rumpled suit made Lance assume this was a vagrant who had wandered in off the street.

"Lance Walker?" the vagrant said to him. Lance gulped and nodded. "Octavius Garvey," the man said by way of introduction, and Lance heard his stepfather saying the name Garvey. This was his attorney. Lance looked the man up and down again, trying to see him as a competent professional and not someone who was possibly homeless. "I got here as quickly as I could," Garvey said.

Garvey availed himself of the seat beside Lance and pushed aside some of the sleeping pill boxes to set his briefcase on the table. He unsnapped the latches, opened the case and removed a manila folder.

"You're under no obligation to answer any of their questions," Garvey said to Lance. Turning to the police officers, he said, "Now, where were we, gentlemen?"

"Where we were," Young said in a snide tone of voice, "is we were trying to figure out where Mr. Walker's son is."

"Correct me if I'm wrong, but I believe Mr. Walker has already explained that he does not know where his son is, which is why he engaged the services of the police," Garvey said.

"Actually, it was Mrs. Walker who contacted us,"

Marley said with a hint of a grin. "We had to track down Mr. Walker ourselves."

"Well, perhaps in the interest of clearing things up," Young said, "Mr. Walker would be willing to explain to us what he was doing in Culver Creek, Pennsylvania, last weekend."

In an attempt to make it look like he had nothing to hide, Lance answered quickly. "I took my son to play miniature golf."

Garvey made a little throat-clearing noise.

"You are under no obligation to answer any questions," the attorney reminded him, and after considering both the question and his quick reply, Lance wondered how the police even knew he was in Culver Creek. Perhaps his mom's friend Pamela had been gossiping to them as well.

"Pretty far to go to play miniature golf," Young commented.

"I grew up around there," Lance said.

Garvey cleared his throat again because he was too polite to shout, *Shut up, you damn bastard!* or so Lance assumed.

"You having an affair?" Young asked.

"What? No," Lance said.

"Might I advise you, Mr. Walker, that you please refrain from answering any further questions," Garvey said. Then to the police he added, "Gentlemen, if you're just going to waste everyone's time with this wild, baseless speculation, then I think we should consider this interview concluded."

Young continued as if Garvey hadn't said a word. "Because the way I see it, is you went out there for some sort of lovers tryst. Because I'm pretty sure if we contact the owner of this Culver Creek phone number, which called you repeatedly immediately following that weekend, we'll discover the young woman with whom you had intimate relations. Or perhaps it was a young man. Is that the way you swing, Mr. Walker?"

Lance opened his mouth to talk, but Garvey beat him to the punch.

"A series of phone calls?" Garvey asked. "I assume you have a warrant to examine Mr. Walker's phone records." He paused, but Young and Marley neither confirmed nor denied this. "I must say I'm a little curious. Young Adam went missing all of seven hours ago now, so how is it that you were able to obtain both a search warrant and a copy of these phone records?"

"It's a matter of official police business," Marley said with a sneer, but Lance noticed that Young looked decidedly uncomfortable. Well, that was point one for Octavius Garvey. The man might have looked like a bum, but he had already turned the tables on the cops, so he might just be worth his retainer, however exorbitant it was.

"So let me get this straight," Garvey said. "Adam goes missing from a parking lot in New Jersey, while his father is at work, and you think the fact that the previous week his father took him on a miniature golf outing in Pennsylvania somehow makes him a suspect in his son's disappearance?"

"Don't forget the sleeping pills," Marley said, pointing at the brightly colored boxes spread out on the table.

Garvey regarded them with distaste.

"And Jacob Pinochet," Young said. "If we wanted to, we could arrest Mr. Walker right now for assaulting Pinochet, but we're nice guys and we're taking pity on a man whose son is missing."

"Pity," Garvey muttered. "Interesting way of showing it."

～

F ifteen minutes later, Lance sat across from Garvey at a tiny table in the corner of the coffee shop down the road from the police station. After taking several sips from an extra large glass of iced tea, the lawyer took out a pen and a yellow legal pad and, there being no room on the table, did his best to balance it on his lap.

"Ideally, I would have liked to have spoken to you before our little tête-à-tête with the police, but it is what it is," Garvey said.

"I shouldn't have spoken to them," Lance said. "I thought maybe they had found out something about Adam."

"No, I understand," Garvey said as he sipped more tea. "Your son is missing, and you don't want to appear uncooperative. Unfortunately, I believe you're presently the prime suspect in your son's disappearance. So it's definitely time we got some facts straight. First things first, tell me about Culver Creek."

At first, Lance was impressed. He thought Garvey must have really done his homework to know that Lance was from that Pennsylvania town, and he was about to launch into an explanation that would capture the essence of the down-on-its-luck town. He stopped himself just in time. Garvey didn't want to know about Culver Creek's stagnating economy or its geography. He wanted to know why Lance had been there last weekend.

"I took Adam out there to go to a miniature golf place I remember from my childhood," Lance said. That statement was maybe two-thirds true, which he didn't think was bad at all, and he figured busybody Pamela could always back him up.

"This will all go a lot smoother if you're completely

honest with me," Garvey said. "So let's try this again. What were you doing in Culver Creek? Are you having an affair?"

"No," Lance said. "I wouldn't even consider it."

"Word of advice," Garvey said. "When someone, especially but not limited to the police, ask you a yes/no question, a one-word response is probably best. You aren't helping yourself with these little comments of yours, and it makes me wonder if you're a liar, because even the most faithful husband has certainly entertained the idea of an affair now and then."

"I took my son to see a dream whisperer," Lance said sullenly. He surprised himself by saying this out loud. He hadn't intended to share this information because he realized that it painted him as a bit of a kook, but maybe if they just cleared the air about things, everything would get back to normal.

"A what whisperer?" Garvey asked, scribbling notes on his pad.

"Dream whisperer," Lance said. "Adam was having nightmares. She was recommended by a work acquaintance. I was desperate, and I figured it was worth a shot. I changed my mind once I got out there. It was all too woo-woo, and I didn't want to subject Adam to that. Then the woman started calling me repeatedly. That's the phone number they referred to."

"Right, well, I wouldn't worry too much about that. I don't think that's ever going to be legal to use in a court of law thanks to dumb and dumber's heavy-handed police work."

Talk of Adam and his nightmares reminded him of Caitlin ransacking Adam's room. A strange, uneasy feeling passed through him as he saw that piece of paper she was waving around, the one Adam had drawn based on his nightmare. It was the same nightmare he had described to Phelicity Green, the dream whisperer. He saw the crude crayon drawing in his mind, horrifying in its graphic depiction of a murder. Where had his innocent little boy gotten such a disturbing idea from?

He heard an echo of his wife's voice in his head. *Adam had a dream about this. He knew this was going to happen.* Why would she say that? He reminded himself that Caitlin wasn't thinking clearly, that those damn pills had her messed up, and on top of that the stress of Adam going missing, because that's all it was.

Adam was missing. No harm had come to him, despite what Caitlin said. Maybe he had wandered out of the car on his own, and some sweet old lady had taken pity on him and he was sitting in her kitchen drinking tea and eating graham crackers. Lance tried to hold this image in his mind and to banish that nightmare drawing from his head.

"What I'm more concerned about is Jacob Pinochet," Garvey said. "You had some sort of altercation with him apparently. Is he someone you did business with?"

Lance came back to reality.

"I've never in my waking life laid eyes on the man," Lance said. It was the truth, but he could see Garvey was not satisfied.

"It was outside some bar," Garvey said. "Do you have a drinking problem, Lance?"

"No," Lance said, and for a moment he was fourteen years old again, sitting in the chair outside the headmaster's office, his stomach in knots because he knew he was going to be expelled. Lance never really knew if it was Tucker's money, the sheer unpopularity of Eric Pitt, or the testimony of his fellow students who saw Lance as a sort of savior for taking on a bully, that had saved him.

Maybe it was some combination of the three. What he knew was that none of those things could save him now. "It began when I was away at boarding school," Lance said.

As soon as he spoke the words, he knew they weren't true. He caught another glimpse of a memory. Standing in the kitchen of their small Culver Creek home with no memory of how he had wound up there. It was the middle of the night, and there on the table in front of him was a bowl of cereal floating in apple juice. Judging by the amount remaining in the bowl and the peculiar taste in his mouth, he had already eaten a fair amount of the strange concoction.

Then his mother was there, washing dishes in the sink, telling him everything was going to be okay but that he must never tell anyone about this. Some people might not understand that he had a condition that made him do things while he was asleep. They might think he was crazy. *The police won't understand*, he heard Raquel say, but no, that was a different memory, a different time.

"Or maybe before," Lance said. "I'm not really sure. The first time I hurt someone when I was asleep was at school. To be fair, he was a bully, and he probably had it coming to him. Anyway, I have no conscious memory of the event. When I woke up, I was leaning over him with an aching fist and he lay there on the ground, his face bloodied."

"You're a somnambulist," Garvey said, "a sleepwalker." Garvey set down his pen and rubbed his temple. There was a heavy sigh as he considered this new information.

Lance had never told anyone about this before, and he thought of his mother's words.

"You think I'm crazy," Lance said.

"What I think doesn't matter," Garvey said. "It's what a jury thinks that matters."

It was that day outside the headmaster's office all over again, only this time it would be far worse than expulsion. They would send him to jail. He would lose his job. They might lose the house. Hell, Caitlin would probably leave him, and he couldn't really blame her at all. Lance pressed the backs of his hands to his forehead and buried his face in his wrists.

"Did the police say how badly he was hurt?" Lance asked. "I didn't mean to do it. He must have tried to wake me up or something."

"Who?" Garvey asked.

Lance pulled his arms away from his face.

"Pinochet," Lance said. "Whoever the hell he is. They're going to send me to jail, aren't they?"

"For an assault?" Garvey asked. "A first offense? I doubt it. From what I can tell, the guy hasn't even pressed charges."

Lance waited for relief, but it never came. Maybe it had something to do with the way Garvey was looking at him.

"But that isn't what we're talking about here, is it?"

"I don't understand," Lance said.

"Lance, did you ever hurt your son? Did you ever hurt Adam when you were asleep?"

Lance's mind went immediately to the other morning. The day he awoke in Adam's room, his hands around his son's neck. He could feel his heart racing as he relived the awful experience. What would have happened if he hadn't woken up when he did? No, he couldn't bear to think about that.

He looked up. Garvey was still waiting for an answer.

"I would never hurt Adam," Lance said.

"Intentionally," Garvey added. "I understand. Look, here's what we're going to do." He picked his pen back up. "You're going to walk me through everything that happened today, starting with when you got out of bed. Can you do that?"

Lance began by describing getting up and going into their bathroom to get ready.

"Your wife didn't wake up when you got out of bed?" Garvey asked.

"Caitlin's a very sound sleeper," Lance said. "She takes these sleeping pills."

Garvey jotted this information down.

"Go on," Garvey instructed.

Lance described getting dressed, then heading down the hallway and poking his head into Adam's room to see that the boy was still asleep in bed, but even as he described this, he felt uncertainty. His schedule was so similar from one day to the next that sometimes the days blended together. Was that this morning he had stuck his head into Adam's room, or was that yesterday? He remembered he had been in a hurry. He had to get to that meeting, the one that was cancelled. Maybe he hadn't wasted time checking on Adam because he was worried about being late.

"And that was the last time you saw Adam?" Garvey asked.

The finality of the sentence bothered Lance, but that wasn't the only thing. He wasn't even positive he had seen Adam at all that day.

27

CAITLIN STEPPED INTO HER BEDROOM. Luanne was right behind her. Caitlin wanted to escape the tense scene in the living room and appease her mother, who insisted she go to sleep, but Luanne apparently wanted to make sure Caitlin really was going to try to sleep.

Lance still hadn't returned from the police station, and Caitlin didn't like it. She should have gone with him. When the cop had shown up at the front door, she was sure it was to say they found Adam and everything was going to be okay. At least, that's what she wanted to hear. Instead she had been waiting anxiously to learn whatever development had been significant enough to require him to go down to the police station.

"I can understand that you don't feel tired," Luanne said. "I mean, I know I can hardly think about sleep at a time like this, but you agree it's probably the best thing, right?"

"What if it's too late?" Caitlin asked.

"No, no, don't talk like that," Luanne said. Caitlin sat on the edge of the bed, and Luanne stroked her hair. "Do you have any Tylenol PM or Benadryl or something? Maybe that would help."

Caitlin wasn't about to explain that drugs were what had gotten her into this predicament in the first place. If it wasn't for Pacifcleon, she probably would have had a dream about this. She probably would have had some useful information to give to the police, which was when she remembered she did have useful information for the police. She stood up from the bed.

"I have to go to the police station," Caitlin said.

"Sweetie, Lance is fine," Luanne said.

"No, it's not that," Caitlin said. "There's something I need to tell the police. Something I just remembered."

"Something you dreamed?" Luanne asked, but Caitlin didn't answer her as she headed down the hall. "I'm coming with you."

The reception desk was empty when Caitlin and Luanne stepped into the police station. Caitlin craned her neck to try to see someone in the office area.

"Hello?" she called. "I need to talk to Officer Young! Hello!"

"Do you think something happened?" Luanne said. "Maybe they've found Adam."

A door opened at the other end of the building, and Officer Young stepped out.

"Mrs. Walker," he said, surprised to see her. "Are you looking for your husband?"

"You need to look for Adam in Culver Creek!" Caitlin said. The words flew out of her mouth. She knew she sounded hysterical, but she didn't care.

"What?" Young asked.

"Culver Creek, Pennsylvania," Caitlin said. "You need to look for Adam there."

"Were you following your husband?" Young asked.

Caitlin had no idea what he meant.

"She had a dream," Luanne explained. "That's how she knows Adam's in Pennsylvania. She has psychic dreams." Then the full import of Caitlin's words hit her, and she turned to look at her daughter.

"Culver Creek?" Luanne repeated. "What are the chances?"

"I know," Caitlin said, and she had a dizzying feeling again. For a moment, she was ten years old walking beside her mother as they stepped into the bustling Culver Creek police station, nervous and terrified.

History was repeating itself. Caitlin saw her mother as she had looked all those years ago, proud, head held high as she marched into the police station. She had been dressed up for the television cameras and basked in all that extra attention from the media, from Officer Brighton. While Caitlin had been trembling with fear, her mother was in her glory.

Of course, she had never told Lance the story. He knew nothing about her psychic dreams or the freak she used to be. She had always thought it was for the best, but now the unthinkable had happened, and it was all her fault.

"I didn't have a dream!" Caitlin shouted at Officer Young.

"Caitlin, dear." Her mother placed her hand on Caitlin's arm either to restrain her or to console her. Maybe a little of both.

"I didn't have a dream," Caitlin repeated. "I was out

there. I was in Culver Creek. Please don't tell Lance. I mean, let me tell him."

Young nodded as if he understood perfectly.

"You suspected him," Young said. "Maybe you saw a call come into his cell phone or it was something he said. So you followed him out there last Saturday. Is that it? Do you think that's where he took Adam?"

Caitlin frowned. What Young was saying didn't make any sense. Why was he asking if she had followed Lance? Lance wasn't the one to go to Culver Creek. She was.

"Last Saturday?" she asked.

Young looked uncertain.

Then Caitlin remembered Adam in the backseat this morning, asking if they could go get ice cream. He hadn't recognized the ice cream place from a dream. Adam must have gone there last Saturday with Lance—their boys' day out. But why on earth would Lance drive Adam all the way out there?

"I went there this morning," Caitlin said. "Adam and I were there this morning."

"The FBI has already been in contact with the local police in Culver Creek," Young said, "but if you'll excuse me, I'd like to let them know this additional information. If you can wait right here, Mrs. Walker, I won't be a moment."

Caitlin watched Young's retreating back as he headed into the office he had come out of. Luanne tried to steer her to one of the waiting area seats, but Caitlin remained standing as she tried to take in everything.

She hadn't had a dream about Culver Creek, but what if something else, some strange psychic force had drawn her back to that town. Her thoughts twisted in her head. The ghost of a murdered little girl cried out for vengeance. A dark monster bubbled up from the dark creek water. That wasn't the only thing bubbling up.

Caitlin bolted for the front door of the police station. She flew out the door and nearly flung herself into the scrubby bushes that lined the side of the building as she threw up her omelet dinner. Her mother was close on her heels, and then it seemed a spotlight was shining on her and she heard voices. She looked up and saw a television news crew descending on her.

"Mrs. Walker?" someone shouted. "Caitlin Walker?"

Oh God. It was Culver Creek all over again. She waited for her mother to do her thing and start primping for the cameras, so she was surprised when Luanne held up an elbow to ward off the reporter and cameraman.

"Please give us some space," Luanne said. Then, using her body, she shielded Caitlin from the cameras and led her back to the car.

"We're supposed to wait for Officer Young," Caitlin said as her mother forced her into the passenger seat of the Land Cruiser.

"I'm taking you home," Luanne said. "If Young needs to talk to you, he knows where to find you."

Luanne got behind the wheel, then fished around in a giant handbag before locating a bottle of water. She passed it to Caitlin, who gratefully did her best to wash the bad taste from her mouth.

Luanne drove slowly in the unfamiliar car as they made their way back to the house.

"Is it true what you said back there?" Luanne said. "That you didn't have a dream about Culver Creek?"

"I haven't had a dream in nine years," Caitlin said.

"It left you," Luanne said quietly, "your gift."

"I sent it away," Caitlin said.

Luanne might have said more, but she was trying to navigate a busy intersection.

"Back there," Caitlin said, "with the news crew, I was surprised you didn't jump at the opportunity to play the celebrity."

Her mother gave her a funny look before turning her attention back to the road.

"Why would you say that?"

"Oh, come on, Mom. I know what your priorities are."

"You're my priority," Luanne said. "Adam's my priority, not those vultures from the television station."

"Age has changed you," Caitlin mumbled.

"My looks maybe," Luanne said as she pulled into the driveway, "but not my priorities."

28

SAGE HAD SAT in the book-filled office of his academic advisor. The small, cramped room had smelled of dust and microwaved lunch. Professor Andrews shoved the plastic tray of tortellini into the last space available on his cluttered desk and fixed his attention on Sage.

"Do you want to be here, Sage?" Andrews asked. There were flecks of tomato and cheese in the professor's scrubby beard.

"In your office?" Sage asked, confused.

"At the college," Andrews clarified. "At school."

"Yeah," Sage said, "I guess."

"You guess?"

Sage regretted adding those two words, but he honestly had no idea why this meeting had been scheduled. It was Wednesday afternoon, and Wednesday afternoons he usually hung out in Evan's dorm room and played video games. This whole thing was messing with his schedule.

"You had a marketing class this morning," Andrews said. "Were you there?"

If Andrews was asking this question, then Sage

figured he already knew the answer. He hated when teachers did things like that. Did they think they were being clever?

"I overslept," Sage said.

"What about on Monday?" Andrews asked. "Did you oversleep on Monday, too?"

"It's just a couple of classes," Sage said.

"But it's not, is it?" Andrews asked. "Your academic performance has been below par, and you've been identified as at risk."

"At risk," Sage repeated. He was sure this was a case of a professor overreacting. He went to classes, not all of them, but most of them, a lot of them anyway. He may not have been some super-genius, but he felt pretty sure he was holding his own.

"At risk means you still have time to turn things around, but here's the thing, Sage, you've got to start shaping up. Because if you don't, they will kindly ask you to not return next semester."

"Wait, what?" Sage said. "Just for missing a few classes?"

"Well, that's where it begins, then your grades go into the toilet, and well, when your record gets reviewed, it just looks like you don't really want to be here."

Andrews folded his arms across his desk, and to Sage the professor's expression looked smug.

"I don't know what anyone even wants from me," Sage protested.

"Well, lucky for you, your professors were kind enough to put together this list of the assignments you haven't turned in." Andrews picked up a piece of paper and handed it to Sage.

The number of items on the list surprised him. Could

this possibly be right? Had he really missed this many assignments?

~

S age skipped video games that day, went back to his own dorm room, and sat down with the admirable intention of catching up on all his missed assignments, but it was a long list, and the problem with long lists was where did one begin. Starting at the top of the list wasn't an option. It was a five-page research paper. He couldn't start there. What he would do was ease himself into things by starting with a less difficult assignment. He scrolled down the list and decided he could start with a one-page essay. That wouldn't be that hard. That was doable. One page. He could do one page.

He opened up a document on his computer and sat there staring at the blank screen. Well, of course he couldn't write. He had to decide on his topic first. What he needed was inspiration. He tried Google. Then somehow, five minutes later, he found himself watching a video of a guy recklessly weaving his motorcycle in and out of traffic on a congested roadway. The video led to another, and then another, and then his stomach rumbled and he decided there was no point trying to write on an empty stomach. He would be able to work better once he had a full belly.

Wednesday turned into Thursday, which turned into Friday, and by about noon on Friday, Sage was no further along and he had reached the conclusion that he was never going to complete all the missing assignments and so what was the point in even trying to tackle any of them? The stress of the whole thing was making him a little crazy, and so he decided he was going to spend his night completing a task that he was pretty sure he could handle: he was going to do his best to drink himself into oblivion. Getting drunk wouldn't fix his problems, but it would, however briefly, help him forget about them, and that was all he wanted.

He spent the rest of the day preparing for his personal pity party and gathering all the supplies he needed. By the time eight p.m. rolled around and his sister had driven all the way to the college, he was only three or four drinks into his sad celebration, but it was enough.

He blinked in confusion at Melodie standing in the dorm hallway.

"What are you doing here?" he asked. "Are you supposed to be here?" He wondered if his assignments weren't the only thing he had missed. Maybe Melodie had scheduled a visit and he had somehow missed that too, but then his alcohol-thickened brain attempted to use some logic, and he reached the only conclusion that made sense. The school must have informed his parents about his academic failures, and they had decided to send Melodie out here as some sort of emissary. They were sending her to do their dirty work. Typical. "Mom and Dad sent you, didn't they?"

"What?" she said. "No." But the fact that she had said "what" first instead of "no" bothered him. "Uh, can I come in, or what?" She was still standing in the dorm hallway.

Sage shrugged and pushed the door open a little wider so she could walk in. She wrinkled up her face in disgust at the messy room. Technically only half of the mess was his. The other half belonged to his roommate, who had gone out with his girlfriend.

"What's with you?" Melodie asked.

"What's with you?" he countered. It wasn't exactly brilliant, but he was still trying to wrap his head around his sister being here and what exactly it meant for his evening's plans.

"Are you drunk or something?"

"And what if I am?" He felt like this admission freed him from the need to pretend to be sober, and he went over to his desk where he had set up his stash and refilled the plastic tumbler he was drinking from.

"Sorry," Melodie said. "I should have called first." She watched him refill his drink and then take a long sip. "There's something I need to talk to you about."

"Look, you can't just barge in here without notice. I got a life, you know."

"Clearly," she said. Her eyes went to the alcohol bottles lined up on his desk. "You expecting company, or are those all for you?"

Picking on him and his shitty life choices seemed to be the theme of the week. He was pissed off at Melodie. How dare she show up here unannounced? He wanted to drink enough to forget about all the things that were bothering him, and judging by how bothered he felt, he clearly had a long way to go.

"I'm willing to share," he said, "but it's BYOC. Bring your own cup." This struck him as a killer line, and he laughed at it.

Melodie didn't. She just glared at him. What right did she have to show up here and judge him? She had no right to judge him. This wasn't how this worked.

"I need to talk to you," she said.

"So talk." He took another sip of his drink.

"Not like this." She looked around at the sad, ugly dorm room. She might have been looking for a place to sit down. His desk chair was piled high with dirty laundry and other random stuff. His bed wasn't much better, and the sheets were long overdue for washing. "Maybe we could go get coffee or something," she suggested.

"Don't want coffee," he said. "I would think you would be sick of the stuff." He took another sip from the tumbler and was surprised he had emptied it already.

He went over to the desk and started to refill his cup.

"Sage, stop it!" Melodie screamed. Her voice was loud and shrill in the little room.

It made him pause for a moment before he continued pouring his drink. He looked over at his sister, who paced back and forth in front of his bed. Her eyes looked glassy like she was about to cry.

He didn't understand what she was doing here, and he still wasn't convinced that this didn't have something to do with his slipping grades. She hadn't actually come out and said anything about that, but she hadn't really said anything. If his parents were behind this visit, he was pissed at them, but he was disappointed in Melodie. She was old enough to know she didn't have to do their bidding.

Suddenly Melodie stopped pacing. She reached out and knocked the nearly full cup from his hands. Vodka splashed down the front of his clothes and onto the floor. At least the clear liquid wouldn't stain, but he couldn't imagine it would do much for the already unpleasant odor in the room.

"What the hell?" he said to her. Before he knew what was happening, she grabbed all the bottles from his little makeshift bar. She cradled them in the crook of her arm, and with her free hand, she worked open the window. She glanced outside, then dropped all the bottles three stories to the concrete walkway below. They exploded with an epic crash.

"Hey!" he shouted at her. He wasn't exactly awash in

money, and his afternoon's purchase had nearly drained him of his financial reserves. "You've got no right—"

"I need to talk to you about something." She looked like she was about to cry, but in that moment he wasn't thinking about her feelings. All he cared about was himself, all he cared about were his evening's plans, which were now ruined. The last thing he wanted was to have some heart-to-heart chat with his sister. Not tonight. Another time, when he was in a better mood.

"I'm going out," he said.

"But—"

"You can stay here," he said. "You can use my bed if you want."

"Sage—"

"You should have called first," he said. "I've got to go."

He swapped his vodka-soaked T-shirt for a more or less clean hoodie and headed out the door. His plan, insomuch as he had one, was to find some party somewhere on campus where he could get wasted. It shouldn't be hard. It was Friday night. Then maybe in the morning, or whenever, he would be more in the mood to sit down and shoot the shit with Melodie.

"Lock the door," he said on the way out. "Don't let anybody in."

The rest of that night was an alcohol-soaked blur. He traded what could have been a nice evening with his sister for some worthless night of partying. He remembered that Melodie was asleep on his floor when he returned. It was the last time he would see her alive. He'd crawled into bed without waking her and promptly passed out. It was past noon when he awoke Saturday morning. Melodie was long gone. She hadn't even left a note.

The police files spread out on every flat surface and the assortment of takeout containers now filling his apartment reminded him of his messy college dorm room. If he squinted in the dim early morning light, he could almost make out his sister sleeping on the floor in a corner of the room. Of course, it was nothing but a jacket he had tossed carelessly on the floor, but for a brief instant it filled him with a flicker of hope.

Why couldn't he have just gone out and had some coffee with her that night? There was that funky place with the ratty couches just a block from the campus. They could have hung out in there all night while she told him whatever it was she wanted to tell him.

"What did you want to tell me?" he asked his empty apartment, but there was no reply.

A feeling of futility filled him as he surveyed the files spread about his apartment. He was wasting everyone's time. What made him think he could find out the truth about the murder of a girl he'd never met in a town he didn't know that had happened nineteen years ago, when he didn't have the first clue about who had killed his own sister?

He began gathering up the folders and files, quickly shoving things back together as he worked to reclaim his apartment from his useless examination. He cleared off a spot on his table and began to stack everything related to the case there. A photo slipped out of one of the folders and landed at his feet. He bent down to pick it up but froze as he stared at the grisly image. Craig Walker's body lay at the bottom of a flight of stairs, but *lay* was too gentle a word for the contorted way this man's body had ended up.

Rod's words came back to him, *Why did I always think*

the guy had been pushed? Sage had read through the file. The conclusion had been that Craig Walker just took a bad tumble down the stairs. The wife had been out of town, and the guy was home alone with his five-year-old son.

Sage stared at the grim photo. The man had landed on his back, his feet closest to the stairs, which was a weird way to land if you fell while walking down the stairs. Could he have actually tumbled head over heels? It seemed unlikely.

Still holding the photo, Sage sat down on his couch and tried to visualize a man tumbling down his stairs. He had trouble wrapping his head around a way Walker could have landed on his back, unless he hadn't been facing the stairs when he fell. And if he wasn't facing the stairs, did that mean he had been pushed? The man was cold by the time the police arrived on the scene. That left plenty of time for a murderer to make a getaway.

Sage let out a rueful little laugh, which seemed completely inappropriate considering the photo he was staring at, but he was alone in his apartment, and he couldn't help but appreciate the fact that not only was he no closer to finding Lily Esposito's killer, but now he had added another murderer to track down to his to-do list.

Maybe he would get lucky and they would be the same guy. Yeah, like that was going to happen. He couldn't think of any instance of a murderer who started out his killing career shoving men down stairs, who then moved on to bashing little girls over the head.

Craig Walker was killed seven years before Lily Esposito was. He double-checked the dates. She wouldn't even have been born yet. He looked again. She wouldn't have been born, but she would have been conceived. What if Craig had an affair with Honoree? What if he was Lily Esposito's real father?

Rick Esposito could have found out about the affair. He shows up at Craig Walker's house, confronts him, things get heated and he shoves the other man down the stairs. He might not have meant to kill Craig, but when he realized what he had done, he would have hightailed it out of there. Who knows? Maybe that was when he started drinking too much.

Then what? Seven years later, he realizes Lily wasn't his real daughter? Maybe he recognized Craig in her features, maybe it drove him crazy seeing the face of the man he had killed in the girl, maybe that was why he did it. Jade was too young to be Craig's kid. She might have been Rick's real daughter, and that was why he hadn't touched her.

Lily Esposito wouldn't have been scared of Rick, she would have trusted him. And Jade? If Jade had seen her father murder her sister? What must that have done to the girl? No wonder she hadn't been able to talk about it. But if he was right, she certainly would have been able to identify the killer. He wished so desperately that he could talk to her. It was like Melodie all over again. He wondered what it was that Melodie needed to tell him. Had she witnessed something like Jade had? Was that what had gotten her killed?

Why did she stop her car that night? Why had she gotten out of it? He tried to imagine the scene and what could have possibly made his safety-conscious sister pull off the road late at night and get out of her car. The car.

That was the whole thing that had led him to the Craig Walker file. It was Raquel's description of the suspicious car. What was it Arlo said? It belonged to a friend or a relative. Well, Rick was a relative, wasn't he?

29

WHEN CAITLIN and Luanne stepped into the living room, Lance was there. He still had his jacket on, which made Caitlin think he probably hadn't gotten back much sooner than they had.

"Where were you?" Lance asked when he saw her.

"At the police station," she said. Had Tucker and Raquel not told him that? But then she wasn't sure if she had told Lance's parents that was where she was headed. "Where were you?"

"I was talking with Garvey," Lance said, but she just stared at him blankly. Was Garvey one of the other officers? "The attorney," Lance explained.

And now she remembered Tucker saying something about that. Wasn't it weird that Lance needed an attorney when his son had been abducted? This all felt very wrong to Caitlin. What was going on? Did it have something to do with what Young said about Lance taking Adam out to Culver Creek?

"Can I speak to you?" Caitlin asked. She could feel

Raquel and Tucker and her mom and Stu staring at them. "Alone."

"Of course," Lance said.

They went into the kitchen. She wished it had a door, but she hoped that whatever dumb video Stu was entertaining the others with would be enough to drown out their conversation. Lance took off his jacket and folded it over the top of a kitchen chair.

"What is it?" Lance asked.

"What were you doing in Culver Creek?" Caitlin asked. Lance didn't answer right away, and she was too on edge to stay silent. She rephrased her question, "Why did you take Adam out to Culver Creek?"

"I don't know," he said. "I was thinking of going out to see my parents, so we started heading out that way, but then I changed my mind."

Caitlin's knowledge of Pennsylvania geography was limited. Was Culver Creek near Atkins? It might have been. She wasn't sure, but still, something about Lance's explanation felt off to her. Was it her imagination, or was he avoiding looking her in the eye?

"It's just strange that you didn't mention that," Caitlin said.

"I meant to," Lance said, "but then you were telling me about your mom and her shotgun wedding—Stu's cool, by the way—and I guess I forgot about it."

But that wasn't right, was it? Caitlin was pretty sure they hadn't had that conversation about Luanne and Stu until later, after they had put Adam to bed, wasn't it? She searched her memory, but everything was such a jumbled mess in her head. After they had put Adam to bed, Lance had gotten a bit frisky and they had gone upstairs to their room. So maybe they had been talking about Luanne before that. She wasn't sure.

What was it Young had said at the police station? He asked her if she had seen a phone call on his cell phone. A call from a woman. That was what he meant, wasn't it? He had asked her if she suspected her husband of having an affair, but were those his words? And who took their son on a romantic rendezvous?

"What were you doing out there?" Caitlin asked.

"We played miniature golf," Lance said.

"We who?" she asked.

"Me and Adam," Lance said. "What the hell?"

And this time he looked her in the eyes. So maybe she was freaking out over nothing, but he was acting so strange. Maybe it was this whole awful situation. She wanted to find some quiet corner somewhere and curl up and have a good cry. It wouldn't solve anything, but this was all so heavy and overwhelming.

"Are you having an affair?" she asked, her voice so meek and quiet it was practically a whisper.

"No," Lance said. "No, of course not."

And he went over to her and wrapped his arms around her. He held her tightly and rocked her gently, and for a moment or two it felt like everything was going to be all right. But then she remembered Adam was out there somewhere, and for some reason Tucker had hired a criminal attorney to represent Lance.

"Where is he?" Caitlin asked. "Where's Adam?"

"I don't know," Lance said, "but they're going to find him. He's going to be okay. Everything's going to be okay."

She got the sense that he was lying to her again. His words sounded hollow to her. She was reminded of the way she had spoken to Adam about his nightmares.

She pulled away from Lance suddenly.

"He dreamed about that place," she said. "He had a dream about Culver Creek."

"He said that?" Lance asked. "He said that was the town he dreamed about?"

Caitlin shook her head. "No, I recognized it from what he said."

Lance looked puzzled.

"Why did you really take him out there?" She waited, but he remained silent. She repeated the question louder, all but shouted it at him. "Why did you really take him out there?"

Her shout brought in the calvary. Raquel peeked her head through the doorway. Luanne was right behind her. Caitlin didn't see any reason to send them away. Maybe Lance would feel more compelled to be honest with her, now that they had an audience.

She flinched when he reached into his back pocket. For a moment she thought he was going to draw out some sort of weapon, but instead it was only his wallet. Raquel and Luanne decided they didn't need an invitation and stepped into the kitchen to get a better view of the action.

"What's going on?" Luanne asked.

"I took Adam to a dream whisperer," Lance said. "Are you happy?"

He shoved the card into her hand. Caitlin stared down at it. Raquel peered over her shoulder, then let out a little gasp before taking a shaky step backward and bracing herself against the counter. One thing her mother-in-law and her mother had in common was a tendency to be dramatic.

"What's a dream whisperer?" Caitlin asked.

"You said no shrinks, right?" Lance said. "Well, Adam's nightmares just kept getting worse, and I didn't know what else to do. She's just some new-age quack. The whole thing was a waste of time. We were only there a few minutes. I didn't tell you about it because I knew it would piss you off."

Caitlin stared at the cheesy business card. It did seem to match with what Lance had described, but could she trust him? Then she noticed the dark red blotch on the corner of the card. At first she thought it was part of the printing, but no, that wasn't what this was at all. It looked an awful lot like blood.

The memory of standing there in the bathroom looking down at the bloody sock on the floor of the linen closet came back to her in vivid clarity. Was the blood on that sock the same blood that was on this business card? Whose blood was it? And what did it have to do with why Lance had taken Adam out to Culver Creek?

"Did you say Adam's been having nightmares?" Luanne asked. "But you know what this means? He might have the gift too."

"Gift?" Raquel repeated, still leaning against the counter.

Caitlin let go of the dream whisperer's business card and watched as it fluttered to the ground.

"I need to use the bathroom," she said as she started out of the room.

"Are you going to be sick again?" Luanne called after her, but Caitlin waved her mom off as she left the room.

~

Caitlin locked their bathroom door behind her. There was a bathroom downstairs, but she didn't really need to use the facilities. She just needed some space and some quiet to try to think.

She opened the door of the linen closet, pushed the hamper aside, and stared at the spot on the floor where the bloody sock had been. It was long gone. She remembered now that she had thrown the thing out. Why had she done that? Why hadn't she asked Lance about it?

Because you were afraid of what he would say, a little voice in her head said. She shook off the thought. She wasn't sure if it was true.

She had found the sock the day Lance had taken Adam to Culver Creek, so it couldn't have anything to do with that trip. Or could it? Theories began to race fast and furious through her head. What if he was having an affair? Maybe the woman was married or had a jealous ex or something, and Lance had been involved in some altercation with the man. That could explain the bloody sock and Lance's unexpected bathroom cleaning spree. The theory grew legs in her head. Then what if that guy, the husband or jealous ex or whatever, had seen Adam when Lance took him to Culver Creek that day. What if he had kidnapped him as revenge? Caitlin felt dizzy. She had unwittingly driven her son out there, so that this crazy man could steal him away.

She reminded herself she didn't know this for sure. Maybe Lance hadn't been having an affair at all. Maybe he really had taken Adam to some wacky dream whisperer, and she was being paranoid. Something was eating at her, though, and she knew what it was. It had been in the back of her head since Young asked if she had followed Lance to Culver Creek because she was suspicious.

~

Raquel had been the one to tell her about the Rixby family vacation. Like so many of her mother-in-law's calls, it had come in the middle of the workday, but she and Lance had been married less than a year and she was still trying to be a perfect daughter-in-law, so she said nothing as Raquel prattled away. Raquel seemed to be suggesting that Caitlin was the reason she and Lance weren't going on the big family vacation.

"It's more like a reunion really," Raquel said. "It would be such a shame for you two to miss it. Especially after the Rixbys were so generous with their wedding gifts."

Tucker and his brothers had rented some posh ocean-front mansion for a long weekend, and all their children and grandchildren were going to be coming out for the event. Raquel assured her the place was huge and there was plenty of room for them. She didn't seem to believe Caitlin's explanation that Lance hadn't told her about the reunion.

Caitlin asked him about it when he came home from work, and he made excuses.

"Honestly," he said, "these things are not much fun. The Rixbys are a bunch of spoiled, rich brats."

"Your mother seemed to think I was the reason we weren't going," Caitlin said.

"I'm sure I didn't say that," he said. "I forget what excuse I used."

"Is it because you're ashamed of me?" she asked. "Am I not good enough for you and your fabulously rich family?"

"Stepfamily," Lance corrected her, "and no, of course not. They're the ones who aren't good enough for you."

She stood there with her hand on her hip, staring him down.

"Fine, you want to go? I'll call my parents and let them know we'll be joining them after all, but I'm warning you, it's not going to be much fun."

~

Aﬁter a day spent in the company of the Rixby clan, Caitlin realized with some chagrin that her husband's description of them might have been pretty accurate. They weren't completely unbearable, just not especially likable.

Then, despite Raquel's promise that there was plenty of room for everyone, Caitlin and Lance ended up having to sleep on an air mattress on the sunporch. When Lance had asked his stepcousin if her two daughters really needed their own separate bedrooms she had responded, "Well, you weren't even going to be coming, and I'd already promised them their own rooms."

So an air mattress in a not exactly private room it was.

"I'm sorry," she said to Lance as they tossed and turned trying to get comfortable that night. "You were right about this weekend. We shouldn't have come."

"Well, the house is pretty amazing," he said, "and we're right on the water. We can spend the day off on our own tomorrow, if you want—stroll along the beach, have lunch in town. What do you think?"

"Sounds nice." She attempted to roll over and rest her head on Lance's chest, but that sent the whole air mattress rocking like a ship on a storm-tossed sea, and they both lay back down on their backs and did their best to remain motionless and keep the waves at bay.

Things had seemed good that night, when they went to

sleep, hadn't they? As she drifted off with the help of Pacif-cleon, she had been full of happy thoughts thinking of the fun day together they had planned.

Even with her magic sleeping pills, Caitlin woke up early. The sun was only just starting to rise. Her back ached. The air mattress must have had a slow leak, because it was half deflated. There was no air between her body and the floor. Lance's side of the bed still had some air, but he wasn't there.

She figured he hadn't been able to sleep in their uncomfortable bed, and got up to try to find him. She wandered through the living room, the kitchen, the dining room, the library and the game room. Maybe he had decided to ease his aching back with a hot shower. She checked, but none of the bathrooms on the main floor were occupied. The hot shower idea appealed to her, though.

By the time she got out of the bathroom in a somewhat more awake and revived state, some of the Rixby clan were milling around. There was still no sign of Lance. She grew concerned. Could he have driven somewhere? She went out to the sunporch, but his keys, wallet and phone were all there. It was as she was tidying up their makeshift bedroom that movement caught her eye outside the window. She was relieved and surprised to see Lance staggering toward the house. He looked confused and disoriented. Had he been drinking? Part of her wanted to run out there to him, but she remained rooted to that spot of the sunroom floor as she watched him. Something felt very off to her.

Caitlin was still in the sunroom when she heard Lance talking to some of his Rixby relatives in the kitchen, and she wandered out there.

"There you are, sleepyhead," he said to her. It was a

strange remark. He was the one who looked like he had just crawled out of bed. She was all showered and dressed.

"Where were you?" She expected him to smell of beer or liquor, but the only aroma she caught was that of the outdoors.

"I couldn't sleep," he said. "That damn air mattress. I ended up sleeping on that couch in the library."

Her blood went cold. She had checked the library. He hadn't been there, and she had seen him just a minute earlier staggering around outside. Why was he lying to her? She felt the others watching them, and didn't challenge his explanation.

There was a spread of bagels and fresh fruit for breakfast, and Caitlin picked at a pumpernickel bagel while Lance showered and the Rixbys talked about European vacations and exotic sports cars.

After Lance got ready, she told him she had changed her mind about the day's plans. She didn't feel that well, and she just wanted to go home. He made their excuses to their family, and well before noon they were on their way home.

As she stared out the window on the drive back, she had come up with her own logical explanation. Lance had gone and slept on the library couch, but he had woken before she did and decided to go for an early morning stroll on the beach. It was probably peaceful at that hour. It was weird that he hadn't told her about that, but maybe he didn't want her to get upset that he had gone on the promised beach stroll without her. Of course, she could have cleared all this up with a simple question, but she didn't ask and never told him she had seen him wandering around outside.

∼

Even on a half-deflated air mattress, Caitlin had slept through the night thanks to her miracle pills. For all she knew, Lance could have been throwing wild parties in their bedroom every night. She knew he wasn't, but wasn't it entirely possible he could have been slipping out of the house to carry on affairs? How many other women had there been over the years?

She shook her head. Lance was kind and attentive, he wouldn't cheat on her. *People fall out of love*, a little voice whispered in her head. She thought of that awful night in the motel when her mother and Officer Brighton were sharing the bed beside hers. Her relationship with Lance had definitely changed over the years. They were both busy with work, and of course, Adam, despite all the joy he brought to them, had changed things as well.

Adam. Just the thought of her sweet boy made her heart break all over again. Where was he? Was he scared? Was he hurt? She would give anything to hold him in her arms. She would give her life if it meant he would be safe.

Deflating air mattresses and wild parties might not have been able to disturb her sleep, but there was something that could. More than once, Adam's nightmare-induced wails had woken her from the deepest of slumbers. They were one thing that could rouse her from Pacifcleon-sleep. She had never made the connection before, but now that she did, she wondered how she hadn't seen it before—Lance's strange insistence on locking their bedroom door was a sure sign he was up to something, wasn't it?

He didn't want Adam to barge in there and wake her up because that meant she would discover Lance was nowhere to be found. He wanted to keep his midnight dalliances a secret from her, and Adam threatened that.

Something gnawed at the back of her head, an itch she couldn't quite scratch. In her confused and chaotic mental state, though, she couldn't see the faultiness of her own thinking.

30

"THERE'S BEEN A DEVELOPMENT!" Stu shouted. "Turn on the television!"

Lance ran out to the living room and grabbed the remote for the TV. He flipped through the stations until he saw a reporter standing in a highway rest area parking lot, a battalion of police cars behind her. Lance heard footsteps on the stairs and looked up to see Caitlin coming down.

"What's going on?" she asked.

"The police think they've located Adam!" Stu said excited. "Everything's going to be okay!"

Lance looked around at the tense expressions in the room. Stu seemed to be the only one assured that this was good news.

"Where are they?" Luanne asked. "Does it say where this is?"

"Wait, I recognize that place," Tucker said, pointing at the television. "That's that rest area along the way home. It's about halfway between here and Atkins."

Raquel nodded in agreement, but her face was grim.

She turned and caught Lance's eye, and there seemed to be a question in her expression that he couldn't read.

Caitlin came over and stood near him, but not next to him. He reached to hold her hand, but she shied away from him, her eyes riveted to the image on the television screen. It seemed like everyone in the room was holding their breath. Without warning, the image cut back to the television studio, where a newscaster said, "We'll update you with any developments, but now let's go to chief meteorologist Stan Dorsey, who has all the details on a major thunderstorm moving into the area."

Oblivious to their plight, Stan Dorsey launched into an excited description of the major weather event, which brought with it the potential for flash flooding.

Caitlin voiced the question that was on everyone's minds. "What's going on?"

Lance pressed his hand to his chest, where his heart felt like it was going to explode at any second.

"Thank God the doc gave me a clean bill of health at my last checkup," he said, "or else I would be worried about following in my father's footsteps."

"What? Falling down the stairs?" Tucker asked.

Lance made a face at him. His stepfather could, at times, be full of wisdom. However, he also had the tendency to be a big buffoon. This was a buffoon moment.

"I meant how he died," Lance explained. "He had a heart attack when I was five years old."

"Heart attack?" Tucker said. "He broke his neck falling backwards down the stairs in the middle of the night."

"I think you're a bit confused," Lance said.

"Not in the slightest," Tucker said. "That was back when your mother was working for me. You don't forget a story like that."

Lance silently agreed that it would be pretty hard to forget a story like that. The problem was that he had never heard that story. He looked at his mother, who gave him what seemed to be a sheepish smile.

"Is it true?" he asked her.

"I might have let you think it was a heart attack because that's more common, and not really preventable," she said. "I didn't want you to grow up with a fear of stairs."

"No, instead I grew up thinking I had a family history of heart disease!" Lance roared. He couldn't help the outburst. "I've been getting an annual stress test every year since my early twenties!"

"Is that such a bad thing?" Raquel asked.

"I just can't believe you never told me the truth," he said.

"I'm telling you now," Raquel said defensively.

Caitlin rested her hand on his arm. Sure, *now* she wanted to be near him. He knew she was just attempting to comfort him and calm him down, but he wasn't sure he wanted to be calm.

"Come in the kitchen with me a sec," she said.

Lance looked toward the television, which had cut to a car commercial.

"I'll shout if there's more news," Stu said.

~

In the kitchen, Lance took a glass from the cabinet and filled it with water, but before he took a sip, he set it back down on the counter. It wasn't quite a slam, but it was hard enough for the glass to make a ringing sound as it met the granite.

"Can you believe that?" Lance asked. "My whole life

she's told me my father died of a heart attack, and now, *now* I learn that he fell down the fucking stairs and broke his neck? Jesus."

"It's awful," Caitlin agreed in a murmur. "Lance, there's something I need—"

He didn't let her finish. He couldn't get over his mother's sudden revelation.

"What other bullshit stories has she been feeding me my whole life?" he asked.

"She was probably just trying to protect you," Caitlin said. "Like when Adam has a nightmare."

"That's different," Lance said. "It's not like we're lying to him."

Caitlin's expression grew pained, and she looked away from him. He knew she was probably thinking about Adam. Could they really have found him at that rest area? Why hadn't the police called them about it? Shouldn't they be the first to know?

He wrapped his arms around Caitlin and pressed her head to his chest as he stroked her hair.

"He's going to be okay," he promised her, and he wondered if lying to loved ones was something he was genetically predisposed to, unlike heart disease.

He remembered he and his mother in their old bathroom with the peeling wallpaper, and the worry in his mother's voice as she said, "The police aren't going to understand." It all made more sense now. It hadn't made much sense when he thought his dad died of a heart attack, but breaking your neck falling down the stairs—backwards, no less—well, that was freakish, wasn't it? It did seem a bit odd, and maybe even suspicious.

Well, crap. If the police suspected him of somehow kidnapping his own son because of a few bad mistakes on his part, they must have had some suspicions about his mother when her husband died in such a bizarre way.

As he consoled his tearful wife, he realized he had some suspicions of his own. Why had his mother lied to him about his father's death for years? To protect him from a fear of stairs? I mean, okay, maybe when he was too young to understand, but certainly at some point she should have told him the truth. He thought of how peculiar she acted right after Lily was killed and the police were canvassing the neighborhood. He thought she had been freaked out that a neighborhood kid had been murdered, but what if she was worried they would somehow find out she murdered her husband? Wasn't it strange how his mother barely talked about his dad unless he prompted her? Maybe he had been abusive and she had pushed him down the stairs in self defense.

The police won't understand, he heard her words in his head. He saw that old, ugly bathroom with the peeling wallpaper, and he saw the two of them reflected in the mirror. He gasped.

Caitlin froze and looked up at him.

"What is it?" she asked. "Did you hear something from the television?"

She was silent, her head cocked to hear from the other room, but they were only reporting the scores of hockey games.

"That couldn't have been when my father died," Lance said aloud.

"He didn't die when you were five years old?" Caitlin asked.

"No, he did," Lance said. "It's just something my mom said to me. I always thought it was right after my father died, but it couldn't have been, because I was older. Much older. It must have been right before I went to Ryerson."

And it was like that one realization opened a floodgate, because memories suddenly rushed at him. The night his father died, he remembered finding his dad at the bottom of the stairs. Dear God, what an awful, traumatic thing to go through at any age, but especially at five years old. He remembered touching his dad's face, and it was cold. The memory must have been buried all these years, and no wonder. It was frightening and dreadful.

Then something else, he remembered being in Mrs. Drummond's kitchen. Mrs. Drummond was the old lady who lived next door to him. She babysat him sometimes when his parents went out. Probably his mom had sent him over there while the police came to the house. That would make sense, except, no, he could remember very clearly sitting at Mrs. Drummond's kitchen table eating those cookies that were shaped like windmills while she talked to two police officers.

Well, of course, he reasoned, they would want to interview her. They must have already suspected his mother, right? So they were probably asking Mrs. Drummond if she suspected Raquel was capable of such an act. Maybe they wanted to know if she had ever witnessed any arguments between his parents. That sort of thing.

And his mother? Where was she in all this? Why was his mother absent from all his memories of his father's death? Was there something else he had buried? Something he buried far deeper than his memory of finding his father dead? Maybe he had heard them quarrel, or worse, maybe he had actually witnessed her shove him down the stairs.

"How long have you been cheating on me?"

He heard the question faintly, like it was coming from

another dimension. He returned to the present day, to his kitchen, to Caitlin looking at him like she barely recognized him.

"What?" he asked.

"How many women have there been, Lance? Be honest," she said.

"One," he said.

"Who is she?" Caitlin asked. Tears ran down her face.

"No, I mean there's only one woman for me. You're the only one for me," he said. "I told you, the only reason I went out to Culver Creek was to take Adam to that damn dream whisperer. I'm so sorry. It was a dumb thing to do. I just felt so helpless. God, what if this is all my fault?"

"No," Caitlin said. "It's all my fault. I should have seen this coming." Her trickle of tears turned into a torrent.

"This is because of what your mother said? Look, if I've learned one thing tonight, it's that maybe listening to our mothers isn't the best thing."

Caitlin shook her head and wiped at her tear-streaked face with the back of her sleeve.

"Lance," she said, "there's something I need to tell you."

31

CAITLIN TOOK a deep breath before she began. She wanted to tell Lance the truth, but she didn't want him to think she was crazy. She realized it might be too late for that.

"I used to have these dreams," Caitlin told Lance.

"You?" he asked. "You never have dreams."

She held up a hand to silence him. This wasn't easy to do. She wasn't sure she would be able to get the words out if he kept interrupting her.

"I used to have nightmares like Adam, but mine came true," she said. He frowned, but she was grateful he didn't say anything. "It was usually about people I knew or people who had crossed my path at some point, and the scary dreams were about something bad that was going to happen to them. Once I dreamed about a little girl who was killed. In college I had a dream about a woman who was attacked. I went to the campus security office, but they didn't take me seriously. They failed to stop the attack, and the woman was killed. That's when I decided I couldn't go on like that. The dreams were too much of a burden."

Lance took in all that she had just said.

"Caitlin," he said, "I'm sorry. I never knew—"

She held up her hand again because she wasn't done.

"I experimented with some different sleep aids, until I discovered Pacifcleon. It worked like magic. I slept through the night, and I never had nightmares or any dreams at all. It changed my life. I felt like I could finally be a normal, functioning human."

"You haven't had a dream since college," Lance murmured.

She nodded to confirm this was true.

"I never really saw this as a bad thing until now," she said.

"You can't possibly think that a dream would have changed anything," Lance said.

"It would!" Caitlin insisted. "The campus police might not have listened to me, but I would have listened to myself."

"You don't even know that you would have had a dream about Adam," Lance pointed out.

"Of course I would have," Caitlin said.

Lance seemed unconvinced, but that was her fault. If she hadn't been taking those pills all these years, there would have been other dreams over the years, other portents that she could have warned him or others about, and then he would see that when those things she dreamed about really did come true, that this was a gift she had. Like her fender bender the other day. She would have dreamed about that, and maybe she would have been extra alert and avoided it. Of course, she wouldn't have had the fender bender if she wasn't taking her pills, because that was what caused it in the first place.

"There's another reason I'm to blame," she said.

"Would you stop saying that?" Lance said. "This is not your fault."

"It is," she insisted. "Because the whole reason I drove out to Culver Creek was because of Pacifcleon. I went out there to buy more."

"They stopped making it years ago," Lance said.

"There was a pharmacy out there that had gone out of business. The old woman I spoke to said she had a case of the stuff in their unsold inventory, but she was mistaken." The thought that she had caused all of this filled her with such dread and horror. The fact that Lance didn't seem to hold her responsible bothered her. She slapped her hands on his chest to make her point. "I drove all the way out there to buy some drug, and now Adam is gone."

Lance grabbed hold of her hands and once again did his best to comfort her, but she didn't feel like she deserved to be comforted.

"Do you know it's where I'm from?" Lance asked.

"What is?" Caitlin asked.

She stepped away from him and went to the refrigerator. The doors were filled with snapshots. Adam was in most of them, and her heart broke again looking at his cherubic face.

"Culver Creek," Lance said.

She frowned and looked at her husband. If this was his weird way of trying to comfort her, she didn't understand it.

"You're from Atkins," she said.

"Well, not originally," Lance said. "Before my mom got married to Tucker, we lived in Culver Creek. That's where we lived when my dad died."

This information surprised her. She supposed she

vaguely knew Lance and his mother had lived somewhere before moving into Tucker's palatial home, but in her mind it was just somewhere else in Atkins. His mother met Tucker while working for him, and in her head that all happened in the same town, but if Lance had actually grown up in Culver Creek, then that would have meant he lived there when Lily Esposito was killed. Lance was barely two years older than Caitlin. The town wasn't that large. He might even have known Lily.

"Lance, did you ever—" Caitlin began, but she didn't get to finish.

"Come quick, the news is on!"

Caitlin and Lance turned to see Luanne in the doorway, waving them back out to the living room. They followed her, and on the screen was more footage from the rest area. The reporter now stood under an umbrella as rain fell around her.

"We've learned that a police raid on a vehicle in this parking lot earlier this evening was in conjunction with the kidnapping of Adam Walker, the four-year-old child who was reported missing earlier this afternoon. Unfortunately, the police have said the raid was a false alarm, and that they have not located Adam. The public is urged to call this hotline if you see young Adam." A hotline number flashed on the screen along with the snapshot Caitlin had emailed to the police earlier.

The news report was over too quickly and contained frustratingly little information. If they were raiding a car at a Pennsylvania rest area, then maybe they had picked up some sort of trail in Culver Creek, but had she waited too long to come forward with the information that she had driven Adam out there?

She looked over at her mother for confirmation, and her

mother knew what she was asking without Caitlin having to say a word. Luanne nodded. Standing here watching useless news reports wasn't going to bring her son home. There was only one thing she could do that would have any hope of saving Adam, and she knew she must do it now.

"I'm going to bed," she announced.

32

SAGE HAD NOT BOTHERED to look at the clock before jumping in his car and driving over to Brighton's, and he realized it was not quite seven thirty in the morning. Maybe it was a bit early to be showing up at a retired man's front door, but there was a light on inside the house.

It was Mrs. Brighton who answered the door. She frowned when she saw him.

"Is something wrong?" she asked.

"I need to speak with your husband about something," he said. "I'm sorry about the early hour."

"Oh, I'm a cop's wife," she said. "I'm used to it."

Brighton was sitting in an armchair in his living room, drinking his morning coffee while watching the birds eating their breakfast at his backyard feeder.

"You crack the case?" Brighton asked without taking his eyes away from the window.

"Why didn't you look more closely at Rick Esposito?" Sage asked.

"You would have to be a monster to brutally murder

your daughter like that, and then you have to ask yourself, why would he kill one daughter and not touch the other?"

"What if Lily wasn't really his daughter?" Sage asked.

Brighton finally turned away from the window long enough to give Sage a skeptical look.

"What makes you say that?"

"It's a fact of life," Sage said. "Sometimes husbands and wives aren't faithful to each other."

Brighton set his mug down on a coaster.

"That nasty blue jay is back," he said. "Come with me."

Sage followed Brighton out onto the patio. They stood there in silence for a minute or so. Brighton's eyes were fixed on the feeder, but he didn't really seem to be seeing it. Sage, for his part, never saw the alleged blue jay.

Brighton glanced back at the closed patio door before speaking. "I knew you would figure it out. I heard about you. Rayanne said you were super smart. *Astute* was the word she used. Thank you for that bit of misdirection back there." Brighton nodded toward the house. "I appreciate it. That bit about Rick Esposito."

"I'm not sure I understand," Sage said.

"My wife never knew about it," Brighton said. "I think she always suspected, though. She's astute like you." He smiled briefly, then a stoic expression returned to his face as he stared in the direction of the bird feeder. "I'd never cheated on her before, but I guess we were going through a rough patch, and well, I just made a really shitty decision."

Sage tried to wrap his head around what Brighton was telling him, and before he could stop himself, he burst out with, "You're Lily's father! You should have taken yourself off the investigation!"

And was that why he had never seriously investigated Melodie's murder? On the one hand, it would seem that being related to the victim might give you special insight, but it could also complicate things in so many ways.

"Lily?" Brighton looked horrified. "No, I meant the psychic's mother. Isn't that why you came here?"

Sage thought of that psychic reading place above the lawyer's office. Did Brighton mean he had an affair with that woman's mother? Why did he think Sage would have found out about that?

"The Lily Esposito case was a national news story," Brighton said. "People were coming out of the woodwork with their theories and speculations, and of course there was a whole slew of people who knew who the killer was because the Virgin Mary had told them in church, or because they had read it in their tarot cards or whatever. I wouldn't have given that girl and her psychic dreams more than a passing notice if it wasn't for her mother. She was a looker."

And at last Sage knew what Brighton was talking about. The girl who had given the description to the sketch artist. The man she had seen in her dream.

"Luanne was vivacious," Brighton recalled, "and she really believed in these psychic dreams her daughter supposedly had, so then I started believing in the daughter's dreams. The murderer got away because I was too busy screwing around with a woman who wasn't my wife and chasing the bogeyman a little girl had seen in her nightmare." Brighton shook his head at the memory. "You know what it's like living with this guilt?"

"I can imagine." Sage thought of the look on his sister's face when he abandoned her in his dorm room. "You don't happen to remember what kind of car Rick Esposito drove, do you?"

"Rick Esposito," Brighton repeated. "What, you don't

really think . . . You don't really believe what you were saying about Rick, do you?"

"Right now he's the best lead I got," Sage said. "You wouldn't happen to know anything about Craig Walker's death, would you?"

"Walker? That was the guy who fell down the stairs, wasn't it?" Brighton asked, and Sage nodded. "Not really, no. But I wonder what ever happened to his kid."

"What do you mean?"

"Well, imagine how something like that would have fucked you up, right? Finding your dad dead like that when you were just a little kid. That sort of thing could really mess a kid up."

Sage had forgotten about the kid. If his theory about Rick Esposito was correct and there had been some sort of heated argument, then the boy almost certainly would have heard it. It would have woken him. Why would Rick leave the child untouched, but then years later murder Lily? Maybe Rick hadn't realized the boy was there. Plus, it would have been different with Lily. She represented the living, breathing proof of his wife's infidelity. Well, maybe. It was only a theory.

Sage sat at his squad room desk, Facebook open on his browser.

"Goofing off on social media is a big no-no," Rod said as he peered over Sage's shoulder.

"It's for an investigation," Sage said. Whatever camaraderie had developed between him and Rod at the rally seemed to have melted away.

Rod leaned in a little closer to get a better look at the

search bar that read "Jade Culver Creek." Sage had tried every variation he could think of to pull up something on Lily's sister, but it was like the girl had ceased to exist.

"Oh, shit, are you stalking some broad," Rod said, then he announced to the room at large, "We got a regular old horndog here!"

"It's not—"

Rayanne cut him off. She leaned her head out of her office, and in that no-nonsense way of hers said, "Sage. Office. Now."

He exhaled loudly through his nose as he resisted the urge to shove Rod through the wall, and stood and walked into his boss's office. There were a few stray catcalls from his fellow officers.

"It wasn't what you think," Sage said after Rayanne closed the door behind them. "It was for the Lily Esposito case."

"Yeah, about that," Rayanne said as she sat down behind her desk. "You're officially off that investigation as of right now."

"But I think I might have something."

"Lily Esposito's been dead nineteen years. It can wait. Meanwhile, we've got a kidnapped child and the FBI looking for our help. I'd like you to be the official liaison."

"What?"

Rayanne passed him a fax that had just come in. He scanned through it quickly.

"The child was kidnapped in New Jersey," Sage said. "How do they expect us to help?"

"Apparently the parents gave them some conflicting information. The mother originally said the child had been kidnapped in New Jersey, but then changed her story. Said she was out here earlier in the day and that's when the kid was taken. Look, most likely the parents are lying, but right now there's a kid missing, and if he's out there alive somewhere, we're going to do everything in our power to bring him home safe."

"Of course," Sage said.

"An Agent Henderson is going to be calling you shortly with more information," Rayanne said. "He'll catch you up to speed."

"Should I return to my desk to wait for his call?"

"Yes," Rayanne said. "Henderson will give you further instructions, and of course you'll receive overtime pay for any extra hours you put in."

Sage stood to go, but before he left the office, Rayanne added, "I wanted you on this because you're the best we have. If that kid's here somewhere, I know you'll find him."

Sage thought of the impasse he had come to with the Lily Esposito case and wondered if the praise was warranted, but he nodded his appreciation before leaving Rayanne's office.

The pharmacy Agent Henderson wanted Sage to check out was outside the city limits, but he wasn't about to quibble over that detail. He was relieved to get the hell out of the station. Word had spread quickly that he was working with the FBI, and this caused a bit of an uproar with the other officers, who considered it tantamount to making a deal with the devil.

Apparently it wasn't the first time the feds had rolled into town and thrown their weight around. Sage wondered if his skillset wasn't the only reason Rayanne had chosen him to be the FBI liaison. Maybe she knew no one else on the force would agree to it.

"Can't say I'm surprised," Steve Arlo said as Sage was on his way out to his car. "I knew you were disloyal."

Sage hadn't bothered to respond, but the remark was still taking up real estate in his head as he sped out to the state road toward the pharmacy.

The memory, like too many of them, was a hazy one. He had been in his early teens. His parents had gone out to the store, when one of his friends had come over with some fireworks. For some reason, Sage had thought it would be a good idea to use their new plastic patio table to launch the fireworks from. As fireworks displays went, it was pretty lackluster. Sage at least had the good sense to clean up all the evidence from the lawn so his parents didn't flip out when they returned, but there was nothing he could do about the weird melted spots the fireworks had left on the tabletop. He hoped his parents wouldn't notice. They noticed.

When they asked him about the marks, he claimed ignorance. Then they asked Melodie. She had seen the whole sad fireworks spectacle from her bedroom window, and she could have easily ratted him out, but she didn't. She said maybe it was hail damage from that storm they'd had a few days back.

Late that night, after his parents had gone to bed, he went into her room to thank her.

"You didn't have to do that," he said.

"Yeah I did," she said. "You're my brother. We look out for each other, right?"

"Right," he agreed.

Melodie had always been loyal to him, but when the ball had been in his court, he let her down in her hour of need and hadn't done a thing to save her from being murdered. The least he could do was bring her murderer to justice, but he hadn't even done that. Steve Arlo had him pegged.

He pulled his car into the empty pharmacy parking lot and sat there for a few minutes as the guilt of his disloyalty weighed on him.

The pharmacy was closed—not closed for the day but closed for business forever, and it looked like it had been for a while. Certainly there was no way it had been open earlier in the day, when the mother claimed to have been shopping there.

Rayanne was most likely right. The parents were lying. Probably they had murdered their kid and were now making up some bullshit story to try to save their necks. It was like Rick Esposito all over again, only this time they weren't going to get away with it. Sage would make sure of that.

33

AS LANCE DRIFTED BACK toward consciousness, the first thing that seemed peculiar was how loud the rain was. It pounded the roof above his head, which didn't seem right. Even during torrential downpours, he had never heard it so loud. The attic and all that pink fiberglass insulation meant the sound of the rain always had a muffled quality. But he wasn't in his bed, was he?

He was sitting in a chair, but as he blinked open his eyes, he realized that wasn't quite right either. He was in a seat, specifically the driver's seat of his wife's Land Cruiser. *Please let me be in the driveway,* he silently wished as he squinted at the rainy landscape outside the windshield. He was scared that he would find himself looking at the smashed front end of her vehicle, and if that was the case, he prayed that all he had hit was a telephone pole or fire hydrant or some other inanimate object.

It came as a pleasant surprise that the car did not appear to be at all smashed, and instead looked to be parked legally and competently on some unfamiliar road. He had no memory of taking the car for a drive, but was it possible he had simply forgotten about this? Maybe he had found himself getting drowsy and pulled off the road to get some sleep. None of this felt vaguely familiar.

To the best of his knowledge he had never driven a car in his sleep before, though he wasn't sure how he had gotten to and from the bar the night he had his run-in with Jacob Pinochet. He supposed there was a first time for everything. Stress tended to bring on his sleepwalking bouts, and the past twelve or so hours had been remarkably stressful. So he shouldn't have been surprised that his disorder had been triggered. But the car thing, well, that was a surprise. A big one. Where the hell was he?

He started the car up and switched the wipers on. It wasn't the first time he had woken up and not known where he was. Usually when something like this happened, it was because he had been sleeping in an unfamiliar place. A locked door tended to be enough to keep him from getting into too much trouble, but bunking on someone's living room couch, outside in a tent, or that time he and Caitlin got stuck sleeping in the sunporch during the Rixby family vacation could lead to trouble. He remembered that morning waking up in a patch of scrubby grass near the beach with sand in his mouth. No way he wanted to embarrass himself in front of the snobby Rixby clan. So he had done his best to slip into the house unnoticed. Caitlin was the only one who suspected something might have been amiss, but she didn't say anything.

He almost confessed the whole thing to her that afternoon when they stopped off somewhere on the way home for lunch, but he chickened out. What if she freaked out when she found out the truth about him? If she left him, he didn't know what he would do. Of course, the longer they were together, the harder it became to slip into casual conversation the statement, "Oh, by the way, I'm a sleepwalker."

So Caitlin never knew, and his secret remained his and his alone. Well, and now Garvey knew about it as well. He realized how remarkably wrong it was that his defense attorney now officially knew more about him than his own wife.

The police won't understand. That damn memory of him and his mother came back to him again. What was it about that memory? It struck him now how much it reminded him of the day he awoke in the bathroom after what he now knew was him beating the crap out of Jacob Pinochet. His mind went back to the bathroom of their old Culver Creek house. He saw his dazed reflection in their cloudy bathroom mirror. His clothing looked to be stained and dirty. Was that mud or blood? His face had blood on it. He must have cut himself at some point. Could he have fallen down the stairs? The thought gave him a chill, but this would have been years after his father's death. It must have been right before he went away to Ryerson. What was it the police wouldn't understand?

And as if they could read his thoughts, a cop car approached in the dim morning light. Was he going to get a ticket? Had he even remembered to bring his wallet? The car slowed as it approached, and Lance's palms started to sweat, but then the cruiser made an abrupt left turn, and Lance saw that it had pulled into a parking lot full of police cars, which was when he realized he had parked only feet from a police station. Smooth.

What had he been thinking? He didn't have time to figure out an answer because he had realized where he was. The street wasn't unfamiliar at all. It was insane, but it also made perfect sense. He had driven to Culver Creek.

He looked out the windshield at the torrential down-pour and thought about Adam being out there somewhere. He wondered if the police had tailed him from New Jersey, but no. He had been parked here awhile. Nobody seemed particularly interested in him.

But how would it look when they went to the house and he wasn't there? When nobody there knew where he was? He needed to call Caitlin or his mom and let them know where he was. What would he tell them when they asked why he had driven to Culver Creek in the pre-dawn hours? He wanted to look for Adam? He had felt helpless just sitting at the house, and he couldn't sleep anyway? He decided it was a perfectly reasonable explanation, but when he reached for his phone, it wasn't in the cupholder where he normally left it. He checked the glove box and under the seats as well, but he already knew his phone and his wallet were probably still in his bedroom. It was interesting that in his sleep logic, he had the foresight to grab the car keys but nothing else.

He turned off the ignition as he sat and tried to figure out his next step. The voice of reason told him that what he should do was go home, but he thought of the excuse he had fabricated about driving out here to look for Adam. It wasn't a bad idea. He could maybe drive around to the different places he and Adam had been on their boys' day out. Maybe he would see some clue the police had overlooked. The rain might make things more difficult, but if there was even a chance that he could do something that would bring Adam home safe and sound, he had to try. He watched the rain cascade down the windshield and was reminded of the night his father died.

He saw the policemen standing in Mrs. Drummond's kitchen, their sopping wet jackets dripping onto her linoleum floor. They left damp footprints as they walked back to the door. Mrs. Drummond followed behind them to let them out.

"We're on sandbag patrol," one of the police officers said, and Lance remembered thinking the police were playing with those little beanbags they had in his preschool classroom, but the other policeman said something about the creek flooding.

This seemed to be important, but Lance couldn't figure out why at first. After she had seen the policemen out, Mrs. Drummond came into the kitchen. She mopped up the puddles with an old dish towel.

"Don't worry, Lance," she said. "Your mother is on her way home. She'll be here as soon as she can, but it's a long drive and the weather isn't very good."

A long drive? As Lance played the memory back in his mind, it didn't make any sense. A long drive from where? Lance had assumed his mother was at the police station or maybe at their house, but neither one of those places qualified as a long drive. The police hadn't even mentioned his mother. They were off to go deal with the creek.

Lance had a sudden flash of inspiration. The police had taken down a statement from Mrs. Drummond. That meant there had to be some sort of official police report on his father's death. Surely that would be able to supply the information his memory was lacking.

He made a mad dash through the pouring rain to the front door of the police station. It was only as he gratefully entered the dry vestibule that it occurred to him it was a strange and suspicious hour to be going to a police station to get information on a death that had occurred twenty-six years ago.

So he wasn't surprised that the officer on his way out of

the building paused to give Lance a strange look. The cop was dressed in plain clothes with a flimsy windbreaker that would be no match for the downpour outside, but Lance could tell straightaway that he was law enforcement. He had that look.

"Can I help you?" the cop asked.

"I need to get a copy of a police report." Lance hadn't even considered what he was wearing, and he glanced down, relieved to see that he was at least in clothes and not pajamas. His khakis and shirt were beyond rumpled, but his short run to the police station had left him so drenched he doubted it mattered.

"You'll need to go see the clerk at the window," the cop said. He held the door for Lance but narrowed his eyes at him. "I know you from somewhere, don't I?"

Lance had a panicked thought—had the police already found out he was missing from the house? Caitlin hadn't taken any sleeping pills before bed. It was possible she had woken, found her car and her husband missing, and called the police. They might have been posting his photo along with Adam's on all the news stories.

"Don't think so," Lance said, and then for good measure, "I'm not from around here."

The cop shrugged it off. He seemed to be in a hurry to get somewhere, and Lance proceeded down a narrow hallway to a window with a little counter attached to it and one of those little speaking grates, but when he glanced back, he noticed the cop was still in the vestibule, a frown visible on his face. He nodded at Lance before turning to head out into the deluge.

The clerk at the window didn't seem too troubled by Lance's appearance or his early morning request. Unfortunately she was also unable to help him.

"Anything more than a year old is in our archives," she said. "You have to go fill out a request at the courthouse for that, but the records office doesn't open until ten." She jotted down the address on a piece of paper and passed it through the little opening in the bottom of the window.

"Thanks," Lance said. "Do you know how quickly I would be able to get that? Like would they be able to give it to me today?"

The clerk laughed at this. "Two to three weeks, if you're lucky. That's if they even have it. About ten years ago, some of the archives were lost in a big flood."

Lance's heart sank. He doubted he would even bother to make a request at the courthouse. The best thing to do would be to head home.

"You know they're saying the creek might flood today," the clerk said.

Lance got the impression that this shift didn't give her the chance to talk to many people, and she was probably glad for the company.

"Is that so?" Lance didn't really care about the creek, but he was doing his best to be polite and not arouse suspicion.

He remembered the police officers in Mrs. Drummond's kitchen talking about sandbag duty. Had the creek flooded that night?

Lance felt dizzy as another memory came back to him. He had been sitting with his dad on the couch in their old living room, watching a show on the television. Lance didn't quite remember the show, something with car chases and explosions that his mom never would have let him watch.

"Our little secret," his dad had said to him with a wink.

The memory was fuzzy, but he had the vague sense that his mother had gone away for the weekend. Had she gone to his aunt's house in Connecticut maybe? Or on a trip with some of her old school friends? He seemed to remember something like that happening when he was a kid. What he remembered was that it was just him and his dad.

"A boys' weekend," his dad had said. They had eaten French toast with sausage for dinner, and his dad hadn't cared when he flooded his meal in a sea of syrup.

A loud sound drowned out the explosions on the TV, and a yellow banner started to scroll across the bottom of the screen.

"What's it say, Daddy?" asked Lance, who was old enough to recognize the look of letters, but who hadn't yet mastered putting them together to form words.

"Says there's a flash flood warning in effect," his dad said. "But don't worry, kiddo, we're far enough from the creek here that it won't be an issue."

"I moved a bunch of stuff upstairs."

Lance looked up with a start. For a moment he had forgotten he was still inside the police station talking with the clerk.

"What's that?" Lance asked.

"My place is less than a block from the creek," the clerk said, "so I always end up moving the important stuff upstairs when we get a lot of rain, just in case."

Lance nodded and thanked her again for the courthouse information.

"Hopefully it doesn't flood," he said as he backed away from the window and headed toward the exit door.

Something she had said had made him uneasy, but he was too distracted to place what it was until he got back in the car. He turned on the car and blasted the heat to try to dry himself off, but the car had been sitting too long and the chilly air that blew on him made him shiver.

She had been talking about stairs, and that was how his father had died. He fell down the stairs backwards Tucker had said, and now Lance was very sure of something. The night his father died, his mother hadn't been home. It had been their boys' weekend. She was away somewhere. That was why Mrs. Drummond said it would take her a while to get back.

So if his mother hadn't been around that weekend, then that only left two explanations for his father's strange and terrible death. The first was that somehow his father had accidentally stumbled backward down the stairs. It seemed such an unlikely scenario. Could his father have been very drunk? But Lance had no recollection of this. Sometimes his dad had a beer or two with dinner, but he had no memory of his dad stumbling around in a drunken way. Still, he was so young, would he have even recognized drunkenness? he wondered. Then there was the second possibility, the one that really frightened him—that his father's death was not entirely an accident, that he had shoved his father down the stairs. Why would he do that when he loved his dad? A more recent memory came to Lance, the morning he awoke to find his hands around his son's neck. He wasn't the same person when he was sleepwalking, and when someone tried to rouse him, he turned violent. He knew this from his incident at Ryerson. Jacob Pinochet had been on the end of one of his sleepwalking attacks, and so maybe had his own father.

The thought left him so numb and bewildered, he didn't know what to do. He remembered his plan to drive straight home. He pulled out onto the road, but when he came to the first intersection, he didn't make a right and head out to the highway. Instead he drove through his hometown as thoughts tumbled through is head.

His mother had known, hadn't she? When had he first started sleepwalking? He must have started very young. She knew better than to try to wake him, he supposed, but his father didn't know that secret, maybe, or else Raquel had warned him, but like her rules about no violent TV shows and not too much syrup, he had decided to ignore her instructions.

That was why Raquel always said his father died of a heart attack. She wasn't trying to protect him from a fear of stairs. She wanted to protect him from remembering that he had, in a sleeping state, killed his own father. He thought of how distant she had seemed to him as a child, and it made so much sense. She loved him, because he was her son, but she must have been fearful of him and considered him to be something of a monster. It was why she had sent him away to Ryerson, wasn't it? She wasn't worried about a neighborhood bogeyman. He was the bogeyman she feared. Certainly she must have lived with the knowledge that any night he might break into her bedroom and strangle her in his sleep.

His heart was heavy as he drove down half-familiar streets. The elementary school building looked unchanged from when he was a kid, but there was a newer townhome development just down the block from it that he didn't think had been there before. He let memory guide him and was surprised how easily he found his way back to his old house. The old asbestos siding had been replaced by modern vinyl siding in a tasteful taupe, but otherwise the little house looked just the way he remembered it.

He idled at the curb as he stared at the house and the secrets it kept hidden in its walls. If only there was some way he could go back there and save his family from that tragic night.

"I'm sorry, Dad," he whispered to the empty car as he wept. "I'm so sorry."

A light flicked on in the house, and he remembered it was still early morning, and he was an unfamiliar car on a residential street and drove away as the rain and his tears continued to fall.

34

SAGE STEPPED out of the police station into the pouring rain. The icy cold water did little to revive him. It had been a long, sleepless night and everything had a fuzzy, surreal feeling. He glanced back over his shoulder at the guy he had passed in the hallway. He was pretty sure he knew him from somewhere. It could have been his sleep-deprived mind playing tricks on him. Most likely he just worked somewhere local, but Sage couldn't place him.

He jogged through the rain to his car and was drenched by the time he sat down behind the steering wheel. Water dripped onto the upholstery as he leaned his head back against the headrest while the events of the hectic night passed through his mind.

The FBI field agents had shown up shortly after Sage scoped out the shuttered pharmacy. The feds commandeered the squad breakroom as their field office, much to the annoyance of the Culver Creek police force. Sage reported to Henderson on the closed-up pharmacy, though Henderson had barely seemed interested in what he had to say.

Sage stared at the photo that had been taped to the pillar in the room—the allegedly kidnapped little boy, Adam Walker. The kid was from New Jersey. What would he have been doing all the way out here? It was probably just a coincidence, but Sage had to say something.

"Walker," Sage said. "Are his parents from here? Is that why they were out here today? There were Walkers that used to live over near the creek—"

"Atkins," Henderson snapped without bothering to look up from his phone screen.

"What?" Sage asked.

"The father's from Atkins," Henderson said.

"It's just I'm working on this cold case, and there was a Walker family that used to live—"

"It's a common name," Henderson said. "You got a Starbucks in this shithole town or what?"

"There's a coffee shop on Main Street that's pretty decent," Sage said.

"Cool, do me a favor and grab me a mochaccino," Henderson said. "Two sugars. Biggest size they got."

Which was how Sage went from liaison to glorified gofer. It had been a very long night.

As dawn spread its rosy fingers through the grimy squad room windows, Sage had come around to sharing the Culver Creek police force's low opinion of the FBI, and that was before they had curtly told him his services would no longer be needed as they were shifting the focus of their investigation.

"The kid's not here," Henderson said. "He was never here."

"Are you sure?" Sage asked. "You haven't even—"

"Trust me, we've got everything under control, Officer Dorian."

"Detective," Sage corrected before storming out of the building.

Sage shivered as he sat dripping in his car. What he should do was go home and go to sleep, but he felt too wired to sleep, and it seemed a shame to waste this restless energy. He could take another look through the Lily Esposito files. There had to be something he was missing. Except he had left the files he needed back in the squad room. The thought of going back out in that pouring rain filled him with dread. Lily Esposito had been dead for years. What difference did a few more hours make either way?

He had been hanging around Agent Henderson too long. That wasn't how he worked. Besides, he was already soaked to the bone anyway.

The other officers didn't hear him come in. They were too busy flipping through the folder from the Lily Esposito case that he had left on his desk. Well, Steve Arlo flipped through it while the two other officers peered over his shoulders. Sage thought Henderson had beat too hasty a retreat. The way the Culver Creek police force shirked their duties, it was very likely a little boy could have been kidnapped here in broad daylight. It was a small miracle there wasn't an epidemic of kidnappings.

Sage was about to clear his throat to get their attention when he heard Steve say his name and instead eavesdropped in silence.

"He's just running around talking to loonies," Steve said. "It's a fucking waste of taxpayer dollars."

Sage thought that was ironic considering how hard at

work Steve and the other two officers were at that very moment.

"I saw him in the coffee shop one day interviewing that crazy lady that works at the grocery store," Steve continued.

"The one with the blue hair and all the tattoos?" one of the officers asked.

"Nah, the older one. She's always going to that psychic place," Steve said.

Sage thought of Brighton and his affair with the psychic girl's mother. Something tingled at the back of Sage's mind. He tried to focus on it, but it evaporated before he could even grasp it.

"What psychic?" the other officer asked.

"You know," Steve said, "the whatchamacallit, dream whisperer. She's always going over there, bringing her offerings of food. She's a total weirdo. These are the sort of people this nitwit is going around questioning."

This time it was more than a tingle. A jolt of inspiration hit Sage.

Left where? Maura had said that afternoon in the coffee shop before she caught herself. What if all this time Jade had been right here under his nose? He had a dream whisperer to visit.

35

CAITLIN AWOKE, and the feeling of being completely refreshed was so foreign it was disorienting. There was something vaguely familiar about this feeling. This was what it was supposed to feel like when you woke from a deep sleep. Normally she awoke in a groggy state, and it was only after a couple of cups of coffee and a hot shower that she finally began to feel human. To feel exceptionally human on waking was a joyous occasion, but the moment was fleeting.

With wakefulness came consciousness and the memory that her son was out there somewhere. She needed to find him, and she lay there trying to remember if she had dreamed last night. She was so out of practice that maybe she wouldn't even have remembered how to dream, but she caught the glimpse of something at the corner of her memory. The dream was elusive, but she fought to relax her mind, and the all-too-familiar details of the dream bubbled up to the surface of her consciousness.

"No!" she screamed as she sat up with a start. She

looked over to see if she had woken Lance, but he wasn't in bed.

Instead of giving her answers about Adam, her subconscious mind had forced her to relive a dream she had relived far too many times already. Last night she had her old Culver Creek nightmare again. Details had morphed and twisted in the intervening years, with some aspects of her present life working their way into the old dream, but it was still the dream about the murder of a long-dead little girl. Adam hadn't been in the dream at all, and she still had no idea where to find him.

She climbed out of bed. It was after nine, and she could hear movement and voices downstairs. Probably she was the last one up. She pulled a sweatshirt over her T-shirt and decided the yoga pants she had slept in were presentable enough for a family breakfast.

Caitlin moved quietly down the stairs and paused outside the kitchen when she heard Luanne and Raquel talking.

"What we should do," Luanne was saying, "is hold a press conference. Ask the public for information. Remind everyone they should be looking for Adam. Caitlin could say a few words and hold up a picture of him."

"I don't see any reason in making a spectacle of our grief," Raquel said. "Besides, do you even think Caitlin is up for talking to a bunch of news cameras?"

Caitlin was reminded of her run-in with the press outside the police station the previous day. She doubted she was up for talking to the press, but she was still annoyed that Raquel didn't think she was capable.

"Well, if she doesn't want to talk, I can do it," Luanne said.

Typical, Caitlin thought. That had probably been what

Luanne was gunning for all along, another chance for her to be the star of the show.

"This all reminds me of back when Caitlin was still a girl," Luanne said. "She was always having these psychic dreams, and this one time she had a psychic dream about this little girl who was murdered in Culver Creek."

Caitlin decided now would be a good time to make an appearance and put an end to Luanne's story.

When she stepped into the kitchen, she was struck by how pale her mother-in-law looked. Well, the last several hours had been extremely trying. She ventured a guess that her mother-in-law hadn't slept anywhere near as well as she had.

"Well?" Luanne asked eagerly when she saw Caitlin. "Anything?"

Caitlin shook her head, and noticing there was still some coffee left in the coffeemaker, she poured herself a mug.

"I was just telling Raquel about that time we went out to Culver Creek to try and help with that murder investigation," Luanne said. "We were on the television and everything. Do you remember?"

"Couldn't forget it if I wanted to," Caitlin muttered as she sipped the hot coffee.

"What was so strange about that dream of yours is normally you only ever had dreams about someone who was connected to you in some way or that you had met or something, right?" Luanne said. "But here you were dreaming about some girl all the way out in Pennsylvania somewhere. But what if the reason you had that dream was because of right now, because of Adam going missing in Culver Creek. Maybe that's the connection."

"I'm not sure I follow you," Caitlin said.

"What if the connection is that the person who killed that little girl is the same person who took Adam," Luanne said. "They never caught him, remember?"

Two things happened at once. The first was that the mug of coffee slipped from Caitlin's hand and crashed on the floor with chips of stoneware and coffee splattering all over the place. The second thing was that Raquel gasped, pressed a hand to her mouth, and sprinted toward the first-floor bathroom.

"Seriously, Mom?" Caitlin asked as she tried to mop up the coffee and clean up the scattered shards.

"Well, it was just a theory," Luanne said as she squatted and helped Caitlin with the cleanup effort.

Tucker stepped into the kitchen and in his stentorian voice asked, "Does anyone know where Lance is?"

Caitlin realized it was strange that she hadn't yet seen her husband. Luanne shook her head, but Stu stepped into the kitchen and asked, "Do you mean he hasn't come back yet?"

"Back from where?" Caitlin asked.

"I was awake late last night," Stu said. "All the excitement, and I guess I'm still on Vegas time. Anyway, I saw Lance head out in the SUV." Stu pointed toward the driveway.

All of them, including Raquel, who had just emerged from the bathroom, turned to stare at the front window, where it was obvious that Caitlin's car was missing from the driveway.

"What time was this?" Caitlin asked.

"Was he awake?" Raquel asked.

Caitlin dismissed the bizarre question as Raquel being under a lot of stress and not thinking clearly.

"I asked him if I could help him," Stu said, "but I don't

think he heard me. I was trying to be quiet because I didn't want to wake anyone."

"We have to go to Culver Creek," Caitlin said.

Everyone turned to look at her in surprise. Even she was surprised by her declaration. She didn't know where it had come from, but suddenly she felt the unshakeable conviction that she needed to go to Culver Creek.

"Did your dream just come back to you?" Luanne asked.

Had it? Caitlin felt fleeting glimpses of it floating around in her head, but she didn't think that was what led to this sudden belief. "I have to go to Culver Creek," she repeated.

"Well, I'm going with you," Luanne said.

"Me too," Raquel said.

"I'll drive," Tucker said.

"Wait, someone has to stay here at the house, just in case," Caitlin said.

"I guess that leaves me," Stu said. "If you're okay with that."

"Of course," Caitlin said. She considered showering first, or making some more coffee, but decided there was no time. She needed to get to Culver Creek as fast as possible.

The windshield wipers sped back and forth, but even at full blast they couldn't keep up with the downpour. With the visibility so lousy, Tucker had no choice but to drive below the speed limit and keep to the right lane.

Caitlin sat in the backseat beside her mother, who had been unusually quiet so far on the journey. Nobody had much to say. Caitlin watched Raquel fidget nervously in front of her, and Caitlin's stomach protested the fact that she'd provided it with no more than a few feeble sips of coffee. She stared out the side window at the rain pouring down and thought of Adam. She hoped he was somewhere safe, dry and warm. Safe, though, that was the important part. She didn't care if he was drenched to the bone as long as he was okay.

As if she could sense her thoughts, her mother reached over and gave her arm a squeeze, and Caitlin gave her a grateful smile. Maybe they didn't have a perfect relationship, but Caitlin was thankful to have her mom here with her right now.

"Hard to believe we're headed back to this town after all these years," Luanne said to her.

"It makes me sick to think about," Caitlin said.

"You'll get to be a hero all over again," Luanne said, and she squeezed Caitlin's arm again.

"I honestly have no idea what you're talking about," Caitlin said.

"Well, like last time when you gave the police that information to help them."

"Mom, it didn't help them at all. They never found the murderer, remember?"

"Well, you can't be held responsible for police incompetence," Luanne said.

"And in case you don't recall, it was my psychic dreams that destroyed your marriage," Caitlin said.

Luanne let out an inappropriate bark of a laugh. "You don't really believe that, do you?"

"Mom, I know about your affair with Officer Brighton," Caitlin said.

"Well, that didn't have anything to do with you,"

Luanne said. "And I don't know if *affair* is really the right word. *Fling* might be more appropriate."

"The semantics hardly matter." Caitlin turned and looked out the window, but her mother wasn't done with the conversation. She reached over and tucked a strand of Caitlin's hair behind her ear, forcing Caitlin to turn and look at her.

"Listen to me, you had nothing to do with why your father and I got divorced, do you understand?" She waited for Caitlin to respond, and when she didn't, Luanne continued, "I married the wrong man. Raymond and I, we didn't belong together. I was never happy. That was all on me."

Caitlin felt something inside of her release. She had been holding on to this pain and shame her whole life, and now in an instant it seemed to melt away. What her mother said made sense. She saw her home life growing up, her wildly different parents who sometimes seemed more like bickering roommates than soulmates. They had argued over her dreams, it was true, but they argued over everything. If it hadn't been Officer Brighton, it would have been someone else, and Caitlin spared a glance at her mother beside her. Considering what she knew about her mother's more recent love life, there might very well have been several someone elses long before Officer Brighton. A fling was what she had called it, and didn't people who had flings often have multiple flings?

It made her think of Lance. When she told the story of how they met, she always used the phrase "love at first sight." Maybe it wasn't entirely accurate. She couldn't say for sure that it was love at first sight, but she felt something the moment she laid eyes on him in that coffee shop. He had been younger then, and with his preppy haircut and country club clothes, not at all the sort of guy she normally went for, but there was just something that drew her to him.

She had never been especially forward when it came to guys, but when she saw Lance sitting there, she went right up to him. When she told the story, she always ended it with something along the lines of "and I'm so glad I did." She wondered, did she still feel this way? She thought of everything they had endured in the past twenty-four hours, and she felt a longing ache in her chest.

She loved her husband, and she wished that he was sitting here beside her. Instead she closed her eyes and pictured him sitting there that day in the coffee shop. In her imagination his face went from young and boyish to the way it looked today, wiser and a little doughier, and she gasped.

36

SAGE POUNDED on the dream whisperer's door. The sign read "By Appointment Only," and it looked dark inside, but he hammered anyway.

"Can I help you?"

Sage looked around and saw that the voice belonged to a man in a business suit, standing near the bottom of the stairs. It was the dream whisperer's neighbor. The lawyer whose office was below hers.

"I'm looking for the dream whisperer," Sage said.

"Did you have a nightmare?" the lawyer asked with a chuckle.

I'm living in a nightmare, Sage thought, but he shook his head.

"It's about an important matter." Sage ran down the stairs. "Do you know where I can find her?"

"If she's not there, no," the lawyer said. "She must be out somewhere. Oh, but I think she did have some family visiting from out of town."

Family? As far as Sage knew, the only family Jade had alive was Rick. Could he have come here to visit her? What if he had come to finish what he started all those years ago when he murdered Lily? Sage glanced back at the dark door of the dream whisperer's building. No, he was jumping to conclusions. He didn't even know for sure if Jade was the dream whisperer.

"What's her name?" Sage demanded.

The lawyer blinked in surprise.

"I'm sorry, I didn't quite catch who you were."

Sage pulled his badge from his pocket and flashed it at the lawyer.

"Her name's Phelicity," he said. "Phelicity Green."

He took out a pad and pen and had the lawyer spell it for him.

Sage's hopes sank. He found himself at another dead end. He thanked the lawyer for his time and started to walk back to his car.

Phelicity Green. What the hell kind of name was Phelicity anyway? It sounded like the name of someone who would choose "dream whisperer" as their occupation. In fact it sounded exactly like the sort of name that someone who considered themselves a dream whisperer would choose for a name. He stopped and spun around. The lawyer pushed his now unlocked office door open.

"Do you know if that's her real name?" Sage shouted.

"Pardon?" the lawyer said, even though he had clearly heard Sage's words.

"Is Phelicity Green her real name?"

"It's her legal name," the lawyer said.

"What's her real name?" Sage asked.

"By real, do you mean—"

"What's the name she was born with?" Sage demanded. His patience was wearing thin.

"Jade Esposito," the lawyer said softly, and Sage felt a

current of happiness run through him. He had found her! Well, sort of. It would have been a bit more of a thrill if she had actually been there. "You can't blame her," the lawyer said.

"Blame her for what?" Sage trembled with excitement for what the lawyer was about to say, or maybe it was the shakes from sleep deprivation.

"For changing her name, of course," the lawyer said. "I mean she couldn't exactly walk around this town with a name like Jade Esposito, could she? She would never have any peace. It would be like having your name on a wanted poster."

The tremble changed to a flash of recollection that rattled his whole head.

The wanted poster. That was where he had seen that man who walked into the police station earlier. He was the guy from the psychic girl's sketch artist drawing.

Even as he thought this, he could see how it made no sense. That drawing was from nineteen years ago, but he didn't have time to worry about that.

37

CAITLIN FELT the car start to slow, and she realized where they must be. As Tucker drove down the exit ramp, unease swept over her. She was still dizzy from the fragment of last night's dream that had come back to her a few minutes ago. Was it just her mind playing tricks on her? Or maybe last night's dream, which had seemed in nearly every other way to be an exact repeat of the nightmare she had when she was ten years old, was actually a revised version of that dream, peopled like Dorothy's dream of Oz by the people closest to her. She wanted so desperately to cling to this idea, but something about it didn't feel right, and she knew what it was.

It was the bolt of electricity that seemed to go through her the day she laid eyes on a young guy sipping a cappuccino and reading a newspaper in a crowded coffee shop. She had never laid eyes upon him before, but some part of her subconscious must have recognized something familiar in his face. Foolishly, she had believed that jolt of electricity was destiny. She thought the universe was telling her, "Here he is. Here's the guy you've been searching for your whole life," and she supposed in a way that was exactly what the universe was telling her. It was she who had misinterpreted the message.

But how could it possibly be? How could Lance be the man she had seen murder a little girl in a dream she had nineteen years ago? It didn't make any sense. Lance was her age. He would have been a boy then, but she felt a chill pass through her as she thought of what she had learned just last night, that Lance was from Culver Creek. How was it that she had been married to her husband for seven years and was just now learning where he had grown up?

She thought of something else she learned last night, and she grasped at it like a drowning woman grabbing a life preserver.

"How old was Lance when his dad died?" Caitlin asked, but she was so excited that it came out as a startling shout in the silent car. The others jumped.

Her mother gave her a puzzled expression, and Raquel turned around and frowned.

"Oh, he was just a little boy," Raquel said. "About Adam's age."

No, that doesn't make sense, Caitlin thought. If Caitlin's theory was right, then it would have needed to be when Lance was older, twelve at least. That was when Raquel had sent him away to boarding school, Caitlin remembered. Sent him away to boarding school, sold their house and married her wealthy boss. The story had always seemed so bizarre to Caitlin, and she couldn't help but see her mother-in-law as some cold, calculating woman, but what if it wasn't that cut and dry?

For years Raquel had lied to Lance about how his father died. So was it that much of a stretch to think she might have lied to him about when? Maybe he hadn't died at all, but she threw him out of the house or they separated or something, and she made up a story about him dying to spare Lance's feelings. Except death seemed a far more emotional thing than a separation, unless, like her lie about the nature of her husband's death, the lie had been meant to protect Lance from the truth.

What if Raquel had learned what a monster her husband was back when Lance was just a young boy? Caitlin had a sickening thought. What if Lily Esposito hadn't been the first time Lance's dad had murdered a child? If he had killed or otherwise shown his true colors, she wouldn't have wanted someone like that in her or her son's life. She would have kicked him out. Maybe she assumed that would be the end of everything, but then seven years later, Lance's Dad could have murdered Lily Esposito, and to protect her son, Raquel had sent him away to boarding school, sold their house and married a man with enough money to keep her safe.

There was something else. Caitlin knew Raquel had not wanted Lance to marry her. Raquel hadn't exactly tried very hard to mask her feelings. Caitlin assumed her future mother-in-law's disapproval stemmed from the fact that she didn't think Caitlin was good enough for Lance, what with his boarding school education and his country club membership, but what if that wasn't it at all? If Lance's father had murdered Lily Esposito, then Raquel would have followed the case closely. Surely she would have seen at least one of the news reports about the supposedly psychic girl from New Jersey who was working with the local police. When she realized who Lance's girlfriend was, of course she would have worried that Caitlin would say something that would reveal the truth to Lance. Raquel had no way of knowing Caitlin wanted to put as much distance as she could between herself and wretched Culver Creek and had no intention of revealing that ugly bit of her past even to the man she loved.

It fit, she supposed, but now she wondered, had she ever seen a picture of Lance's father? She must have at some point, but she couldn't pull up anything in her memory. Well, it would make sense that Lance would look like his dad, right? Enough so, that their faces in a shadow-filled dream might look more or less identical? Caitlin thought this might be true. She could see glimpses of Raquel in Lance, but only glimpses. So it stood to reason he probably looked a lot more like his father.

Caitlin leaned over and whispered to her mother, "Do you remember what the police sketch looked like? The man I described to Officer Brighton?"

"You've been thinking about that too, haven't you?" Luanne said.

Caitlin felt like she had been stabbed in the chest.

"You mean you knew all this time that he looked like Lance, and you never said anything?" Her voice rose above a whisper as the emotion crept into her voice, and she noticed in the front seat the way Raquel cocked her head as if she was trying to hear their conversation.

"Lance?" her mother said, not even attempting to whisper. "What are you talking about? I meant that going back to Culver Creek is making me think of when we came out here to try and help catch that killer."

Caitlin's face grew hot with embarrassment. Her mother stared at her with concern, and Raquel peered over the back of her seat at them. Tucker at least had his eyes on the road as he navigated the streets leading into town.

"Who looked like Lance?" Raquel asked, and then a nearly deafening sound filled the car.

Four cell phones blared a dire klaxon warning that made it sound like the end of the world had begun. Everyone jumped. Tucker jerked the wheel in surprise. Caitlin thought it was another Amber Alert for Adam, but Luanne was the first to glance at her display.

"Flash flood warning," Luanne said, reading the message. "Streams and creeks could flood."

Caitlin stared out the window at the endless rain. Maybe it was the end of the world. Certainly that was what it had felt like since that horrifying moment yesterday afternoon, when she found herself staring at Adam's empty car seat.

"Where do we go?" Tucker asked. They had come to a four-way intersection, and now everyone turned to look at Caitlin as if she had the answer.

"Maybe we should go to the police station," Luanne suggested.

"No!" Caitlin and Raquel said at the same time. Caitlin was surprised that her mother-in-law was as fervent as she was in her objection.

Caitlin tried to determine where they should go. She hadn't thought things through. Did they go to the shuttered pharmacy—the last place she knew for sure she had seen Adam? Maybe they should try to retrace her route, but this didn't feel right to her.

Luanne's suggestion that they go to the police station was infinitely more practical, but that was the last place Caitlin wanted to go, and then she knew without a doubt where they had to go.

"The creek," Caitlin said. "We have to go to the creek."

"But what about the flood?" Luanne asked.

"It might not be safe," Tucker agreed.

"No, Caitlin's right," Raquel said. "Make a left here.

There's a community park with access to the creek up that way."

Caitlin was surprised that her mother-in-law was taking her side. She couldn't remember a time that had ever happened before.

38

LANCE HEARD the creek before he saw it. Even with the windows closed and the driving rain outside, somehow he heard that familiar sound. He parked in a little pull-off that he remembered being a popular spot with fishermen and looked out at the stream. It was bigger than he remembered, more like a river than a creek. His memories of standing in ankle-deep water on a summer day didn't seem to jibe with the raging torrent he saw before him. Could his memories be that off? But then he realized the stream's transformation was probably due to the pouring rain.

Anyone who attempted to wade out in the water today would probably be swept right off their feet by the rushing water. For a split second an image flashed into his head. He saw a little girl lying in the stream water. He blinked, and it was gone.

The image frightened him. His heart raced. He closed his eyes and tried to summon the image. Then he saw it in the hazy, uncertain way of a half-remembered dream. Was that what he was looking at? Something he remembered from a dream? A nightmare. The word sent a shockwave down his spine, and he didn't have to puzzle over why. Of course it made him think of Adam.

There was a tickle at the back of his head. He felt like there was something important he was forgetting. *Caitlin.* He felt like it was something important about Caitlin that he was forgetting. Had she said something? Done something? He puzzled over this confusion. Did it have to do with Adam? Could she have done something to hurt Adam? Was that what his subconscious was trying to tell him?

The memory of Caitlin feverishly ransacking Adam's room came back to him, and he shuddered. It hadn't been easy to see his wife in what seemed to be the midst of some sort of psychotic breakdown. Was that what was nagging him? Was his head trying to tell him that in some sort of psychotic episode, Caitlin had done something to hurt Adam? He didn't want to believe it, but her behavior had been so strange and erratic. She said she had driven here yesterday, to Culver Creek. Wasn't that such a strange coincidence?

Had she really driven all the way out here? Couldn't she simply have imagined she did? He couldn't shake that image of her ransacking Adam's bedroom. He saw her frantically going through his doodles and drawings, and the shockwave hit him again.

That piece of paper Caitlin had been holding—one of Adam's crayon drawings. Did it look just like the image that had flashed into his head? The little girl lying in the stream, and he remembered seeing it yesterday and having the queasy, sickening sensation that he recognized it.

He was being ridiculous. Adam was no Picasso. His crayon scribbles were barely recognizable. Half the time Lance couldn't tell the difference between houses and rocket ships or dogs and people when he looked at one of

Adam's masterpieces. So wasn't it a stretch to think one of his doodles, the one in Caitlin's hand that she said had come from one of Adam's nightmares, matched some picture in Lance's head? And where had that picture come from? Was it his subconscious mind turning that glimpse of Adam's drawing into something real? He had been under a tremendous amount of stress, and maybe this was his mind's way of coping with it.

Was that all it was? Because now he felt sure that when he looked at that drawing clutched in Caitlin's hand, he had felt a shockwave of recognition. Well, of course he had. Adam had drawn the picture from one of his nightmares. Lance had been there when Adam was telling the dream whisperer about his nightmare. It made Lance form a picture of what had happened in his head, and then he saw that picture yesterday and it was like everything was coming full circle. That was what it had to be. There could be no other explanation.

The police won't understand.

His mother's long-ago voice echoed in his head again. Won't understand what? He thought of the afternoon the police had come over to ask them questions about Lily Esposito, his mother's weird nervousness.

The shockwave struck again. Because he realized now that the vision he saw in his head was not just any little girl lying in the stream. It was Lily Esposito. He hadn't seen her in nineteen years, but he knew without a doubt this was true. What he didn't know was where this image had come from. Was it something he had imagined? Had he dreamt about it? Of course they all knew that was where they had found Lily, but the realness of the picture in his head frightened him because it felt more like something he had seen than something he had dreamed or imagined.

He felt like he was suffocating in the car, and he flung open the door and staggered outside into the pouring rain.

At the edge of the little parking area was a short path that led to the creek. He walked over to it and down the slick mud until he was standing at the very edge of the creek. The rushing water was brown and muddy. The sound was loud, almost deafening.

The kids in the neighborhood used to have a path they took to get down to the creek. If you stuck to sidewalks and paved roads, access to the creek was blocks away from his neighborhood, but all you had to do was cross the road and cut through a backyard and then follow a little dirt path to get to the water. It was as close as the school bus stop.

The backyard they cut through was a rental property, and the guy who lived there was mean and nasty. When he was home and he caught kids sneaking through his yard, he would shout and curse at them, but most of the time he wasn't there.

If the mean guy was there, you had to run through a stand of trees where there were pricker bushes to get back to the road or incur his wrath. The pricker bushes were thick, and they snagged on clothing and tore exposed skin, but Lance considered them preferable to a run-in with the nasty guy.

He wondered if suspicion had ever fallen on that guy after Lily was killed. It must have. Where she was found was only feet away from that guy's backyard. Yet Lance couldn't remember anything happening to that guy after the murder. Could the police have overlooked such a likely suspect?

Lance recalled a feeling of pure terror as he and his childhood friend were walking back up from the creek one afternoon and were surprised by an angry shout. They looked up to see that nasty guy on his back deck. He hurled a beer can at them and began shouting. They scrambled back into the cover of the trees and took the treacherous pricker bush route back to the road.

Lance remembered his mother making tsking noises later as she cleaned all the scratches and scrapes on his arms and legs in their bathroom.

The police won't understand.

Lance shook his head. He was confusing memories now, he knew it. He had the distinct feeling that when his mother had uttered the words that forever imprinted themselves on his brain, it had been nighttime. He could see the darkness outside the window. That couldn't be the same time he and Allen had made their pricker bush getaway, but something nagged at him.

That night in the bathroom, an image, like his mother's words, seemed to be forever burned into his mind. He remembered in a state of surprise staring at his reflection in the mirror. He was disoriented and confused, unsure of how he had come to be there in that room. It was a feeling he now knew all too well—the feeling of waking up in a strange or unexpected place after sleepwalking. That was the sense he had in the bathroom that night, and he was startled by his reflection. There was dirt and blood on his clothes and his face, but that wasn't all. He remembered now seeing the scratches on his arms. A lacework of tiny scratches crisscrossed his forearms. He had seen such scratches before, the last time he had cut through those pricker bushes.

Had he been down by the creek and gotten yelled at by the nasty man? But it was pitch black outside. What would he have been doing by the creek at this hour? How would he have even found his way in the dark? Maybe that explained the scratches on his arms.

He felt strange and sad, but it was his mother who was the one crying. Tears ran down her face as she wiped dirt off him with a wet washcloth.

"The police won't understand," she said.

What won't they understand? he wanted to ask his memory, but before the question was fully formed in his head, he knew the answer. The sleepwalking, the scratches, the mud, his mother's distress and the late hour revealed a truth so horrifying that he must have locked it away in some vault in his mind all these years. Maybe he hadn't even been totally aware of what happened. Not then, anyway, but now it was all too clear.

"Oh, God," he said as horror gripped him, and he fell to his knees on the hard ground. He nearly toppled into the raging stream waters but steadied himself by clinging to a clump of dead weeds on the bank.

It wasn't his mother who was a murderer, it was him. He had murdered his own father, and then seven years later, he had murdered a little girl. It hadn't been deliberate. He hadn't even been awake, but he must have taken a walk down to the creek in his sleep on the very same night Lily and her sister had gone down there to play in the water late one night. Perhaps Lily had tried to wake him or disturbed him in some way, and then his sleep self had lashed out violently.

It wasn't cold-blooded murder, even though it looked that way, but what his mother had said was one hundred percent true. The police wouldn't understand. How could they?

So she had done her best to protect him. She sent him away to school. She moved away from the neighborhood where the tragedy had occurred. Lance felt dizzy as he knelt on the creek bank. He had murdered at least two people, but were there more?

Where was Adam? The police seemed convinced he knew more than he was saying about his son's disappearance. What if they were right? What if in a sleep state he had hurt or killed his son? It was something he couldn't bear to think about, but he couldn't ignore the possibility that he had done something to Adam.

The wet ground soaked through the knees of his pants, and as he looked down, he noticed that the water level was climbing. The bank was shrinking at a frightening rate. He scrambled to his feet, slipping on the muddy ground with his shaky legs.

He would turn himself in, he decided. He would go back to the police station and tell them what he now knew to be the truth: during a sleepwalking episode when he was twelve years old, he had murdered Lily Esposito. He would tell them about his father and his fears about Adam, and they would lock him up and throw away the key, and he would never be able to hurt anyone ever again. This plan frightened him but also brought him a sense of calm. For years he had been living in fear of his sleep disorder, but he would come clean, and he wouldn't have to be afraid ever again.

He turned and started back up the path to the parking area, but he saw something out of the corner of his eye. He spun back around in surprise. Someone was out there in the middle of the creek. He stared at a child in a bright green jacket out in the middle of the water. *Adam has a jacket that color.*

Had he become delirious? Was his weary mind playing tricks on him? As he stared, though, he realized it wasn't just a child. There was someone else out there, an adult, though they were too far away to really see. At first they looked like they were standing in the middle of the water, but now he realized this was not the case. The two figures stood on a small strip of land, an island in the midst of the surging creek, but like the bank where Lance stood, their island was rapidly shrinking.

He needed to do something. He felt instinctively for his phone before remembering he didn't have it with him. The police. He could drive back to the police station and have them send help. He took another look at the fast-moving water. There was no time for that.

He stepped into the angry stream and gasped at the ice-cold water. Even with the water only up to his ankles, the current was so strong he almost lost his footing. Would he even be able to make it out to that little island? He had no other choice.

Lance took one deliberate step after another as he traversed the raging waters. It took every ounce of his strength to remain upright, but somehow he managed. He was thankful the water didn't rise above his chest, because if he was forced to swim against the current, he would be swept too far downstream.

~

"Daddy!" The word was so faint when it reached Lance's ears that he couldn't tell if he had imagined it or not.

The treacherous walk through the flooded stream had left him panting with exertion, but now as he looked up from where he had collapsed on that shrinking strip of land, he saw a sight that filled him with joy.

"Adam," he said with awe and wonder.

He forced himself up from the ground and wrapped his arms around his son. He hugged him tightly as he blinked back tears.

He still had his arms locked around Adam when he looked up at the other person on the island. It took him a moment to place the drenched figure in her hooded jacket, but with a jarring start he recognized Phelicity Green, the dream whisperer.

"I tried to call you," she said.

He remembered blocking her number when her calls to reschedule Adam's appointment had become borderline harassment. He had so many questions, but they had to wait. He needed to get Adam to safety.

"We have to get back to the shore!" he shouted at her over the roar of the rain and creek.

Worry etched itself across her brow as she looked over the rushing water to the shore. The water was still getting higher. They didn't have much time.

Lance lifted Adam over his shoulder and held him tightly as he stepped back into the creek. "Hang on," he told his son as much as himself as he struggled with the extra weight in the strong water. He turned back to see Phelicity Green nervously eyeing the rushing water. "Come on!" he shouted at her.

The current was strong, and she was small and slight, but he thought she should be able to make it.

His muscles trembled with the effort to wade across the stream while carrying Adam. He felt Adam shivering with the cold and looked forward to getting him back in the car where he could blast the heat to warm him back up.

"Just a little bit further," he reassured Adam.

He forced his aching legs to keep moving as the water pushed against them. The brown water was full of sticks and debris that slammed into his legs. He pushed forward, but as he stepped down, his foot landed on a rock. The unexpected obstacle sent him teetering. He needed his arms to steady himself, but they were clutching Adam. He stumbled through the rough water as he fought to stay upright and get to the shore. A second later, he felt himself going down, but they were close enough to the shore. He flung Adam onto the solid land as he went down, landing on his chest on the rocky ground. It left him wheezing and gasping for air, but Adam was silent. Lance's heart raced.

"Adam?" he said with what remained of his voice. He heard a murmur and looked up. Adam was sitting on the ground in front of him shivering, his eyes wide with fear. "Adam, are you okay?"

The boy nodded. He didn't speak, but he pointed back out at the water, and Lance summoned the energy to turn around and look where he was pointing. Phelicity Green. In his desperation to get Adam to safety, he had almost forgotten about the woman.

He saw her, just midway across the raging creek. The water was nearly to her shoulders and she was struggling. Lance looked at Adam. He needed to get Adam to someplace warm and dry, but he couldn't leave the woman out there.

"Climb up the bank," Lance told his son. "Wait by the car."

The boy just stared at him. Lance pointed up toward the little parking area and waved his hand. At last Adam rose and began to walk up the little path, but he kept looking over his shoulder. Lance nodded encouragement.

"Wait there for me," Lance said. "I'll be back."

He turned back to the water in time to see Phelicity knocked off her feet. She went under, and he thought she was gone, but she bobbed back up, gasping, and managed to grab hold of a fallen tree that had been washed down the stream. She clung tightly to the tree, but the rushing creek water was strong and still rising.

Lance stepped back into the water on legs already shaky with exhaustion. The tree Phelicity clung to was closer to the shore, but further downstream than the little island. It shouldn't have been as difficult to walk with the current, but with each step Lance felt like the water was going to push him right over. He made it to the tree, struggling to climb around branches to get to Phelicity. She stared up at him, her eyes large with fright. He reached his arm out to her.

"You have to let go of the tree!" he shouted.

She showed no signs of having heard him.

He struggled to maneuver through the tangle of branches to get to her. The wood scraped against his shredded pants. It reminded him of pricker bushes. He reached for her but tripped on a branch. He fell, and the side of his face smashed into the trunk of the tree. Numb from the cold and with his body full of adrenaline, he barely felt it. He shook off the injury and reached for the struggling woman. Phelicity finally let go of the tree, but the current was so strong it started to sweep her away. He splashed through the water after her and caught her when her jacket snagged on a tree branch.

He cradled her in his arms as he fought his way back to the shore.

"I'm sorry," she said through chattering teeth. "I tried to call you."

He gritted his own teeth as he carried her toward safety.

"When I found him in the car, I thought I was meant to find him," she said. "I thought it was what the universe wanted."

He really wasn't in the mood to listen to her new-age mysticism right now, but he couldn't tell her to shut up.

"The universe brought him to me," she continued, "because he has the gift. He can see things. He knew about my sister."

He didn't have a clue what she was talking about. She was crazy. He knew that from his earlier dealings with her. She had kidnapped Adam because of voices in her head or the universe or whatever the hell she was babbling about. She could have killed him. If he hadn't come out here and seen them on that island, they could have both drowned. Well, the police would take care of things, lock her up somewhere, maybe get her the help she clearly needed.

The police won't understand.

No, not that again. He didn't need to hear that anymore, but it was crazy that he was back in this creek, that his own son could have been killed here just like that little girl. They were almost back to the shore, but his arms were trembling with exertion and his mind felt woozy. He looked down at Phelicity Green in his arms, and with her wet hair plastered to her head and her face washed of makeup, she looked like a little girl, but not any girl. She looked like Lily Esposito.

"Lily," the name left his lips as a hoarse whisper.

He saw a look of recognition in her eyes.

"Jade," she said. "I'm Jade. I changed my name."

It came back to him then. There had been two Esposito

girls. Lily, who was killed, and her younger sister Jade, who had survived.

Lance froze in the water as the hazy dream memory of that awful night flickered in his consciousness. The full weight of what he had done pressed down on him.

"I'm sorry," he said, his voice trembling with emotion as well as the cold. "I'm so sorry." A slim metal pole came out of nowhere. Picked up and carried downstream by the floodwaters, it had cruised unseen beneath the muddy water until it collided with Lance's legs. There was a look of shock on his face as his legs buckled. He let go of Phelicity/Jade as he toppled over backward. He watched her as she crawled through the last few feet of water onto the shore. The water carried him downstream, and he splashed around for something to catch hold of, but there was nothing but choppy water in his reach, and his legs did not seem to want to work.

He watched as first the shore and then the fallen tree shrank in the distance. His head seemed to be sliding lower and lower in the water, and then it washed over him. Dirty, metallic-tasting water filled his mouth. He sputtered and tried to stay above the surface, but he didn't have the strength. As the water pulled him below the surface, he saw Lily's face.

39

SAGE RACED back to the police station. His wipers flew across the windshield in an effort to keep up with the deluge. The police radio crackled with conversation. A tree and wires had come down out on the state road, and a different road was underwater. Sawhorses were at a premium.

It was an all-hands-on-deck situation. Sage would need to get out there and pitch in, but first things first. He parked in front of the station and ran inside. Of course the man was long gone, but he ran up to the intake desk.

"I need to know who the man was who came in here before, the one looking for old records," Sage said.

The officer glanced down at the log in front of her.

"Lance Walker," she said.

Lance Walker? Sage shook his head. That didn't make any sense. He knew that name. He had been hearing it all night. That was the kidnapped kid's father.

"No," Sage said. "You must be looking at the wrong piece of paper. There was a guy in here a little while ago who wanted to see some records."

"Yeah," the officer said, annoyed. "Lance Walker. See for yourself."

She slid a clipboard across the counter, and Sage stared at the name written in a shaky hand on the sign-in sheet as water dripped off him onto the paper: Lance Walker. Sage's heart raced as he stared at the paper.

"Where's Arlo?" Sage asked. "I need to talk to him."

"He's out putting up sawhorses," the officer said.

"Where?" Sage demanded. He hadn't meant to slam his palms on the counter.

"I don't know," the officer said. "Somewhere down by the creek. It's flooding."

Sage didn't have time to waste. He ran back to his car. He tried to raise Arlo on the phone and the radio but couldn't get through. It would be easier to just drive around looking for flooded roads.

Sage raced off in the direction of the creek. He caught a glimpse of red-and-blue lights and spun the wheel. He took the turn too fast, sending up a spray of water and fighting to keep the cruiser under control. He saw Arlo out in the road next to the car, trying to haul a large tree branch over to the curb.

Sage stopped his car and ran over to help. Together they were able to get the branch mostly out of the road.

"Please tell me you have sawhorses with you," Arlo said.

"No," Sage said. "I need to ask you something about the Craig Walker case."

"You fucking kidding me?" Arlo said. "In case you haven't noticed, we're in the middle of an emergency situation here."

"What was the kid's name?" Sage said. "His name wasn't on the file."

"Jesus," Arlo muttered. "Now? You gotta do this now?"

"Was his name Lance?" Sage demanded.

"What you have to understand," Arlo said, "is he didn't know what he did. He was just a little kid."

"Was his name Lance?" Sage repeated.

"You know how they say you should never wake up a sleepwalker? It's true. Growing up, my sister sleepwalked sometimes, and yeah, if you tried to wake her when she was having an episode, she got kind of violent. Never hurt anyone but herself though."

"Arlo," Sage said. Whatever patience he had was long since gone.

"What did you want me to do?" Arlo said. "Send the boy away to prison for accidentally pushing his father down the stairs? What kind of life you think the kid would have had?"

"But—"

"Yeah, I know. I realized as soon as his mother started telling that bullshit story about seeing the car. Well, I couldn't do anything about it. If I started investigating the kid, it would have all come out, how I never said anything when the father was killed, how it was my incompetence that got a little girl killed. Look, it wouldn't have changed anything. He wasn't some cold-blooded killer. He was sleepwalking again. I'm sure of it."

"Yeah, well it's happened again," Sage said.

"What?"

"The alleged kidnapping? It's his kid who's missing, Lance Walker."

"God damn it!" Arlo slammed his hand on the edge of his open car door.

The radio screeched. Even over the pouring rain they could both hear the frantic voice that shouted, "All units report to creek between Juniper and Lawnside Roads! Reports of multiple people stranded in creek!"

Arlo jumped into his cruiser, and Sage ran back to his. His mind was reeling.

Had it happened again? Had Lance Walker killed his son while sleepwalking? If that was the case, then what was he doing back here? Sage wasn't sure if he bought the whole sleepwalking thing. Arlo had come to that conclusion because of his sister, but what were the chances that someone who suffered from sleepwalking would accidentally kill someone twice, let alone three times? What if Arlo had it all wrong and Lance Walker was some sort of sociopath?

Henderson. He had to call Agent Henderson.

As he sped down the wet Culver Creek roads, Sage slipped his phone from his pocket and managed to dial Agent Henderson. He waited impatiently for the FBI agent to pick up, praying he didn't get voicemail. When Henderson finally answered, Sage skipped the pleasantries.

"It's Lance Walker. It's the father," Sage said.

"Sage? Is that you? I was just going to call you."

"Lance Walker's a murderer," Sage said. "He's killed at least two people before."

"No, we've had more than one report. They've seen the boy with a woman. We think it's the father's girlfriend. She lives out your way. She's some sort of dream interpreter. Has some weirdass name." Henderson turned away from the phone to shout to someone there, asking what the woman's name was.

"Phelicity Green," Sage said quietly.

"That's it," Henderson said. "You know her?"

"Look, I think she might be in trouble," Sage said. His

car hydroplaned slightly as he drove through an unusually large puddle. He fought to keep things under control.

"I'd say she is," Henderson said. "She kidnapped a little boy."

"I don't know anything about that," Sage said, "but Lance killed her sister, when they were just kids, and I think he might have come back here to kill her as well. I saw him here this morning, but I didn't realize who he was at first."

"What? That bastard! The cops here in Jersey instructed him to stay put."

Sage saw another big puddle up ahead, and this time at least he had the foresight to slow down before entering it. The puddle was even bigger than the last one, and as he moved through it slowly, he realized his mistake. It was more than a puddle. The road was flooded. He tried hitting the brakes and cranking the steering wheel, but it was too late. The front end of the car was in too deep.

"Sage!" Henderson's voice barked in his ear. "Sage, you there?"

"Yeah." Sage checked his rearview mirror to see if Arlo was still following behind him, but he didn't see his head-lights. He looked up and noticed the street sign on the cross street. He had missed the turnoff that led to Juniper.

"Sage, I want you to find her, goddammit!" Henderson bellowed.

"I might have to swim there," he said.

"What's that?"

"Nothing," Sage said. "I gotta go."

Sage opened the door and stepped out into ice-cold water. His feet and ankles were numb by the time he walked back to the comparatively dry road surface. He took off at a jog back toward the turn he had missed, his feet sloshing with each step. He saw a pickup truck approaching and flagged down the driver. The driver rolled down his window.

"Road's flooded," Sage said.

"Well, the cops should be out here directing traffic," the old man behind the wheel said.

"It's been a busy morning." Sage fumbled his badge out of his pocket to show the driver. "I need you to give me a lift."

"Shouldn't you be setting up sawhorses?"

"We're fresh out of those," Sage said. "And right now we got some lives to save."

The driver shrugged and popped open his passenger side door. Sage walked around and got in.

"Where to?" the driver asked.

Sage had to make a decision. The rest of the force was already at the creek for the rescue operation. Meanwhile Phelicity and the boy might still be out there somewhere, and it was only a matter of time before Lance Walker tracked them down, if he hadn't already.

His unanswered knocks on Phelicity's door and the darkness that lay beyond came back to him. It was possible she and the boy were in there hiding. It was also possible Lance had already found them and they were in there dead, but Sage didn't want to think about that. No, Phelicity Green had lived in this town her whole life, and she knew a thing or two about hiding. She wasn't going to be easy to find, which meant she might be able to evade Walker. It also meant she would be able to evade Sage.

"Left here," Sage said suddenly as he recognized the turnoff that would lead to Juniper. He would pitch in with the rescue, then get Arlo or someone else who knew this town better than he did to help him find Phelicity.

"Ah, shit," the truck's driver said as they neared Juniper. "Is that the creek?"

Sage couldn't believe what he was seeing. The once peaceful stream had become a raging river. He thanked the driver and dashed out of the car toward two police cruisers.

Arlo and Rod had a neon-yellow rope tied to a tree and were trying to fight against the current to get to what looked like a piece of debris out in the middle of the swollen creek. He caught sight of movement out on the water and spotted a couple of the guys from the volunteer fire department trying to pilot a Zodiac with a motor on it through the engorged creek.

"He's that way!" Arlo shouted, and he pointed at what Sage had mistaken for debris. He recognized it now as a person. Whoever it was did not appear to be moving.

A whimpering noise caught his attention, and Sage looked around expecting to see an injured animal. Then he caught sight of a woman and child clinging to a tree root at the edge of the stream, trying to climb up the muddy bank. He ran over and grabbed the kid, effortlessly lifting the boy to safety. The hood on the kid's jacket fell back, and Sage recognized the face of Adam Walker. He went back and pulled the woman up to solid ground. The last photo he had seen of Jade Esposito had been from her high school yearbook, but he had no trouble recognizing her as well.

40

THE ROAR of the rushing water filled Caitlin's ears as she burst out of the car. She looked all around as she tried to get her bearings. None of this looked familiar. Her heart pounded in her chest. Was this the right place? Had she made another mistake?

Then she noticed the blue of police lights in the distance up ahead, and she took off at a run. Dimly over the roar of the water and the rain she heard the others shout after her, but she didn't have time to stop.

Her shoes were no match for the waterlogged grass. They became drenched and muddy in no time. Her cold, numb feet stumbled over the uneven ground, but she kept running until the grass turned to asphalt, and she suddenly skidded to a stop as she came to a small parking area. There was a police car here, but that was not what made her stop. Her Land Cruiser was here, parked haphazardly in the tiny space.

"Lance!" she tried to yell, but she was winded from her run, and it was barely more than a gasp. She took a moment —she could spare no more—to catch her breath and try again. This time the word "Lance!" rang out louder, but there was no reply. The SUV was empty, and there were no police officers in the squad car, but she could just make out the sound of shouting from the creek. As she came around the cars, she saw a man as soaked as she was perched on the small strip of land that remained between the parking area and the raging creek. It wasn't Lance. She could see that at once, but she called his name again, just because she had to at least try.

Fear gripped her. Images from her dream danced in her head, and she found it difficult to distinguish what was real from what she had dreamed. Of all the places he could be, that Lance was here terrified her. The thought made her dizzy. This was Lance, after all, her Lance. How could she be frightened of her own husband? He had never once tried to hurt her or Adam, but was that true? Adam had tried to warn her, and she hadn't listened to him. She was as bad as the campus security officers, as bad as everyone who had ignored her warnings. Anxiety swelled inside her.

Without thinking, she scrambled down the embankment toward the creek. Her shoes slipped down the muddy bank. She grabbed at the twisted branches to keep her balance, the rough twigs tearing her flesh. Her foot slammed into a jagged rock and she let out a yelp of pain, but she tried to use the rock to stop her rapid decent. Instead, her soggy shoe came off, and her foot with nothing more than a drenched sock to protect it took a stumbling, painful step closer to the roaring creek.

She looked out toward that rushing water that was now frighteningly close, and what she saw filled her with a heavy, foreboding feeling. It was Lance. She recognized his jacket. He was way out there in the water, and there was a rescue boat trying to get to him, one of those inflatable rafts with a motor on it.

"No!" she screamed at the men in the boat, though there was no way they could hear her. "No! Don't trust him! He's dangerous! You need to find my son! You need to look for a little boy!"

Of course, there was no response from the men in the boat. Her words had been drowned out by the creek, the rain, and the boat's motor. She needed to tell them about Adam. They needed to find Adam before it was too late, but she knew she couldn't rely on them.

Caitlin staggered out into the creek. Adam could be anywhere, but most likely he was near Lance. She could only see Lance's back, and not even that well. For all she knew, Lance was holding Adam down beneath the water as she watched. The image caused adrenaline to surge through her as she waded through the too-deep water. She pushed forward against the strong current as the water crept higher and higher. Then she took a step, and without warning, the ground disappeared beneath her.

The water yanked her under. She saw a swirling mass of bubbles as she struggled beneath the surface, flailing her arms in an attempt to find air. She couldn't tell which way was up, and as she became turned around by the rushing water, she only became more disoriented. The swirling current meant she couldn't stop herself long enough to figure out which way to go. Her lungs began to burn.

Then a weight pressed down on her—a hand, she realized. It was a hand holding her down. Oh God, it was Lance. It had to be. She tried to break free from his grasp, but her strength was fading. She felt weak and feeble. He dragged her, pulling her deeper into the creek. Suddenly everything grew instantly colder, and she sputtered as she sucked in water, but it wasn't water. It was air—sweet, beautiful air. Even as her teeth chattered, she greedily sucked in more of the welcome air.

He still grasped her, but her strength was starting to return, and she fought to free herself.

"Lance," she said, her voice hoarse. "Lance, let me go."

He continued to hold on to her, but she noticed he was dragging her not down into the creek but back to the shore.

"Not Lance," an unfamiliar voice said. "Lance is . . . I'm sorry. We couldn't save him. The current was too strong."

Caitlin cried out.

"I'm sorry," the man pulling her to the shore said. "We tried, but . . ."

"My son!" she screamed. "He had my son!"

"Adam's okay," he promised her. "Come on, I'll show you."

As they crested the embankment, she saw Adam right away. His little face peered out of the big gray fireman's blanket he was wrapped in. She ran to him and grabbed him up in her arms as someone draped another blanket over her own shoulders. Tears rushed down her face.

When she found her voice again, she said to Adam, "I'm sorry Daddy tried to hurt you, but he won't hurt you anymore."

"Daddy saved us," Adam said. She assumed he was confused, like she had been when her rescuer helped pull her from the creek.

"Oh, honey," Caitlin said. "He was a bad man."

"No, he's right," a woman said, and Caitlin looked past Adam to see a woman also wrapped up in a gray blanket. "Lance was the one who saved us."

The words made fresh tears run down Caitlin's face. Someone shouted her name, and when she turned around, she saw her mother. Luanne ran over and clutched Adam and Caitlin in what became a three-person hug. Caitlin spied movement out of the corner of her eye and saw her mother-in-law hurrying toward the creek.

A police officer caught Raquel before she could foolishly climb down the embankment like Caitlin had done, and Tucker came up beside her, pressed his hand on her shoulder and steered her back to him. He embraced her. Caitlin watched her mother-in-law's shoulders heave with her tears. Apparently the police officer had told her about Lance, or else she had already known, through the peculiar ways of a mother's intuition.

41

BY TWO IN THE AFTERNOON, the rain had stopped, the floodwaters had receded, and Detective Sage Dorian could no longer remember what sleep felt like. He sat in the station's interview room across from Phelicity Green. She was dressed in a department-issue sweatshirt and sweatpants that were too big for her.

"Had you met Adam Walker before yesterday?" Sage asked her.

"Yes, he was having nightmares," Phelicity said. "His father thought they were just bad dreams, but I knew they were real. He's got the gift. He's psychic."

Sage tensed up. He thought of Brighton and his affair with the psychic girl's mother. He thought of that sketch artist drawing, which still made no sense to him.

"He told you this was going to happen?" Sage asked, waving his arm around the little interview room.

"He had a dream about me, a dream about me and my sister," Phelicity said. "He could see that night, that awful night. He was the only one who could tell me what happened."

"But you were there that night," Sage said. "You saw what happened."

Phelicity shook her head and squeezed her eyes shut tight. It was several seconds before she reopened them.

"I can't remember anything," she said. "I can't remember that night at all. Do you know what it's like to not know what happened to your own sister?"

The remark made Sage look up in alarm. Had Phelicity been looking into his past, or was this her so-called gift?

"Do you know how he found you?" Sage asked. "How did Lance Walker track you down?"

"Oh, that was fate," Phelicity said. "Fate's an amazing thing. That's what brought Adam back to me."

"Who brought Adam to you?" Sage asked.

"Fate," Phelicity said. "Something, some nudge from the universe, made me pull into the parking lot of the closed pharmacy. Why on earth would I go in there? And then there he was waiting for me."

"He was in the parking lot?" Sage asked. He remembered driving to the pharmacy the day before. It had been an out-of-the-way spot. No way the kid could have just wandered over there from somewhere.

"Yes, he was just sitting there in his car waiting for me," Phelicity said.

Sage blinked exhaustion out of his eyes as he took in what she was saying.

"You took him out of the car?" Sage said.

"Well, I had to," Phelicity said. "I was meant to. That's why he was there."

"He was there because his mother was picking up something at the pharmacy," Sage said.

Phelicity politely shook her head.

"He was there to lead me to the truth."

"And what is the truth?" Sage asked. That was the thing he wanted more than anything—the truth—but would he kidnap a child to get it? No, he didn't think so.

"The truth was that the dark lord took my sister that night," Phelicity said.

"The dark lord?"

"You might know him as the devil," Phelicity said. "That's what Adam told me. He said the bad man had killed my sister. That's his words for the dark lord. He has many names."

"Couldn't it also be his way of saying that a bad man killed your sister?" Sage asked.

Phelicity frowned at this, as if what Sage had just suggested was absurd.

"But there was no man there," Phelicity said. "The dark lord has us under his control."

"Okay, that's one theory, but hear me out: Lance Walker, the man whose son you kidnapped—because, Phelicity, that's what it's called when you take a child who isn't yours out of his car and run off with him—he used to live near you when he was a child. Do you remember him?"

Phelicity stared at him blankly, then shook her head. He couldn't tell if she was following him or not. There was a spacey sort of look to her eyes. He didn't know if that was the ordeal she had been through or if she always looked that way.

"When Lance Walker was a child, he used to sleep-walk. When he was very young, he killed his father when he was sleepwalking, and when he was a little bit older, he killed your sister when he was sleepwalking. He didn't know what he was doing, not consciously, but—"

"That's what I told you. It was the dark lord. He had us under his spell."

"Right," Sage said. "The dark lord."

He excused himself and stepped out into the hall. He rubbed his forehead, then yawned. All he wanted to do was crawl into bed and sleep for days.

"What's going on with her?" Rayanne asked. "We handing her over to the FBI?"

By rights, he knew he should. She had kidnapped Adam Walker. On the other hand, what good would it do? She was unwell, but she wasn't a threat to anyone. Hadn't she endured enough difficulty in her life? Because when a sleepwalking Lance Walker had killed Lily Esposito, he robbed young Jade of her future as well. That trauma had turned her into the sad, broken woman she was today.

Sage looked out over the squad room. Steve Arlo was putting his jacket on and getting ready to clock out after a long, grueling day. Steve had declined to charge a five-year-old with manslaughter, and then protected Lance Walker when he had murdered Lily. Steve's motives hadn't been purely altruistic, but Sage wasn't sure he could fault him for his judgment call. Steve had done what he thought was best for the boy and best for everyone.

"I think we have to understand that any testimony she gives is tainted by the fact that she suffers from delusions and doesn't have a strong grasp on reality," Sage said.

Rayanne raised one eyebrow. "Okay?" she said, turning the word into a skeptical question.

"What she needs is counseling and medication," Sage said. "I think the county facility might be able to provide her with the help she needs." Rayanne nodded but didn't say anything, so Sage continued, "She isn't a threat to anyone. When she took the boy out to the creek, she wasn't aware of the flash flood warning. She didn't mean to put him or herself in danger."

"Detective, I agree with you," Rayanne said. "You don't need to convince me."

Maybe the one he needed to convince was himself. He looked through the door's window at Phelicity sitting there at the desk. What he hadn't told anyone was that he felt a kinship with this woman. Both of them had sisters who had been murdered, but while Phelicity, in her own reckless unstable way, had tried to find the truth, he had not set foot outside his comfort zone to find his sister's killer. Phelicity was a better person than he was. He would make sure she received the psychiatric treatment she needed, and he vowed to do whatever it took to find out the truth about his sister's murder.

42

CAITLIN AWOKE to dim early morning light. Though it had been a month since she had last taken a Pacifcleon she still marveled at how amazing and restful she felt after a good night's sleep. She couldn't believe she had been missing out on that feeling all these years.

She looked over at the empty space beside her. The other thing she was still working on getting used to was the fact that Lance was dead. How many times a day did she pick up her phone to give him a quick call or shoot him a text before she remembered he was gone? Someday, Raquel had assured her, her pain and grief would become tolerable, but it would take a while. She might have bristled at her mother-in-law's advice, but then she remembered Raquel had been about her age when she lost her first husband suddenly.

They had a few heart-to-hearts—Raquel and Caitlin—in the long days following Lance's death. Raquel told her about the sleepwalking episodes that Lance had suffered from since he was a boy.

"He couldn't help it," Raquel assured her. "If anyone

disturbed him while he was in the throes of an episode, he became violent. I was so frightened when he announced that you were getting married. I feared something awful would happen."

"But I never posed a risk of waking him," Caitlin said, "because of the pills I took. I slept like a rock."

"Maybe if I had put him on some sort of medication," Raquel mused. "I should have taken him to a doctor right away."

"They probably wouldn't have been able to do anything," Caitlin said. She didn't know if this was true, but she felt the need to reassure her distressed mother-in-law.

"Instead I tried to hide it, and made him ashamed of it," Raquel said. "He must have thought I was ashamed of him."

That he had been asleep when he killed that little girl made it easier for Caitlin to bear. Since realizing the truth about her husband, she had struggled to reconcile the sweet, caring man she knew with the monster she had seen in her dream. How could Lance have done such a thing? But though it had been Lance's twelve-year-old body that had carried out the horrible act, something beyond his control had been at work. She of all people could understand the helplessness of a sleeping disorder.

To think that for all these years both of them had been suffering and hiding their shameful secrets. It made her want to travel back in time, to hold her husband and tell him that it was all right, that he didn't have to be ashamed. She wanted to confess to him about the dreams she had banished from her life and regretted so much never sharing this with him when he was alive. Maybe if they had both been a little braver, they could have helped each other.

Now she had to be brave for Adam. She heard him stir in his bedroom, and then a minute or so later, she heard his feet pad down the hall to her room. He peeked his head in the open doorway, and when he saw she was awake, he bounded into the room and jumped up on the bed.

"Mommy, I had a dream!" he declared.

She felt herself stiffen. She had resolved, when Adam was a little older, to tell him all about the psychic dreams she had experienced when she was a kid. She didn't want him to ever feel like his dreams were something abnormal or something to be ashamed of.

"What was your dream about?" she asked cautiously.

"I could fly," he announced. "And I had a flying dog, who was purple with green ears, and there were balloons in the air that tasted like gummy bears."

She smiled at his description of the perfectly harmless dream. Since she had started having dreams again, she found them to be pleasant nonsense. She had forgotten what strange things dreams could be.

"It sounds like a good dream," she said. "Where did you fly to?"

"I don't remember," he said. "Can we have gummy bears for breakfast?"

"How about some pancakes instead?"

He gave her a little-boy sigh and said, "Okay."

She tousled his hair and looked over the top of her head to give her husband a smile before she remembered Lance wasn't there. Instead, she glanced up toward the ceiling and silently blew a kiss heavenward.

GET A FREE BOOK!

Hi, this is Alissa. I hope you enjoyed reading *Up the Creek* as much as I enjoyed writing it!

If you enjoy thrillers and would like to learn about new ones I have coming out, I'd love to keep in touch with my The Adventure Continues email newsletter, which I send out each month or so.

Sign up today and get a free ebook copy of my thriller novella *In the Bag*. To sign up and start reading your copy of *In the Bag* today, head over to alissagrosso.com.

A FAVOR TO ASK

I know you're busy, but it would mean a lot to me if you could take a few minutes out of your day to write a review of this book. Reviews help authors by improving search rankings and letting other readers know if this is a book they would enjoy reading.

I am eternally grateful to readers who take the time to leave reviews on the sites of the retailers where they've purchased my books.

DON'T MISS FACTORY GIRLS

A woman is found murdered in Culver Creek and as Sage Dorian investigates the crime he finds disturbing connections to his own sister's murder. Meanwhile a young journalist fears she might be over her head when she goes undercover at the Everluster Paint Factory as she looks into a series of mysterious deaths. Will she wind up the next victim? And will Sage track down his sister's killer? Find out in *Factory Girls* the second book in the Culver Creek Series.

ALSO BY ALISSA GROSSO

For Adults

In the Bag

Girl Most Likely to Succeed

For Young Adults

Unnamed Roads

Shallow Pond

Ferocity Summer

Popular

ABOUT THE AUTHOR

Alissa Grosso is the author of several books for adults and teens. When she's not busy writing she's probably hanging out with her boyfriend Ron or perhaps she's creating some new digital illustrations. Originally from New Jersey, she now resides in Bucks County, Pennsylvania.

For more information visit:

alissagrosso.com